Mighty One Series:

Their children will be mighty in the land; the generation of the upright will be blessed. Psalm 112:2

Burgundy Gloves- 9/2017
Broken Chain- 1/2018
Black Coat- 3/2018

Escape to an era where true love prevails

Escape with short devotionals and extras at juliadwrites.com

Black

Coat

A novel by

Julia David

Field Runner Press

I dedicate this story to the two Graces in my life

Grace (Kingsbury) Ruddy—befriended me as a new neigh-
bor and it changed my path for eternity.
The Grace of God—I've heard about grace hundreds of
Sundays. But until I experienced His Grace firsthand for
myself, I couldn't begin to fathom that love, forgiveness,
and acceptance are truly mine—No matter what.

The **Bridge** of **Grace** will bear your weight, brother. Thousands of big sinners have gone across that bridge, yea, tens of thousands have gone over it.Some have been the chief of sinners and some have come at the very last of their days but the arch has never yielded beneath their weight. I will go with them trusting to the same support. It will bear me over as it has for them.

Charles Spurgeon

1

Carver, Minnesota
1881

Hayes Sullivan peered into the nearly empty Silver Holiday Saloon. He stepped inside. No customers, no trouble. Clyde, the barkeep, nodded at his arrival, a crooked smile rising at what Hayes gripped in his hand.

"The 1810." The grisly barkeep raised his gray bushy eyebrows.

Hayes nodded back, appreciating for one moment the reaction his family's vineyard gave those desiring a fine wine.

Clyde looked over as an older woman came from the kitchen.

"I told you to get Molly out of bed and get these floors done," he barked.

Hayes was just about to place the bottle on the thick oak bar when he froze.

"Yeah, yeah." The woman walked past, ignoring them.

Hayes blinked and swallowed hard. Molly? Could it be his Molly? He realized the bottle still hovered over the bar. He set it down slowly as the barkeep pulled out a tin box.

"Who is Molly?" Hayes snapped.

"What?" The man counted out the bills, never looking up.

Hayes shook his head, looking for the right words. "Is she new? Forget that, what does she look like?" He'd never forget those soft green eyes and that mass of copper curls, those freckles that beckoned his attention.

"Why do you care? Unless you're looking to make a trade." Clyde tapped the bills up and down on the bar. "Let's say… that bottle for some entertainment—more than one night. Maybe say five nights?"

"Just tell me what she looks like." He fought the urge to reach over the expanse of the bar and grab him by the neck.

"Do a trade for that bottle, and I'll have her look like anything you want."

Hayes clenched his teeth and made fists with his hands. His Molly was a domestic but certainly not a harlot. He snatched the cash from Clyde's hand and spun on his heel.

"Come on," Clyde called after him. "You come back tonight, and you can have a dance for two bits. That's a better deal than what I paid for this wine."

He walked out, the bright mid-morning sun catching him in the face. Closing his eyes, he pinched the bridge of his nose and tried to take in a few deep breaths. How could the mention of that name still make his heart take off like a racehorse?

Of course, it's not Molly. He pinched the bridge of his nose harder. It's been five years. If she wanted to find him, she could just walk up to the railroad office. Everyone in this forsaken town knew who he was. He stomped the four blocks back to his office. Most of them despised him for bringing the malicious railroad tracks to their area. Only the ones with half a brain realized it would triple the economy.

He gripped the key and held it in the lock to his office. His shoulders dropped; he wasn't really mad at this town. He tried again to breathe slowly, surprised at himself for allowing anything to disrupt his steadiness. The truth is, he was stung by the mention of her name. He was stung that she allowed his parents to pay her off and return to Ireland. And so they all thought she was gone until a note attached to a baby girl showed up at his family's home.

"Gracie, get those wiggles out now." Mrs. Fox, the housekeeper, tapped the active five-year-old on the head. "It's time to get that napkin in your lap. I won't have any spilled milk on this fine linen I took an hour to iron."

"Mr. Sullivan." Mrs. Fox held out a bowl of soup in front of Hayes.

"Mr. Sullivan…" She ground out his name and set the bowl of soup down.

"Hayes, where *are you?*" his elderly grandmother drawled.

"Hmm?" He finally reached for the bowl. "So sorry, ladies. A lot on my mind."

"I hope no nasty threats from the riff-raff around here." His grandmother sipped her soup.

"No, a fairly quiet day as far as threats." He watched Mrs. Fox step back from the table. "Mrs. Fox, I know you've been working all day. I would prefer for you to sit and not wait on us. Please." He got up to pull a chair out.

"We've already had this talk, mister." She pushed the chair back in and pointed for him to sit.

Hayes gave up. She'd only worked for his parents all her life. Practically raised all seven of the Sullivan children. But for heaven's sake, she was pushing eighty and still worked long days.

"Dear Mrs. Fox," his grandmother said. "Your loyalty and service would never be in question. You have gone above your duty to join Hayes, Gracie and me on this adventure out west."

"It's only Minnesota, Granny." Hayes knew she hated when he corrected her. "Not like Oregon or California."

"I was *trying* to say…" She sounded perturbed. "That Hayes does not have strict conduct when it comes to the line between domestics and the titled." She scrunched up her wrinkled lips and nodded toward Grace. "And, since all need to be more open and accepting." She cleared her throat. "This table seats ten, and there are only three of us, so you are very welcome to join us."

Hayes pulled his napkin from his lap and set his spoon down. Suddenly he had no appetite. His grandmother had poked an open sore. Not wanting to say something he'd regret, he got up from the table.

"Hayes, where are you going?" his grandmother bellowed.

"Just some fresh air. Thank you, Mrs. Fox." Hayes bowed slightly and left. Rounding the corner, he jogged up the polished oak stairs two by two.

He jammed his finger in the underside of his starched white collar, jerking it from his skin. Entering his room, he closed the door and quickly removed the gold pocket watch from his vest. His father had given him the watch at his graduation from Brown University. He flipped it open: seven twenty. Knowing he couldn't just eye the time, he read the inscription. *For Hayes Sullivan, Graduation 1878, with pride, your father.* He snapped it shut quickly, surprised his father didn't want this back after the Molly O'Leary scandal. Setting it down, he quickly unbuttoned his vest and shirt and threw them on the bed. His slacks and shoes he kicked off onto the floor.

Opening the door to his wardrobe, he found his canvas trousers and a flannel shirt. Pulling them on, he felt as if he'd returned to his original skin. After tying his boots, he jerked his gun off the top of the wardrobe. Fresh air, some sharp shooting, and the simple clearing of his muddled mind were all he needed.

"And silence, like a poultice, comes to heal the noise of life," he quoted to the pitch-black night. Unfortunately, tonight's walk in silence accomplished nothing resembling healing. Usually, time alone could help him find his axis. He prided himself in the use of mind and truth over feelings. But today was unusually demanding.

He rarely entered the Silver Holiday Saloon and Hotel unless Clyde asked for a bottle of his family's select wine. Why, today, did he enter and hear that woman's name? She worked there obviously. Why couldn't that clod Clyde just say what she looked like? Hayes realized he probably sounded ridiculous. But just one description of the woman named Molly—how hard is that? Is she a blonde? Old, young? Now it was a distraction just jabbing at him.

He approached the brick steps to the back of his two-story Victorian. He stopped and turned and sat on the second step. It was as cold and dark outside as he felt inside. Five years; five years is a long time. He should have moved on, found someone else to love, someone trustworthy. He should have been thankful that his father arranged for the job as the railroad commissioner. A double degree in Philosophy and Political Science was enough. He'd passed every class with perfect marks. He could read Latin and spar with anyone who knew the writings of Confucius or Buddha.

He rubbed his hands slowly over his face. Not that that mattered in Carver, Minnesota. He could use his intellect for good, but no one taught him the ways of the heart. No book, no philosophy would explain away the real pain of rejection and betrayal. He'd tried to apply his favorite quotes. David in the Psalms often brought comfort. But he knew this God of the Bible looks for the pure. His love for Molly felt pure. She laughed and infused him with a joy he didn't know was possible. He believed they would marry and be together forever. But he was wrong. Oh, how he hated to be wrong.

He looked up to the house, so dark and quiet. Two old women and a child; most nights he could tolerate the tiresome company. But tonight wasn't one of those. He didn't want to be the grandson scolded. He was twenty-seven years old. Now already dressed like everyone else in Carver, might as well go into town and dance with Molly. Two bits was a small price to pay for some elusive peace.

2

Looking side to side, Hayes tied up his horse down from the saloon. The noise and insufferable music flowed out to anyone in earshot. Blowing out a breath, he ran his fingers through his short sandy brown hair. His clothes might disguise him, but he should have brought a hat to be certain. Knowing the staunch suits and ties he generally wore, his everyman denim and flannel might give those who didn't like him cause to provoke him. He didn't care; he was against violence, but not afraid to protect himself.

He walked slowly toward the swinging doors. He looked in and second-guessed his need to see this Molly. The fog of smoke and the smell of alcohol and unbathed bodies was assaulting. She would never stoop to this; what was he thinking? Walking to the end of the boardwalk, he turned down the alley. All he needed was information.

The back door to the kitchen and the one at the top of the stairs to the upper rooms were open. Walking into the kitchen, he saw a man carrying a case of liquor to the front. He went back out and looked up to the stairs and saw a large man coming down the steps. It was dark, but it looked like he was caring a metal bucket. He never looked up, but he reminded Hayes of the big kid who ran the local Feed and Seed with his sister down from his office. Maybe this was the entrance for those who had standing appointments. He might have asked him about Molly if the man wasn't in such a hurry.

A woman appeared at the top of the stairwell. "I smell smoke—you got a fire going down there that's driftin' smoke up here?"

"No." Hayes started up the steps. "Do you know a woman named Molly that works here?"

"Who's askin'?" she said. The light from the hallway illuminated her bright makeup and revealing attire.

"I'm just a friend, but I'm not sure she's the woman I'm looking for."

"Hey love, as strong and handsome as you are, I've got the time to be your new friend. Why don't-"

"I smell smoke, Hazel." Another woman, younger with moppy black hair, walked up to them.

Hayes stepped into the hallway, speaking to this new woman. "Do you know a woman named Molly? Curly reddish hair, around twenty-five?" Hayes looked away from her, suddenly distracted. Glancing down the hallway, he smelled the smoke but didn't see anything coming from the rooms. Like a hound dog, he began to walk down the hallway, stopping at each door to smell.

"Are all these rooms full?" He looked back to the women standing by the exit.

"Some are; some aren't," Hazel said.

Hayes walked up to the last door on the right. "I think it's coming from in here." He went to grab the knob, but someone had tied a leather strap to it and nailed the strap to the door jamb. "What the devil?" He pulled hard twice on the leather strap before it would free from the door jamb.

The door opened quickly to a room full of black smoke. He batted his arms back and forth until he saw red-hot coals sitting in the middle of the bed. He quickly gathered up the bedding and stopped to turn and open the window. One quick toss might save this room from going up in flames. Pulling on the frame until his lungs started to burn, he realized the window was stuck. He put all his back into the lifting and groaned out in frustration. It wasn't going to budge, and he didn't have time to figure out why.

He took the backside of his arm and rammed his elbow, breaking the glass on the window. Turning to grab the mass of smoldering bedding, he thought to heave it out, but his eye caught a large mass of black slumped on the floor. In only a split second the coals found his hands, scorching his skin. He cried out as he tossed the mass out the window. He shook his hands quickly, trying to eliminate the pain. Taking only a few steps, he grabbed at the bulk of the black fabric. He gritted at the searing pain in his hands as he pulled the form toward the door. As soon as the light replaced the smoke, he could see it was a young woman.

"Did you put out the fire?"

"Is she dead?"

"Should I get Clyde?"

"Is this building burning up?" The two women peppered him.

"No. Don't get Clyde." He scooped up the mass of black and the young woman inside. "I'm getting her to the doctor. Watch out." He pressed through where they hovered.

"Your arm is bleeding," one of them pointed out.

Just as he turned to go down the steps, he heard the other one say, "Is that Molly?"

She was a slight thing with dark hair stuck over her face. She was wearing a heavy full-length black coat that was adding to his inability to move fast across the street to the doctor's office. He pressed her against the doc's door and pounded with the fist that held her legs. Two more pounds and the door finally flew open.

"Found her in a room… full of smoke." Hayes panted.

"This way," the doctor urged, holding the lantern out.

"It's going to be a long night, Irene." The doctor shook his head and walked into a small room with a cot.

"Put her here."

Hayes gently lowered her down and for the first time caught a look at her face. She was strikingly beautiful. No bright rouge or lipstick. Like looking at a perfect painting.

"Help me get that coat off. I can't even see if she's breathing." The doctor lifted her head and neck, giving her cheek a few small taps. "Miss, miss…wake up…"

Hayes tried to undo the top buttons while pulling her arm free of the coat.

The woman groaned and crossed her arms. "Nooo..." She began to cough.

Both men stopped and looked at each other.

"Good sign," the doctor explained. "Keep coughing, miss. Out with the bad and in with the good.

"Fred." A haggard voice came from the doorway.

The men quit trying to remove the coat and looked up.

"Yes, Irene," the doctor said, irritated.

"The younger Rollins boy is here. The oldest one's got a knife in the foot. They remembered from last time—you said not to remove it but wrap it until you get there."

"For heaven's sake." The doctor's head fell forward. "Why are they playing with knives again? In the middle of the night? Don't those parents know how to tie them to the bed?"

The doctor turned despairingly at Hayes. "Irene's got Mrs. Harding in the other room. Some simple lancing went wrong. Now I've got to stitch up a foot, and it looks like you need some stitches."

Hayes raised his blood-soaked sleeve. "This can wait. Go. I'll stay with her until you get back." They both looked down at the woman still clutching the coat, eyes closed.

"You're Mr. Sullivan, and you run the railroad office?" the doctor questioned, straightening up.

"Yes, sir."

"Nice to meet you; sorry under such circumstances. Is she someone special?" He moved past Hayes, grabbing a roll of gauze.

"No...no, I've never met... her before." Hayes felt his face flush, stopping the unnecessary information on his reckless night.

"Keep a close eye on her." The doctor handed him a pillow. "Keep her elevated and open the window. If she gets agitated again, you can put three drops of this on this cloth and hold it over her mouth and nose. But only for a count of five."

Taken aback, Hayes opened his eyes wide, looking at the little bottle. He'd done a lot of things, but nursing was not one of them. He nodded as the doctor turned.

"Irene is two doors down if you need her," the doctor said as he left the room.

Hayes shook his head, wondering what he'd just volunteered for.

"I wish it were something softer," he said to the young woman as he lifted her head, pushing the stiff pillow under her.

As soon as he moved her, she began to whimper and clutch her chest. "I can't breathe..." he thought he heard her say. He watched wide-eyed as she wheezed under the strain of getting her breath.

"Hold on; I'm getting some fresh air." He turned to the window behind him and found it lifted with ease.

"My throat...is burning..." she mumbled low and hoarse. Arm and hands stinging, Hayes tried to suck in his own calming breath to no avail.

"Please, miss. Try and hold still; the fresh air is coming." He glanced back at the little bottle and swallowed hard.

"I can't…breathe…" She scratched at her throat, arched her back and wheezed in and out.

"Can you calm down? Miss, please." He bit his lip. Three drops for a count of five. He shook his head; was that right? Or was it five drops for a count of three? He hated when he felt uncertainty.

It must be his first inclination. "Trust yourself, man," he murmured.

Hayes glanced back and forth at the open door, hoping help would suddenly appear.

"Nurse Irene, I need your help," he called over his shoulder. He waited, chewing on his bottom lip. Where could she be? Only a few doors down; she could certainly hear him. He glanced back to find the young woman thrashing and gasping for breath. Jogging to the hallway, he yelled, "Nurse!"

He stalked back to the young woman and grasped her hands to keep her from pulling at her throat. "Miss, please relax. Just breathe slowly."

What a crock, he thought. He was breaking out in a sweat. She pulled up to sitting, her eyelids opening as her eyes rolled back in her head. He pushed her back down on the cot and grabbed the little bottle. Three drops; only three drops he rehearsed, grabbing the cloth. His hands were shaking as he hovered the bottle over the cloth. One, two three, they came out fast. Had he counted right? He dropped on one knee and held her down with his bloody arm.

Securing the cloth over her nose and mouth, he took a quick glance back for the missing nurse. One, she tried to arch her back again. Two, he held her fast with his injured arm. Three, she seemed to relax. Four, the wheezing was subsiding. Five, he felt a bit dizzy. Had he been breathing in this sedative as well? Lost more blood than he thought? Dropping the cloth back on the side table, he saw black spots and fell back onto the floor.

He slapped his hands against his face, only to feel the jar of excruciating pain. He looked to the red and pealed blisters on his hands. In all the commotion, he'd forgotten about the recent burns. He rolled his head back and forth on the rough wooden floor. "A wonderful pair we make." He exhaled, looking over to her. Thankfully, she seemed to be sleeping.

He rolled up on his knees and stood, stretching his head side to side. The fresh air seemed to help his own dizziness. He found the pitcher and poured some water into the basin. Gritting his teeth, he lowered his stinging hands into the water. He rocked his jaw to the side and sucked in more new air. On a small shelf, he noticed some rolls of white cloth. Carefully, he spun the gauze around his palms and fingers. He fumbled with the scissors to cut the cloth and gently tucked the ends into the damp dressings.

"Where am I?"

He turned to the sound of a low wispy voice.

"You're at the doctor's office." He was somehow delighted that her soft brown eyes matched her perfectly shaped face. They slowly closed under the weight of her heavy lids.

"What is your name, miss? Who can I request to come be with you?" He waited, assuming she'd fallen back asleep.

"Nadine," she finally whispered, stumbling over her words. "Call for no one, but thank you, doctor, for your help."

Hayes pulled a chair next to the cot. "I'm not the doctor. He had to run to the Rollins place to get a knife from a foot."

Her thick lashes rose slowly and looked him over. "Who are you?"

"Hayes, Hayes Sullivan." He gave her a small smile. "I found you in a smoke-filled hotel room. Do you remember that?"

Her eyes dropped closed again. "Some, I do," she confessed faintly.

"This thick black coat has been a weight on you. You might feel better with it off-"

"Please," she whimpered, crossing her arms tighter around herself. "Promise me...even if I sleep...don't remove the coat."

3

Hayes' head dropped forward as he woke up with a start in the middle of the night. The lantern burnt low as he looked over the small room. The woman was asleep, her arms still protectively wrapped over her chest. The irremovable black coat didn't make sense. A smoke filled room? This whole night didn't make sense. What degree of insane was he to go to that saloon? Could it have been God's providence to save a life?

He rubbed his eyes for focus and stood up, the chair accidentally scraping the hardwood floor. He stretched his neck side to side. Why hadn't the doctor returned? Surely he would relieve him from her care and send him home.

"Mr. Sullivan, may I have some water?" Her scratchy voice startled him.

"Of course." He turned to the pitcher and poured the water in a small cup. He held the cup up to her lips as she rose up. Lowering back to the pillow, she blinked sluggishly, watching him. "Did you burn your hands...t... tonight?"

He nodded slowly.

"I'm so…" Her chin began to quiver. "s...s...sorry." She pinched her lips together.

"Don't cry over these." He held his bandaged hands up. "They'll be fine in a few days." He sat on the corner of her cot, catching her coat under his leg. "Do you have a hankie hiding under that heavy coat?"

"No." She swiped the lose tears with the back of her hand. She stared at his blood-soaked sleeve. "Your arm—what happened?"

"I used it to break a window." The muscles in his jaw tightened—should he ask questions or just leave well enough alone?

Curiosity, and her innocence, won him over. "When I followed the smell of smoke, I noticed someone had nailed a leather strap to the door frame. It was tied to the door-knob, so no matter how hard you tried, you weren't sup-posed to get out. And the window; I couldn't tell if it was nailed shut, but it wouldn't budge. Someone had trapped you inside. Why would anyone do that to you?"

"And so you used your arm to break the window?" she whispered.

He dropped his chin slightly. "I already said that. So, if you don't want to tell me who was trying to hurt you, it doesn't matter. But I will go to the sheriff, and I will insist he investigate who did this to you."

"Everything's still foggy." She raised her slender hands and rubbed her forehead.

"Mmm." Hayes was sure she was hiding something. "Let's start with an easier question. What's with this unmovable black coat? Certainly you are too young to be a widow."

So many lies. What could one more hurt? "As a matter of fact, I am a widow," Nadine whispered, looking away.

"Humm, I thought the custom was to wear a black gown. I can tell you have a light colored dress under this coat."

Nadine jerked on the coat edge he was sitting on. "Do you mind?"

He stood up and pulled the chair over.

"I promised my l...la...late husband before he died that I would not wear mourning gowns. He did want me to grieve so, out of respect, I agreed. But the coat is about my bereavement state."

"So you wear light colored gowns, but keep the coat on at all times?" He leaned back and scratched his head.

"Have you ever done something unintelligent for love?" Nadine pulled the coat collar together. She noticed he sat up straighter with a dazed expression. He shook his head and raked his bandaged hands through his short hair.

There was a certain discrepancy in him. He was very handsome, with a rugged jaw, yet no facial hair. He seemed astute–almost privileged, but his clothes were a mess. They didn't match his air of control. Even his voice was commanding, yet caring.

"Are you from Carver, Mr. Sullivan?"

"No, from back east. Why would a young widow like yourself be staying at the Silver Holiday?" He went to lean his elbows on his knees and winced, pulling up quickly.

"First, tell me why *you were* there." Nadine raised her eyebrows slightly.

"I can see that fog in your head is still troubling your memory. Yet, it has no problem avoiding my every question." He rubbed his fingertips back and forth across his chin. "Nadine, or I should be calling you Mrs.-"

"Von Keller." She interrupted. "Yes, you may call me Mrs. Von Keller."

"Mrs. Von Keller, I have no problem telling you why I was at the Silver Holiday tonight. Really I, don't. Buddha says, 'We do not learn by experience, but by our capacity for experience.'"

Nadine wondered what she had just heard, this handsome rogue quoting Buddha?

"I was at the Silver Holiday looking for a woman; a woman from my past. I'd heard her name spoken earlier that day by the owner. I made a poor choice to see if the woman from my past was the woman that worked at the saloon. While I was looking for her, I smelled smoke and found it coming from your room." He looked past her. "What I thought was going to be a small issue transformed into a larger, life-saving experience." He tilted his head, smiling at her. "One might say."

"You are surprising." The hushed words were out before she could catch them. His warm smile confirmed her confusion. "Please tell me, what is your trade? What do you do here?"

"I'm the area railroad commissioner." He leaned back in his chair. "If all things go as planned, Pacific Engineering will see the Pungent Sound linked to the Great Lakes in a year or so." He stretched his arms over his head, pulling side to side.

Nadine noticed the edge of his flannel shirt lifted to reveal the taut skin on his waist. She looked away, wondering at the feeling of instant familiarity they shared. "Are you married?" she asked.

"What do you think?" He dropped his arms, squinting at her.

She scrunched her mouth to the side. "I would say... not. You don't seem like the kind of man who would run around looking for lost love if he was happily married."

Hayes nodded once. "Even though I pride myself on not judging, you have judged me correctly."

Nadine wondered for a minute if she was dreaming. Yet she could feel the cool night air from the open window. It mimicked the peace and amity in the small room, somehow tangible. She hadn't felt anything calm for weeks or months. She wasn't even stuttering.

She gripped the coat over her small waist, her immoral secret still tucked away inside her womb. This strange man and his honesty made her feel like she could reveal her every dark mistake. But that was a lie; she'd learned the hard way never to trust a man. He professed he didn't judge. But everyone judged a single pregnant woman. Everyone.

Being a widow was brilliant. Ironically, it was this stranger's idea.

"I can tell you are thinking some deep thoughts." He leaned in. "Even in the dim light, your eyes are beautifully serious. So tell me how you came to be locked in that room tonight."

4

Nadine opened her eyes to the daylight streaming through her sick bed window. She'd been dreaming of Ben Graham, the young man who worked on her parent's dairy farm in Wisconsin. Was there a gentleman here last night? Had she dreamed their conversation?

She looked up to see a woman leaving her room. "She's awake," the woman called out.

Nadine straightened her long black coat over her body and tried to sit up. Slight dizziness and a sore throat seemed to be her only malady. She took a few deep breaths of the fresh morning air coming through the open window.

"There you are." An older gentleman with a black bag came to stand in front of her. He popped the bag open on the small table. "How are you feeling?"

"I guess I'm fine. My throat is still burning."

"People can die in only a few minutes from smoke in their lungs." He tapped his stethoscope and held it under her coat. "Breathe in." She took a few deep breaths. "I think you need to thank the Lord above. Mr. Sullivan saved you and the Silver Holiday from burning down last night."

She looked up, his words registering. Hayes Sullivan was the man in here last night. She wondered if she'd dreamt her shadowy conversations with him.

"Where is he now?" She chewed her bottom lip. Probably getting the sheriff, she thought, her heartbeat spiking. "Am I free to go?" She began to move off the cot.

"Nope. You can just sit back. When your people come for you, I want to tell them what to watch for."

"I have no people coming. I can take care of myself."

"Mmm, no." He grimaced at her. "Irene! Fetch Mrs. Thomason, if you please."

Nadine admitted she needed some time to think. And this morning's breakfast of biscuits and gravy was the best thing she'd eaten in two days. Going back to the hotel from hell was out of the question. She had no money, and no connections anywhere in this state. The thought of Marcus Monroe was making her whole body want to shut down.

She placed the empty tray on the small table and curled up in a ball. A widow in a wedding dress; what a horrid lie. You actually have to be married to be a widow. She'd been so close to saying those vows.

Familiar nausea washed over her; she rolled her eyes and covered her mouth. Ben Graham was willing to marry her, even though the baby was not his. He was kind and genuine. No, she didn't love him, but he would have never left her high and dry as Marcus had.

Suave Marcus had promised her the world. She gripped her face, trying to stop the treachery she remembered in his eyes. He said he loved her, and she'd believed him—until two days ago, when he'd told her he needed her help in recruiting loose women for his own saloon. She refused. She wasn't going to manage the saloon girls. She was carrying his child. A child he had earlier told her she could get rid of. Why did she believe he'd changed his mind?

She just wanted her own home. She could almost forgive what he did for a living as long as she had her own home; something safe and comfortable for her and the new baby. Was that asking too much?

What kind of man wants his woman to enlist poor women needing work? He even tried to make her believe it would be helping the unfortunate ones. Then why did he only want young and voluptuous women? She was not stupid. It was immoral, and they both knew it.

"Oh Lord," she began to whimper, breaking out in a sweat. "Don't think about him, don't think about him…I'm the immoral one," she repeated. Her black coat suffocated her, wrapping her in the lies and depravity.

She heard a woman talking at her doorway before she sat up and grabbed the tin basin. Somewhere from above her she heard, "Hello, Ma'am. I am-"

Nadine never looked up, promptly losing the contents of her breakfast in the basin.

Pushing the basin back on the table, she flopped back onto the cot, covering her hands over her face. Maybe this person would just go away. Hope dashed, she felt a cool rag patting her forehead and hairline.

"There, there, beloved. You've had a rough go, the doctor says."

Nadine contemplated pretending she was asleep. Even though her cloth and words were comforting, she was too bewitched to be friendly.

"I'm sorry, I'm just not well right now," Nadine croaked, moving away from the cool cloth.

"Oh, it's nothing I haven't seen before. I'm not a nurse, but the doctor and I have a little understanding."

"Mrs. Thomason?" Nadine remembered the doctor had asked for her. Glancing over at her, she seemed harmless enough. Sweet faced, maybe in her fifties, with blonde and gray braids tied around the top of her head. "I'm not sure why the doctor asked for you."

"He said you have no family here; no one to help you recover."

Nadine rocked her head back and forth. "I…I…I haven't figured out what to do, if that's what you are asking."

"Well, as the local pastor's wife in, I enjoy helping people. Now I can't take everyone in, but I have ideas." She smiled. "Some folks are wonderfully benevolent in this area."

"I don't want to be a bother to anyone. I just need a few days to wire my family. They will send money to help me get home." Lie number two. She knew she could never face the hurt and disappointment she'd caused her overprotective parents.

"Perfect. I know just the place to hold up for a few days until your family sends for you. You are going to love her. Her name is Nettie Wagner, and she's about your age. She and her brother run the Feed and Seed. They have quite the building; little rooms here and there. Always willing to help those in need."

"I don't want to be a bother." Nadine pulled herself up, wishing this day was over.

"Well, I know she would love to have you. It's your choice, though. The only time the doc sends for me is when he doesn't know what to do." She smiled again, gently rubbing Nadine's back. "I would love to have you for a few days, but my oldest daughter's about to give birth, and I have her four little ones running amuck at my home. I can see by those dark circles you need some place to rest."

Before Nadine could find a rebuttal, the doctor walked in.

"Wonderful, Miss, you've met our godly pastor's wife. She has the hands and feet of Jesus. How's the throat?"

Nadine nodded slightly. She hadn't even had a chance to rinse her mouth out.

"Can you stand for me?" He held his hand out.

Nadine rose from the cot, and he pulled her out and walked in a small circle. "I'm still concerned about your lungs. So nothing strenuous for at least two weeks. How do you feel standing up? Like you're on a rocking ship?"

"I've never been on a ship," she whispered.

"Where is she going to be?" The doctor addressed Mrs. Thomason.

The kind faced woman smiled. "May I introduce you to Nettie Wagner?"

Nadine looked at the ground, shaking her head. "I suppose I don't have many alternatives. Thank you."

"Oh Piddle Paddle. Is this her?" A bright faced young woman clapped her hands together as they entered the long and narrow brick store. Nadine wanted to take a step back at this girl's enthusiasm. She practically bounced to them, her long honey-colored braids swinging back and forth.

"My name is Nettie." With a pretty smile, she offered her hand to Nadine. Nadine was surprised by a gentle hand squeeze.

"I am so sorry to hear about your loss; everything getting burned up and you being so far from home. I know when I lose my purse for a day I almost panic. How frightening for you to wake up in the doctor's office with nothing to your name."

Nadine decided it wasn't worth the effort to tell the truth. She liked Miss Wagner's view on what happened. Lie number three had arrived.

"Mrs. Von Keller, would you feel comfortable if I were to say my goodbyes?" Mrs. Thomason asked.

Nadine gripped the sides of the black coat. "Miss Wagner is a wonderful person to reach out to a stranger like this. I think I will be fine." Nadine gave Mrs. Thomason a weary smile.

"Very well then. Nettie, the doctor wants her to have plenty of water and rest. She's not allowed to help move barrels or feed sacks."

Nettie Wagner dropped her chin. "Certainly not." Nettie and Mrs. Thomason chuckled at the implication.

"He promised he would check on you, especially before you travel." Mrs. Thomason patted Nadine's shoulder before she turned and left.

Nadine felt like she could drop. "Would you mind if I lie down? I don't want to be any trouble."

"Of course I don't mind. When I heard you were in need, I immediately made a bed up. Let me show you." Nettie started walking back to the back of the store. "I'd introduce you to my brother Edgar, but he seems to have disappeared. This back hallway has four rooms. The water closet is at the end. Just a couple steps out the door and to your left." Nettie opened the first door to a simple room, a pink and blue quilt covering a small bed. A wicker chair sat next to a round table. Nadine spied the window. "Does the window lift up and down?"

"Yes, let me show you." Nettie flipped the latch and pulled it up easily. "Here's the key." She handed it to Nadine. "Oh wait, before you rest..." She turned and ran back down the hallway. Nadine watched her come around the corner with a small basket.

"In this little pouch are my favorite tea leaves. I keep the strainer and hot water on the wood stove in the back room. This is a scone and an apple tart to tide you over. Edgar and

I usually eat lunch here. Can I check on you in a few hours and see if you feel up to joining us?"

Nadine, staring at the basket, was suddenly overwhelmed by her thoughtfulness. "I'm sure I smell like a chimney and look...even...worse." She knew her hair hung loose and tangled around her face.

"Well, start with the rest time, and we shall see about a bath and change of clothes when you are ready." Nettie started toward the door, but stopped and looked back. "And Mrs. Von Keller?"

"Please call me Nadine."

"Nadine," she said with a nod. "You are no bother. Since the railroad opened its own store, business has been devastatingly slow. You are not keeping me from anything except maybe chewing my fingernails." Nettie flashed her a smile. "Rest well."

Nadine slowly closed the door and locked it. She brought the wicker chair over and jammed it under the glass knob.

Facing the door, it occurred to her that she never heard anyone enter her room last night at the hotel. She'd fallen asleep, the second night since Marcus had left her. She could hear the people talking in the hallway, so why didn't she hear anyone enter her room? Was it Clyde making good on his threats? Would Marcus have asked someone do such a horrid thing? She didn't want to believe it was him. He was like a hungry rat to get out of there and on to Helena. There was no need to kill her. Abandoning her was enough.

Slowly unbuttoning the black buttons, she removed the dreadful heavy full-length coat. It felt like an oxen yoke was off her shoulders. She let it topple in a pile on the floor.

Sitting gently on the bed, she was confronted by her lovely cream taffeta gown. Only a week ago, she had picked this as her wedding dress and was prepared to marry Ben Graham. She had known by the look in his eyes that he didn't want to. She had pushed and prodded until the honorable young man agreed.

She dropped her elbows to her knees and cradled her head. Her sin had turned her into someone she barely recognized. This silly dress was all she had of her life a week ago. Running away from her sudden wedding hadn't even been on her mind that day. How could Marcus have swayed her?

He'd told her weeks before he would have nothing to do with her and their baby. But he came for her, and she believed him. She believed it when he said they would be married. She believed him, all those sweet-toothed lies and deceit.

She kicked the horrid black coat. Tears began to roll down her face and onto her hands. She kicked the coat again and again. "How could you do this to me?" She moaned, sitting up, clutching her head. "I have shamed my family." She swiped at the tears and stomped on the black coat. "How could anyone be so selfish and cruel?" She muffled her sobs. "You left me with nothing but this dreadful coat. I have nothing...nothing...and nowhere. I...I...have nowhere to go."

5

"Nadine…Nadine?" Nadine jumped up, sleepy and confused. Seeing the door blocked, she silently removed the wicker chair.

"Just a moment; I'm a bit groggy." Nadine quickly pulled the black coat over her wedding dress and buttoned it.

Opening the door, she saw Nettie holding a bowl of soup.

"Please excuse me. I fell into such a deep sleep, I must have missed supper."

"I'm just glad you were able to sleep. I can leave this with you, or if you would like to come out to the back room, you're welcome to. It's just me, and the store is closed."

Nadine hesitated but thought it might help her hopelessness to get out of this little room. "All right."

"Oh, pink punch." Nettie smiled. "Follow me."

They walked down a few steps to the back door of the store, made a slight turn, and entered another room. It was warmed by a large cooking stove. Various cupboards and counters lined a wall, with a stack of wood piled high by the back door. The round table with four chairs was centered over a gray and brown braided rug.

Nettie sat the bowl down on the table and pulled out a basket of bread. "I was hoping you'd come out."

Nadine lowered into a small wooden seat. The smell of warm bread was staggering her senses. "Can you please join me?"

"I ate an hour or so ago, but will have some milk and pudding while you eat." Nettie pulled a small bowl out and poured some milk from a pitcher. It reminded Nadine of the dairy back home. Her family must be worried sick.

"I need to post a letter to my family. Maybe I could borrow some paper and ink if you don't mind?"

"Certainly. I'll get it-"

"No, no...sit, please. I'm sure I can't post it until tomorrow." Nadine tried to remember the strict manners she was brought up with. "Please tell me about yourself, Nettie. May I call you Nettie? Is this store your brother's and you help him?"

Nettie nodded, scooping a rounded bite into her mouth. "Mmm...well...it's a bit untraditional, but the store is mine to run, and my brother works... for me." She chewed.

Nadine swallowed her soup and raised her eyebrows. "Oh, I see. How did that come to be?"

"It's not very obvious, but Edgar and I are twins. I was born first, and they didn't even know another baby was coming. My poor mother; what a shock." She snickered. "There were some complications with birthing him. My mother never had any more children, which she always said was fine with her." Nettie smirked. "He struggled in school and mostly helped in the big store."

"The big store?" It was nice to chat about something besides herself.

"My parents own the Carver Mercantile on Main Street; you can't miss it. They've had the business for over thirty years. They bought this building with the two storefronts about three years ago. About the time they probably expected me to marry, I talked them into expanding. So the Feed and Seed was born. Edgar does all the stocking and lifting, and I do all the sales and accounting.

"But things have slowed down?" Nadine bit into her second piece of mouth-watering bread. "I'm sorry to hear that."

"We keep our head above; God looks out for us." Nettie smiled, looking down at her empty bowl.

Nadine felt the awkward silence.

"And for you, too!" Nettie looked up. "Except, I wish someone besides Hayes Sullivan were your guardian angel." Her eyes squinted with a soured opinion.

"He told me he was the railroad commissioner. I guess the railroad company has taken some of your business?"

"Flowered falsehoods is all you get from him. He tried to tell me that competition is the way we better our businesses. People like choice. Hokey hogwash."

Nadine smiled at her verbiage. Anything that excited her seemed to come out with a matching adjective.

"I'm sure you will make this store work. This is none of my business, so you just tell me to bug off, but do you have anyone special? Any suitors coming by to walk you home?"

Nettie dropped her elbows onto the table and slapped her cheeks. "I wish. Farmers and ranchers are all I see. Most of them are old with a wagon load of grandkids running around the store. It's pitiful."

"Are there some special outings for the young folks in town? Help you find someone closer to your age?"

"Mrs. Von Keller...I mean Nadine." Nettie leaned into the table. "I know I act and look like I am twelve. But I am twenty-three. *Twenty...three.* The last time I went to a corn husking, the oldest boy was seventeen. I lied and said I was looking for a friend." She rolled her eyes and then snorted, shaking her head. "I like my work. I'm thankful my folks are trusting enough of me. I'd go crazy sitting around sipping tea all day."

Nadine stared at her wide-eyed. How many days had she felt the same way? Trapped hour after hour, giving her younger sister music lessons and pining for her own life to begin.

"Would you like some tea?" Nettie jumped up and headed to the stove. "Nothing against sitting around and sipping tea or anything."

Before Nadine could answer, the back door opened and an older well-dressed gentleman entered.

"Hi, Pop," Nettie greeted him. "I want you to meet Mrs. Von Keller. I told you she's staying here a few days until her family comes for her."

He set a large parcel on the table and held his hand out with a warm smile. "So sorry to hear of your misfortune."

Nadine nodded with a weak smile, unconsciously pulling her hair flat to cover her encompassing embarrassment.

"So, Pop, she's not supposed to lift anything, so can you help me with the hot water on the stove?"

"Umm hum." He turned.

"And you, Ma'am, get to look through this." She removed the soup bowl and basket and pushed the large package in front of Nadine, then pulled a large tin tub through the door and into her room.

"Nettie, really, I don't want to be any trouble." She shook her head in dismay. Her father was already carrying the steaming water to the tub.

"It's no trouble." Nettie walked back in. "Look inside the package. My mother packed it, but if anything is missing, my father can run back to the big store." Nettie was already pumping another bucket of water for the tub.

Nadine let out a long sigh and pulled on the twine. The paper fell open, and she saw a hairbrush, bar of soap and a tin of hairpins. She set them aside and pulled the tissue paper back to see new soft white undergarments. Glancing up to make sure Mr. Wagner wasn't watching, she fingered the soft fabric. Her chin began to quiver as she looked below to the large folded woman's dress. It was warm, sturdy cotton with sweet touches of trim and piping. The entire garment was black as the blackest night.

She'd never told them she was a widow. How many circles had her lies turned? At least now she could throw away the sham wedding dress—it only mocked her day and night.

"I shut the win-." Mr. Wagner stopped when he saw her face dripping in tears. "Window." He pulled his hankie from his jacket pocket and handed it to her. "It can get down to freezing this time of year. Say, Nettie…" He turned to his daughter walking in. "Maybe you should stay here tonight and keep Mrs. Von Keller company."

"No…no…" Nadine straightened up, wiping her face. "I've been enough bother to your family. I will enjoy that bath and crawl into bed." She looked Nettie in the eye. "Really, you go on home with your father."

"Are these things helpful?" Nettie asked softly, touching the black dress.

"I'm crying because they are more than helpful." She sucked in a hiccup. "This is without a doubt the kindest thing anyone has ever done for me." Nadine watched as father and daughter looked pensively at each other. She shouldn't have said that. "Please go on. I'll blow out the lights and lock the door."

Nettie turned away and came back with some paper and ink. "Please promise to tell them you are in good hands. Maybe they would be amicable to you staying and making Carver your new home."

Nadine's throat constricted, rattled by that thought.

"Promise you won't touch the tub." Nettie gently touched her shoulder. "Edgar can haul it out in the morning, but not too early."

Nadine finally stood. "You have raised a truly wonderful Good Samaritan, Mr. Wagner. I can't thank your family enough."

They both nodded, and Mr. Wagner helped Nettie into her coat. "Lock this door behind us—Nettie has her own key," he said, stepping out into the dusk with Nettie.

"I think she knows her Bible, Pop." Nadine heard Nettie whisper. "You know I've been praying for someone to study with."

The door clicked closed, leaving Nadine alone without their helpful presence.

6

The tub was half the size of her one back home. No housekeeper Edda to help her wash her hair and keep the hot water coming. She had locked all the outer doors, and left only the lantern in her small room illuminating her bath. She kept her room door open to allow the large cook stove to heat the hallway and her room.

Laying out the new nightgown on her bed, she looked one more time down the dark hallway. It was silent, but she could feel her heart beating hard. Torn, but she wanted to be in the water before it went cold. She took a deep breath and dropped her clothes in a pile. With soap in hand, she stepped in and released a long sigh. It was still warm as she lowered down, her soiled skin tingling. She stared a moment at her bare belly. It didn't seem to look any different.

That Nettie Wagner–feeling herself an old maid at twenty-three. Nadine didn't have the heart to tell her she was only twenty. By twenty-one, she would be a mother. Nettie had an agreeable face and slender build—the right young man would certainly see her pure heart.

Nadine dunked her head and began to scrub her filthy hair. Keeping her eyes closed from the soap she thought she heard something. Did she scrape the tub? What was that sound? She quickly rinsed her hair and face. Cowering down in the water, she heard it again. Was it a door creaking? Now her heart was beating from her throat. Hiding like someone was about to jump out at her, she couldn't take it. She put her arm over her chest and reached for the lantern. She gripped the handle as she saw the door move.

Squealing, she pulled the lantern back to strike. With the swinging lantern in her grip, she looked down at a fat tabby cat leaning against her tub.

"Oh dear Lord…" Her heart was beating so hard she felt dizzy. "You…yes you. You s..sc…scared me." The cat was quite large. It purred, seemingly oblivious to the terror it caused.

Nadine rolled her eyes and finished her bathing. Somehow, the cat's presence was comforting. She talked to it as she dried off and slipped on her fresh smelling nightgown. "I'm assuming you live here?" She took the brush to her wet hair. "I'm just passing through…I think."

Nettie's comment about staying in Carver was interesting. But what if Marcus came back for her? She pulled on the brush as it stuck on a difficult tangle. *It doesn't matter.* She pulled harder. She would never, never be duped by him again. He'd broken every promise he'd made. Even if she had to crawl back to Wisconsin, she would never want him back in her and her baby's life, her clean body somehow supporting her vow.

Grabbing the lantern, the cat by her side, she walked to the back room. Feeling the heat from the warm stove, the familiar wood crackling inside, she set the lantern on the table. Sitting cross-legged on the floor in front of the stove, she began to fluff her hair.

Her mother had never allowed them to go to bed with wet hair. After losing her older brother to influenza, she insisted her three remaining daughters be smothered with every precaution known to man. Her older sister, Margaret, had jumped her mother's grip by going to Northwestern University. A teacher, a missionary and a suffragette and… her list of evangelical work just went on and on.

Nadine dug her fingers through her thick brown hair. Why, oh why, did Margaret have to save the world and yet desert her family? Nadine bit the corner of her lip. She knew perfectly well why. It was the same malady she suffered from. Their mother insisted on controlling their every move. Living with a constant dripping of nagging, fretting and worry, Helga Von Keller was rarely happy. Something bad was always about to happen.

Nadine dropped her hands in her lap. Her mother was right. The first move Nadine had ever made on her own turned into disaster. While all that overprotective harping worked on making Margaret a better person, it had only pushed Nadine off the edge.

In the dim light, she saw the paper and ink sitting where she'd left them, taunting her to find some words of reason—begging her to confess her ruin. She rose up and sat back on the dining chair, reaching for the quill.

Dearest Mother and Father,

Please forgive me for running off as I did. I know you must be sick with worry and all I can do is to beg for your forgiveness. I never wanted to introduce you to Marcus. I know you would not approve of him, but my heart was over-taken by him. He has a good job waiting in the Montana Territory, and we are on our way now. Lie number four. *We are married, and I will be making a home in this new land. I promise to write and understand if you would be inclined to burn my letters. I can only pray one day you may forgive me for running off as I did.*

Your pitiful daughter,
Nadine

Blowing on the wet ink, she eyed the door to the stove. The cat slumped down where Nadine had been sitting earlier. It curled back and forth on its back, finally stretching out. It seemed like the cat was blocking her from burning up the letter. Grabbing the lantern, she walked back into her room.

Cracking her eyes to the soft light coming through the curtains, Nadine got her bearings. She was safe and had slept all night without calamity. The soft nightgown and sheets brought tenderness to her soul. Smelling coffee, she could almost believe this was going to be a good day.

Eyeing the new black dress, she arose and stared at her new things. How could she repay this family for taking such good care of her? Maybe she should just return everything with a note of thanks. She blew out a breath. The Wagner's had no idea she didn't warrant such generosity.

She remembered one of the few times she allowed Margaret to comfort her. It was something about God having many plans far and above what we think. He's not moved by our fear, but He *is* moved by our faith. She remembered shrugging it off as her sister's religious gibberish. Why was it coming back to her now?

She looked down again at the dress. Maybe she needed faith to believe. Could something good be found in this day? Accepting these gifts surely was part of it. Putting on the smoke-filled black coat laying on the floor was out of the question. She'd rather freeze in a snowstorm than put it back on.

Nadine, donning her new dress, walked into the back room, thankful to find Nettie there.

Nettie swung around and clapped loudly. "My oh my to the sky...you are a beautiful sight!"

"Oh, thank you, but it's my messy hair." Nadine pulled her fingers through her thick brown hair. "I've actually never done it before." She sighed. "Well. I mean I can brush it and do some simple things. But I usually wear it up high." She brought her hands up on top of her head to show Nettie. "Two rolls, up like this."

Nettie intertwined her fingers and cracked her knuckles. "Okay...I think...no...probably..." She came to Nadine and circled her, looking and tapping her upper lip. "Oh, nells bells, I think we should ask Alma at home. I mean I can do braids and sometimes twist them into a bun. But you are too...too..."

Nadine watched her struggle for the right words.

"Refined?" Nettie looked innocent. "I just don't think I can get the look you want."

"No, I'm not going to impose on your family any more than I have." Nadine set the brush and pins on the table, determined to figure it out.

In between coffee and muffins, they had tried every way to get her hair up atop her head. Holding the mirror up to the crooked mess, the giggles would begin again. Nettie's snorting was causing Nadine to laugh harder.

"Cow's ears; that's all I see. It just won't stay." Nettie laughed.

Cows, the dairy, and the oil Edda used to get Nadine's hair to stick to her head were all missing from her morning. Just for a moment, Nadine had forgotten her fallen state and was laughing with a friend. Now her lopsided hair didn't seem so funny.

"You look so sad." Nettie took the mirror down. "I didn't mean you looked like a cow or anything. I meant my floppy hair buns; not you."

Nadine touched her arm. "No...no, I was thinking about home. You have been so helpful, and even in our frustration, it has been a balm to laugh again."

Nettie gently pulled the pins out and brushed Nadine's hair. "Is it too painful to tell me how your husband died?"

Nadine froze. She felt like someone had locked her back in the heavy black coat. "He fell from his horse," was the first thing that came to mind. She could feel Nettie pulling large strands of hair together.

"I'm so sorry," Nettie whispered.

"Please continue with whatever you are doing. I need to let you get back to work." Nadine felt her tying something around her hair.

"All right, it's just a French braid down the back. I tied a bow at your neck. I could run home and grab my mother's hot iron and curl the ends."

"No." Nadine rose from the chair. "This is wonderful. Off my face and secure. No saggy buns are falling around my ears." She smiled, hoping Nettie would leave her be. "Could you find a job for me to do? Maybe I could dust or…" Teach music. Flower arranging sounded absurd. "Anything. I'm fairly good with sums—maybe I could help with accounts or receipts?"

"Oh no. You are a fresh flower and have no business in an old feed store."

Nadine tilted her head. "And you are *also* a lovely lady, yet you do not find the work beneath you." She gave her new friend the serious eye. "Please give me something to do to help. Please…"

"You know what I really want?" Nellie looked around to make sure no one was listening.

"Tell me." I'd do anything for her, Nadine thought, her generosity still overwhelming.

"I just long to have someone to read the Bible with. When you saw me as a Good Samaritan last night…I thought-"

"Read the Bible?" This poor, secluded girl. Nadine pulled in a disappointed breath. "I…I…will read the Bible with you, *if* you promise to give me some chores to do around here."

"I don't know; what if Mrs. Thomason stops in to see you and you are working? She'll think dreadfully of me."

"Put me to work back here. I can sweep and dust. Oh, by the way—is there a large tabby cat that lives here? She came to see me during my bath. I need to admit, I almost hit her with the lantern."

Nettie laughed. "That's Boxie Roxie. I just call her Roxie. She's the best mouser I've ever had. Somehow she just boxes the mice that live in the feed store. One punch and she's got them in her mouth." Nettie chewed on her lip and looked around. "If you insist, you can take a broom and dustpan to the little store next door. It's been empty for months, and we'd like to rent it someday, so I guess it might help to make it presentable."

"Perfect." Nadine stood a little taller. "Point me in the right direction."

7

After Nettie had unlocked the back door, Edgar needed her back at the Feed and Seed, and Nadine assured her she'd be fine. She looked around, hoping Boxie Roxie might want to enter with her and do a sweep of any mice. Nadine had never been down to her family's cow barn. Little critters running along her feet were frightening. She preferred freshly swept carpet.

She walked in the back to a back storage room, shelves and large pallets lining the walls. Walking through an open curtain, she saw the span of the store. It shared the long brick wall with the Feed and Seed. Only about half the width was another long red brick wall with a black wood stove against it. A large canvas tarp covered something sitting in the middle of the dark hardwood floor. Stairs ascended on her right, leading to a room of some sort. The front was all windows with curtains covering the lower half.

She walked to the door in the middle and gazed out to Carver. Only four days ago they'd arrived in such haste, never getting a good look at the town. Based on her stay at the Silver Holiday, she had judged Carver scandalous. Today, even though gray clouds hung above, it seemed harmless. She had judged it wrong.

'You judge me correctly,' came back to her, from that man who saved her and stayed with her all night. Besides Nettie's sour comment, she hadn't thought of him. She tilted her head and looked down the street. The railroad commissioner, he had said.

She wondered if there was something appropriate to do to thank someone who saved your life. A plate of cookies seemed an inadequate display of her gratitude. She shrugged. Her guilt would keep her away anyway.

Unfortunately, Mr. Sullivan seemed shrewd, sensing her deception. And his questions were too probing. He had such a strong opinion of himself, but seemed humble in a strange way. She'd been in such a low state that night, but his smile was the most comforting thing she'd ever seen. He'd been at the Silver Holiday looking for a woman; no one on this earth was looking for her. And she didn't blame them.

A few hours later, on her last trip to the waste bucket, she set the broom and dust pan down. Nettie called for her from the back door.

"Yes, I'm here." Nadine came around to meet her.

"Alma just dropped off beef and potatoes. Come, let's eat."

Nadine, famished, followed her next door.

"You must promise to rest. You've spent the whole morning cleaning in there."

"You will think I'm strange." Nadine smiled. "But I enjoyed it."

They entered the back of the feed store as a large bulky man was walking back into the front. "Edgar, wait," Nettie called after him. "I want you to meet Mrs. Von Keller."

Edgar turned toward them and nodded. He stared at his boots, nodded again and walked back into the store.

"He's not usually that shy. Especially when Nick..." Nettie looked wide-eyed. "I almost forgot to tell you. Our freighter, Nick, usually spends Saturday and Wednesday nights in one of the back rooms. Oh my." She giggled. "Sometimes we all play games. Mostly, he plays checkers with Edgar."

"I don't want to be in the way. Maybe there is somewhere else I can go those nights–maybe the pastor's wife?"

"No, no." Nettie cut her off. "Nick's used to sleeping with his wagon. He won't mind while you are here. Please sit down so we can talk about where you would like to read in the Bible tonight."

A full stomach and a quiet bed beckoned Nadine into an afternoon nap. She awoke rested and wondered how one day to the next could feel so different. Just helping clean the smaller store next door made her feel like she was productive, getting her mind off the last few days. She had no money, but this was something she could do. She was accustomed to working in her own way. While her mother fretted over her injured father, she'd taken over managing her little sister's lessons and schooling.

She shook her head, heading back out the door and entering the little store. Why did she despise her place at home? It certainly wasn't that appalling. How could she have allowed herself to be so persuaded?

Nadine dragged in a determined breath, wondering why the large object in the middle of the room hadn't been removed. Expecting a large sales counter of some kind, she pulled on the heavy canvas, exposing instead an exquisite grand piano.

She stepped back and looked toward the back door. Did the Wagners understand the value of this? It was beautiful. Carefully touching the flawless black sheen, she drew her fingers gently over the top. Astounded, she lifted the heavy lid and pulled the arm to reveal the newly felt hammer coverings. With spotless ivory keys, this piano had to be brand new.

The Von Kellers' piano was old and well used, but this was pristine in every way. Pausing, she tried to let her hand rest unaware on the ivory keys. Was something wrong with it? She gently pressed the G chord. The sound was spot on. Looking back again towards the door, feeling like she was trespassing in forbidden territory, she tried a D chord, F chord.

Baffled, she stood back and looked closer. It was indeed a Steinway. Glancing down at the old canvas tarp, it felt almost criminal to conceal such a treasure with the rough, heavy covering. She decided to see if Nettie could come over and explain.

Mind still whirring, she walked back to the back door, turned quickly toward the feed store and ran straight into a large man. The gray clouds flashed off his silver badge.

"Whoa there, Miss."

Nadine almost bounced off his barrel chest. Hoping beyond hope he wasn't going to talk to her, she mumbled her apologies and tried to maneuver around him.

"Mrs. Von Keller?"

She stopped, frozen. What was she to do? The lies were too many to count. *Try to run.* Maybe run to a certain railroad commissioner's office and punch-

"Glad to see you are feeling better. You *are* Mrs. Von Keller?"

Nadine felt herself blinking rapidly, knowing full well she was only Miss Von Keller. "Yes, sir."

"I'm Sheriff Moad. I spoke to Hayes Sullivan yesterday."

Nadine allowed her eyes to roll quickly, grinding her teeth together.

"He mentioned something was unusual about the fire at the Silver Holiday." The large sheriff bent down to see if she was listening. "Can you fill me in? Why would anyone trap you in that room?"

"I really don't know." She spouted, a shiver running up her spine.

"Well then, tell me what you remember."

His words gave her pause. "That's just it—I don't remember anything. I was asleep. I never heard anyone in my room. When I woke up, I was in the d...doctor's office." She scratched the back of her neck.

Sheriff Moad cleared his throat. "All right then; how does a young widow find herself alone and unaccounted for?"

She could feel the steel trap lower. " I...I... w... was..." Her words would not come out without duress. "On..m...m...my...way to..." How could she believe this was a new day? Didn't Nettie's ridiculous Bible say, your sins *will* find you out? She pulled on the collar of her new black dress. " H...H...He...Helena."

"Uh huh." He looked like his patience was running thin. "What ya got in Helena?"

"M...my...hus...late husband's fa...fam...family."

"What kind of family lets a pretty young thing travel alone?"

Nadine shrugged, lips creased.

"So you came to Carver alone, and even though we have a nice hotel a few blocks down, even a boarding house," he dragged the words out, mocking her lies, "you picked the Silver Holiday. Why would you do that?"

"I don't know." Nadine was ready to beg for her freedom. "I...I...thank you for checking on me...but...I'm... I'm ...doing much better." She turned to leave, when she felt him grip her upper arm.

"Listen to me, Ma'am, and listen good."

Nadine willed her knees not to give way. His eyes were boring into hers.

"I already talked to Clyde. He saw the man with you. So why are you lying to me? It tells me there's a whole lot wrong in this story. If he's on the run and you're protecting him, I'm going to find out."

Nadine's throat constricted, her eyes burning with hot tears.

"Please, sir. I will be g…gone soon and you will never s…see me again."

"Sorry, ma'am. You made the mistake of stopping in my town. This is my domain. Nothing gets around me." He finally let loose of her arm. "I'm your old fat daddy from now on. Got that?"

Nadine froze, terrified tears flooding down her face. What was he saying? Was he going to arrest her or help her?

He tipped his hat. "I'll be watching. No one takes advantage of the innocent here." He gave her a bent smile. "As long as you *are* innocent."

8

Staggering back against the door jamb of the little store, Nadine watched the bulky sheriff walk into the back door of the Feed and Seed, obviously on his way to tell Nettie and her family what kind of woman they were lending their benevolence to. She pulled her hands down over her wet face. She wanted to run and run far, but her legs were weak and shaking.

She just needed to hide—somewhere no one would find her. Wobbly legged, she went back inside and grabbed the railing on the stairs. She pulled herself up each step until she reached the door at the top.

"Please be open," she cried, grabbing the knob. It opened, and she quickly ducked inside, closing the door. She pressed her back against the brick wall on the right and slid down the rough interior. Clutching her knees, she sat and buried her head.

For one minute—only one minute, she had actually felt rosy. Nothing good ever lasted long. Maybe she should have died in that smoky room. This fear, this anguish day after day, was more than she could bear. She growled at the thought of Hayes Sullivan, that overconfident busybody. Why didn't he just mind his own business? Maybe he'd enjoy an ad in the local paper telling of his trip to the Silver Holiday? It would serve him right. How dare he be so rude and insidious and-

"Nadine."

Nadine rose quickly—it sounded like Nettie's voice. She might as well face her now. Maybe the pastor's wife could find a barn she could stay in tonight.

She wiped her face and tried to straighten up. "I'm up here," she hollered as she opened the door. Before she could make it down, Nettie was already on her way up.

"You saw the piano? It's amazing, yeah?" Nettie finally made eye contact. "Nadine, new friend, why have you been crying? Did that grouchy gus of our sheriff upset you?"

Nadine nodded slowly.

"Don't worry about him. It's not your job to find out how that fire started; that's his. Let him worry about it."

Nadine could not find any words. How did this simple young woman bring light and comfort into everything she did? Nadine was already feeling better. She'd read the entire Bible with her just to pay her back for being so optimistic.

"Did you have a look around up here?" Nettie walked past her. "It's kind of fun. Did you ever play dress up when you were younger?"

"Yes," Nadine recalled, wiping her face. "With two sisters, it was a favorite play time."

Then you're going to love this." Nettie walked into the upstairs room, and Nadine followed, looking at it for the first time. It held a large bed with a rusty iron bed frame. To the left, a full sink, window and little kitchen area, and a little black potbelly stove and a table and two chairs were down on the right.

"These are fun." Nettie walked past the wardrobe and lifted the top off a large trunk. "The last people that rented this store were the theatrical type. They wanted to start a theater here in Carver. I thought it was a great idea. But to make a living, they sold pianos downstairs."

Nettie sat the top tray of the trunk on the bed. "Look at these." She held the first gown up.

"Oh, my." Nadine touched the striking red taffeta. The piping was red velvet. "A lot of red lace?" She pulled on it, lifting an eyebrow at Nettie.

"I know. Our little town wasn't quite ready for these folks. These must be costumes for plays or…" Nettie snickered, jiggling her chest. "Maybe she wore this just for her husband."

"Nettie Wagner!" Nadine looked at her with lighthearted disapproval. "This one isn't as bad." Nadine held up a white brocade with billowy sleeves. "With a few alterations, your mother could sell these at the big store."

"She just might." Nettie pulled out another one. "Look at the yards and yards of fabric. My mother's upset, because she wants to rent out this space. The last people left almost a year ago, but they weren't too smart. The piano came through the double doors in pallets, took five men to get it in. Now that's it's all put together, there's no way to get it out of the store. But they hadn't paid rent in seven months, so my parents took the piano as back pay."

"Someone could teach piano lessons." Nadine fingered the soft fabric. "We weren't allowed to attend lessons in town—our poor teacher had to come to our house. My mother didn't want us 'out and about.'"

"So, you play the piano?" Nettie stopped folding the dresses and looked at her.

"Yes."

"Do you play well?"

"Very well." Nadine teased while helping her put the tray back on the dresses.

Nettie dropped the lid down and clapped her hands together.

"You!" She bit her bottom lip, bright-eyed. "You could teach piano lessons here, and we could fix up this little room for your own space."

Nadine smiled, walking back to the staircase. "That's very sweet of you, Nettie, but your mother wants more for rent than what a lowly piano teacher can afford."

"Right now, it's bringing in nothing." They descended the stairs. "Why don't I ask her?"

"No, no please don't." They stopped at the polished grand piano. "It *is* a sight to behold," Nadine whispered. "I love the purity of such a beautiful work of art."

"Play something; anything. It's not right for it to sit unused."

Nadine shook her head.

"Please." Nettie pulled out the piano bench. "Just one tune. Anything."

Nadine remembered she'd decided she would do anything for this new friend. "All right."

She sat, wondering what to play. Before she could make a decision, her fingers found the familiar chords to a beloved hymn. Her arms, hands, and fingers moved with grace and affection. Her eyelids closed and she could feel the transparency of her soul playing over anything her mind understood. The sound reverberated off the high ceiling and red brick mortared walls. If she'd been in a real cathedral, it could not have touched her tattered nerves more.

The second time through the chorus, the words finally connected to her heart...*that saved a wretch like me...I once was lost...but now I'm found...was blind...*

The deep connection of soul to song came to a jolting stop. The air in the small store had turned to ice.

"Don't stop." Nettie wiped away a tear. "That was the most beautiful, heartfelt 'Amazing Grace' I've ever heard."

Nadine turned away to rise off the bench—she didn't want Nettie to see how fragile the song had left her.

"Is that how your teacher taught you to play? You must know how extremely talented you are. I think I heard some angels singing along!" Nettie laughed.

Nadine wondered if Nettie Wagner was the angel. "Tomorrow you can dress up in the white baroque from the trunk and dance around the room. Who needs a stage?"

Nettie laughed, doing a pirouette and leaping toward the back door.

"See? You are perfect for the part!" Nadine chuckled, following her.

"This is my favorite part in Luke seven," Nettie repeated numerous times during the reading of her Bible that evening. *"And one of the Pharisees desired him that he would eat with him. And he went into the Pharisee's house and sat down to meat. And, behold, a woman in the city, which was a sinner, when she knew that Jesus sat at meat in the Pharisee's house, brought an alabaster box of ointment, And stood at his feet behind him weeping, and began to wash his feet with tears, and did wipe them with the hairs of her head, and kissed his feet, and anointed them with the ointment. Now when the Pharisee which had bidden him saw it, he spake within himself, saying, This man, if he were a prophet, would have known who and what manner of woman this is that toucheth him: for she is a sinner."*

"Can't you just picture it?" Nettie looked up. "She got down on her hands and knees and cleaned his feet with her tears *and* wiped them with her hair!"

"I guess I can picture it. But you read she was a sinner. Why would Jesus allow such a display? Certainly he was embarrassed by it."

"Exactly; that's why I love this. It's so backward. Jesus actually uses her example to correct the Pharisee. He welcomes her extravagant display. It's somewhere down, oh wait," Nettie trailed her finger down the page. "Jesus is speaking to the Pharisee: 'you didn't give me any water for my feet. You didn't greet me with a kiss or anoint me with oil.' Okay, in verse forty-seven. 'Wherefore I say unto thee, her sins, which are many, are forgiven; for she loved much. And he said to the woman, Thy faith hath saved thee; go in peace.'" Nettie fell back into her chair. "Oh, and when you played Amazing Grace today." She sat back up, her hands moving in the air rhythmically with her words. "So touching. We have a savior that forgives everything."

Everything? Nadine pondered. Sweet Nettie, her childlike faith had yet to run into the harshness of life. Nadine, sucking in a deep breath, hoped it never would.

9

Tossing and turning that night, Nadine could not get her mind to settle down. Piano teacher, the idea was almost believable. To have the little furnished room upstairs all to herself. She could place a cradle between the bed and wardrobe; or maybe closer to the wood stove. How cold did it get in the spring here? She'd heard about the Minnesota winters. The face of the sheriff telling her he'd be watching, chilled her daydreaming.

Flipping to her other side, she wondered why she'd not posted the letter to her parents, besides the fact she didn't have a penny to her name and didn't want to ask Nettie for one more thing. They'd already fed and housed her. How could she pay them back?

Her focus needed to be getting away from here, fast and far. What would her new destination look like? Would it have a pastor's wife lending a hand to the destitute? A Nettie, full of heart and optimism?

Oh, that girl and her love of the scripture. Nadine flipped on to her back. Could Jesus really have forgiveness for a sinner like her? Was Nettie's faith rubbing off on her?

She'd only prayed in church; never thought of asking for anything by herself. What could it hurt? Maybe sleep would finally come.

Dear God,

Since you know everything, You know my older sister is the one who has great faith in You. I suppose I have some. This wasn't sounding like the way people prayed in church. *If you really could save a wretch like me, then please do. Surely if not for me, then for my little babe. Where should we go? Where should we live? I've made a mess of everything, so I surrender to your will to be done. Amen.*
At least the last part sounded better.

Hayes, thinking he heard his name and a sound at his door, flipped off his covers, wondering if he'd overslept. He cracked open the door to Mrs. Fox's stricken face.

"It's your grandmother, sir. When she didn't come down, I went to take her a tray, and she's not... waking up." She grabbed her mouth and covered a loud moan.

"Keep Grace away from her room." He pulled his hand down his face. "I'll go for the doctor."

"Thank you, doctor, for coming—I guess I should have checked on her myself first." Hayes raked his fingers through his tousled hair. "I would have known there was nothing you could do. I never heard her complain or say she felt...ill." He sighed. "She mentioned she was tired last night. But that's not unusual. I just…just…can't believe…she's gone." Hayes rubbed his fingers on his pounding temple.

"She lived a long life. I wish I didn't have to see how so many her age suffer for months—even years—before they pass on. That's how I want to go when my time comes." He slapped Hayes on the back and opened the front door. "I'll have the undertaker send out a casket and see about Pastor Thomason coming by."

Hayes barely listened. "Alright, yes…thank you. That would be helpful."

"I do what I can," the doctor said, going down the wide front steps. "It seems you assisted me a few weeks ago."

Hayes blinked, confused.

"The gal who almost died in the fire? I think you gave up a night's sleep. I'd like to think that's what Christians do."

"Humph." Hayes nodded, unable to connect anything rational in his head.

The next day, the door creaked as Nadine looked up to see Mrs. Thomason enter the little store.

"Mrs. Von Keller."

"Mrs. Thomason. What a delight." Nadine moved from her desk, putting the sheet music aside, and squeezed her hand.

"I had heard from Nettie's mother you are renting this space. Piano lessons? How many students in a small town like this get the opportunity to play such an elegant instrument? It's so beautiful."

Nadine smiled. Everyone who entered was taken aback by its glorious presence.

"And how busy are you?" she asked.

"Well, when you have Nettie Wagner as a friend...she has brought me two families just this week."

"That's wonderful, dear. I was hoping to ask a favor myself."

"Whatever I can do, Mrs. Thomason." Nadine wished she had time to tell Mrs. Thomason how appreciative she was for the generosity shown to her in these last weeks. Her little upstairs room was warm and stocked primarily due to her church ladies and Nettie.

"Well this rarely happens, but we have a funeral at the church Saturday. Our usual pianist, Mrs. Coombs, is out of town and her backup cut her finger slicing carrots. Would you be so kind as to fill in? Just a hymn or two? It will be a small gathering at noon."

Nadine rolled her tense lips together. She'd yet to venture out of her cocoon. Her rapid heartbeat was insisting she decline.

"Nettie has shared how wonderfully you play." Mrs. Thomason smiled. "I know it's last minute, but she said you play many things by heart. What a gifting from God."

Why had she just sounded so willing? "Yes, I can come." She let out a held breath. Surely Nettie would accompany her.

"Silly Nilly, you'll be fine." Nettie shook her head, walking across the Feed and Seed. "Edgar said he'd be back

before noon. But maybe they asked him to stay for supper—I don't know. You know where the church is? Down a
block on the left."

"I know where it is…I…I just don't want to go alone."

"I was the one who didn't want you moving so soon
to the little upstairs room. That's just plain alone." Nettie
wagged her finger.

"I feel safe up there. I didn't want to be in the way of
your freighter friend." Glancing at the clock, Nadine felt
her stomach clench. Eleven forty-five.

Maybe she would just skip showing up. No, she would
never take advantage of Mrs. Thomason's generosity. "All
right." She took in a deep breath. "I'm going."

"If Edgar shows up, I promise to escort you home."
Nettie smiled. "And Nadine." Nettie dropped her chin,
casting those gentle green eyes. "You play better than anyone I know. You look beautiful now that you do your own
hair. The families love having a piano teacher. You fit in
here. Just believe it. God is blessing you."

Nadine tried to let her words sink in as she headed out
the front door. Looking side to side, she put one hurried
foot in front of the other until she looked up to see Mrs.
Thomason waiting in front of the church.

"Everyone's already seated. Let's sneak in the side door
and sit up front." Mrs. Thomason linked arms with her and
they walked in, sliding into the front pew.

Nadine felt that God *had* blessed her. Mrs. Thomason's
company was comforting. She could feel her body calming as Pastor Thompson went to the podium and thanked

everyone for coming. He read the epithet of an elderly woman named Mrs. Helen Burden. She sounded like she'd lived a full life; a widow, her husband a captain in the Civil War, raised a large family, so many grandchildren and fifteen great grandchildren. Goodness.

"I'd like to invite our pianist now to play Mrs. Burden's favorite hymn, appropriately, 'Safe in the Arms of Jesus.' Please rise: page 222."

Nadine's heart gave a jump as she carefully made her way to the simple church piano. Gently she placed her hands on the keys and straightened her back. This was going to be fine, she reassured herself, as she started the notes to the familiar hymn. The pastor nodded at her as he joined his strong baritone voice. *"Safe in the Arms of Jesus, safe on His gentle breast, there His love o'er shaded, Sweetly my soul shall rest…"*

Perfect for a funeral, Nadine thought, wondering if her family had decided it would be appropriate. She glanced to the other side of the row and met a pair of striking gray blue eyes staring at her. Her stomach was suddenly in her throat.

He was…was it? She missed a note and quickly brought her eyes back to the keys. Was it Hayes Sullivan? She could feel the trembling start in her elbows. Her hands, once moving so free from memory of the song, were now betraying her. Why hadn't she opened the hymnal with everyone else? Now her entire arms were shaking.

How dare he stare down at her. And how dare he look so fine in his tailored black three-piece suit and stoic face? Had he come here just to intimidate her?

Oh, heavens; she missed another note! She glanced to Mrs. Thomason with her unspoken request; please come and rescue me. How many more verses?

Clang.

Another sour note. Her hands were trembling so badly. Oh please God… the guests couldn't see it, but they certainly could hear it.

Now her chin was quivering. Why had she agreed to leave her little nest?

"Move over." The authoritative black-suited man came to sit close on the piano bench. In a flawless movement, his hands began to play as hers were freed from ruin. He looked out like she was invisible. Singing, *Only a few more trials, only a few more tears…*

On cue, Nadine rescued a tear before it rolled down her face. Hayes gently closed out the song with perfect execution.

"I'm moved you're overcome with grief for my grandmother," he whispered in her ear. "It was very endearing."

10

Fury has a way of locking someone inside themselves. Hayes never moved, apparently giving himself extended permission to sit on her bench, including the audacity to nod at the pastor and play the closing song flawlessly. Why hadn't he played for his grandmother's funeral himself?

Her fragile emotions were covered by anger, so at least she didn't break down again. He moved out from the bench and began to shake hands with the guests. She looked in every direction, realizing she was trapped in her spot between the casket and the receiving line. It would be a few minutes before it cleared out.

Mrs. Thomason was talking to someone in the far back of the church—she certainly wouldn't be coming to Nadine's rescue. Biting the skin off her bottom lip, she noticed a small girl in a handsome black and gray frock. Her little black silk boots had detailed embroidery on the sides, but it was the sadness in her eyes Nadine observed. She had beautiful cinnamon-colored hair, with soft curls pulled back into a large black ribbon. A short round older woman tapped the little girl on the shoulder, and her heartbreaking eyes rose upward. She slowly took the woman's hand and moved to the back.

"Funny to see you here today."

Nadine looked up to Hayes standing next to her. Over his shoulder, she could see that most of the people had left. She stood and ran her sweaty hands down her black dress.

"Where is your black coat?" His brows creased. "I hope seeing me today wasn't the reason your melody suffered."

"It was not." Blast it. She wasn't going to talk to him. "Can you please excuse me?"

"I can tell you—I was only staring because you look completely different than the last time I saw you. I wasn't sure it was you. I figured you'd left town."

"You know I haven't left town." She hissed. "You sent the sheriff after me."

"After you?" He shook his head, squinting. "A crime, maybe even a murder, was scheduled for that room. You want to act like nothing happened?"

Nadine looked away and back at him. "Who was that darling little child?"

Hayes threw back his head and laughed. "You are the master of redirection. Really, I've never met anyone that can avoid the obvious better than you."

"Should you be laughing at such a time as this?" She pined her pious eyes on him.

"Tell me then—I think you owe me something." His tone beckoned honesty. "Why are you still here?"

"I hardly believe it, but you mentioned you don't judge," she quipped.

"I don't."

"Humm…" She sucked in a breath. "I am alone. I have no money." Her voice was heavy with the short direct words. "I have nowhere to go. And I have never received such forbearance as I have from the women I have met in this town."

"Just the women?"

"Yes, just the women. You may have saved my life, but…" She looked past him. Where had Mrs. Thomason gone?

"But what?" She felt him touch her black sleeve.

"I am grateful for your help." She didn't want to make him angry, his attractive authority intimating her. "It's just that…that…oh my, I think Mrs. Thomason is looking for me." She dodged to the left and felt his warm hand grasp hers. Shocked by his boldness, yet somehow pulled back into the low-lit little sick room. Her vulnerable state was connecting with his strength. His eyes mirrored the same connection.

"Thank you for coming today, Mrs. Von Keller. The child is my grandmother's ward. She lives with our housekeeper and me."

Nadine slowly pulled her hand away. "I am sorry for the loss of your grandmother and my pitiful accompaniment." She swept around him and dashed out the front doors of the church.

Mrs. Fox huffed around the long dining table. Hayes wanted to ignore her, knowing what was coming. His parents had wired to go ahead with his grandmother's service.

They would be out within the month and have a private family service.

"There's a strong possibility my parents will take her back with them," he offered as she marched by.

"Oh, oh oh," Her large frame stopped and sucked in a frightful breath. "I saw them put her in the ground. The Sullivans will dig her up and take her body back home?"

Hayes dropped his head in exhaustion. "No, Mrs. Fox. Not my grandmother. I'm talking about Grace. Can you just bear with me until they come?"

Mrs. Fox untied her apron and threw it on the dining room table. Her head quivered back and forth, her jowls jutting out. "Your grandmother was a saint, Mr. Sullivan. She didn't have to, no, no, no she didn't, but she did; she fought for that tyke." Her finger wagged like a whirlybird. "That poor little babe, left on the front stoop of your parents' fine home. The note *was from* Molly. I read it myself. Your parents wanted to put her in an orphanage." She glared with disgust.

"Mad? Oh, they were mad all right. Where had all that money they gave to Molly gone? She was supposed to go back to Ireland. Your problems were all supposed to just go away. You get that young woman pregnant, and she has to take on all the responsibility!"

Hayes stood. She was going too far.

"I wanted to find her, Mrs. Fox." He tried to keep his voice calm. "I still want to find her. I never knew my parents had paid her to go back to Ireland. I would have taken on the responsibility in a minute, but I was told she was long gone."

"Then why did your grandmother, in her golden years, do it? She knew her own blood. What do you say to that?"

"I don't have anything to say. My grandmother probably did it to spite my parents. How do I even know she is *my child*?" Hayes hated hearing his words aloud that annoyed him daily.

"Because I know Miss Molly. She had eyes only for you. She wasn't like some of the other maids." Mrs. Fox shook her head in defeat. "And in your heart, you know it, too."

Hayes turned on his heel toward the door. This whole day was unnerving. Her confrontation had gotten too personal. His grandmother would never have allowed such frank talk. He contemplated telling her to mind her own business.

Turning back around to face Mrs. Fox, he gripped his forehead. Somewhere deep, beyond all his rational thought, he knew it was wrong to simply tolerate the child. But as long as his grandmother was in charge of raising her, his influence hadn't been needed. Maybe he'd tried to punish Molly long enough.

"What can I do?" He gazed at Mrs. Fox. "Please tell me what to do."

"Late again." George Stevens was older than Hayes, but Hayes was his superior.

"Yes, George. I told you I was under a lot of strain these last weeks at home." Hayes walked past him into his large office and dropped his satchel on his chair.

"The supervisor of the steel and iron works will be here any minute. I can't do my invoice if I don't know what we need to order today," George stated from the open door.

"I worked on it at home." Hayes pulled a stack of papers out of his bag.

"Please tell me you're not leaving early again today. We have a problem with the hay delivery for the teams out on the sites. Our own supplier from the railroad store delivered moldy hay."

"How much do they need to get by?" Hayes rummaged through his messages.

"Just a wagon load, I'd suppose."

"Walk two blocks down to the Feed and Seed," Hayes pointed without looking up, "and order it."

"Can you send Ralph? I have to be out on the site in thirty minutes."

They both looked up to see the supervisor of the steel and iron works walk in. "Send him in." Hayes shook his head. "I'll order the hay later."

Another afternoon in a mad rush and now it was time to pick Grace up at school. He snapped his pocket watch closed and gathered his things to work at home. Looking at the note to order hay, he rolled his eyes. Stalking by the other two men working in his office, he didn't speak to them—he was tired of telling them he was leaving early. He would never tolerate their excuses, but he wanted them to ignore his.

He walked to the school and saw the teacher holding Grace's hand. "Sorry to be late." He looked around. She was the last child left.

"I know, I understand…this is a hard adjustment without Mrs. Burden."

Hayes nodded his thanks to her and reached for Grace's hand. "How did she do today?"

"About the same. Still missing her lovely smile." The teacher looked down to Grace. "But she is taking one of my early readers home tonight. Can you be sure to go over it with her?"

"Yes, of course." Hayes walked away, wondering how mothers did this, some with four or five children.

"Grace, I have only one stop, and then we can get home. Can you help me?"

"Where are we going?" she whispered.

"To order hay for some of the horses that work on the railroad." They walked to the other side of the street and then toward the Feed and Seed. Hayes heard an unusual noise as they approached. The little store front before the feed store was well lit, yellow checkered curtains in the windows.

He slowed down to look over them where he saw a handsome black grand piano. That would explain the strange noise. A child was seated on the bench with…

"Mrs. Von Keller?" Hayes accidentally said out loud. He leaned toward the window, looking closer. Her ridged back, black dress and perfectly featured face. Clearing his throat, he pulled his stiff collar from his neck.

"Is this where we get the hay?" Grace pulled on his finger.

"No, no." He walked on but had to stop and look again. Hanging on the door was a sign.

Piano lessons
Monday through Saturday
Days and Evenings

11

❧❦❧

Hayes thought about taking Grace on all his calls. Miss Wagner, who last time wanted to chew him up and spit him out, was actually kind and helpful. Hayes walked a few steps out, stopping to watch over those yellow checkered curtains. Grace, his new responsibility, was content, sucking a lollypop from Miss Wagner.

A woman entered the little store, and Mrs. Von Keller turned and greeted her. She handed a basket with food to Mrs. Von Keller as she gathered her child and walked out. Hayes moved to the door and stopped short.

A tall young man waved at her from the back curtain. The smiles they both shared seemed a bit more than cordial. He looked up and down the walkway, feeling stupid for watching her. He looked down at Grace, bit hard on his lip, twisted the knob and entered.

Nadine turned from her conversation and froze. Looking back to the tall young man, she thanked him as he nodded his head and left the way he had come in. Hayes wondered why she went from friendly to the man from the back door to spying him like he was the devil. What had he done?

"Mr. Sullivan. It is a surprise to see you today."

"If you would give me a day that I wouldn't surprise you, I'll come back."

She bit back a smile. He'd succeeded in keeping things light.

"I...I... can't think of a day, right off hand. Who is this little beauty with you?" She moved down on one knee, smiling.

"This is Grace, or Gracie. She would like to take piano lessons with you." Nadine appeared about to greet Grace and froze...again.

"With me? Why would she want that, when you play so eloquently?" She stood back up.

"Time." He opened his hands wide. "The thing we all desire, yet somehow eludes us."

"Is that another quote from Buddha?"

Hayes waited to see if she was mocking him, but found it overwhelmingly personal that she remembered their talks in the middle of the night. "No, that's a Hayes Sullivan quote." Why was she smiling again? He felt suddenly nervous; almost flustered. Why was he in here?

"Let me get my tablet and see what might work." She moved over to her desk. Hayes noticed the basket on the piano was full of eggs and bread. "I was hoping for every day after school."

"Every day?" She looked up.

"Not Saturday," He clarified. "Or Sunday."

"I have other children booked on Tuesdays and Thursdays. For the little ones, I usually go only a half an hour."

"I need more, Nadine." The use of her first name slipped out, but it seemed to seize her attention.

"What do you mean?"

"We've always been honest with each other, haven't we?"

She dropped her head to the side, giving him a resigned look for such an ironic statement.

Hayes glanced down at the food basket. "I can pay you a dollar a week."

"What?" She shook her head. "I don't charge anywhere near that."

"Well, I'm about to ask for more than anyone else has, and I want to pay for it." He could tell he was confusing her more.

"Would you agree to have her here every day after school until five thirty? Of course, it would not be about the piano that whole time. She's a compliant child. She could look at books or draw while you teach the other students. It would only be for a few hours."

"You want me to watch her for you?" She put the tablet down. "And I can keep my other students?"

"Of course," He looked to the ground and back up at her. "It seems I am the one in need of help."

She began to tap the pencil on her lip, watching him.

He interrupted her thinking. "I expect my parents in a few weeks. There is a strong possibility she will go back east with them." He wondered if that was helpful.

"Because she is, or was, your grandmother's ward?"

"Correct." The shoes of pretense were certainly feeling snug on his feet now.

"All right. We can try it for a few weeks. I might ask one of the older girls I teach to walk her here after school. Is that all right with you?"

"Yes." He smiled, relieved of some pressure for the first time in weeks.

"Grace, what do you like to be called?" Nadine bent down, observing her face smudged with a sticky sucker. "Grace? Gracie or Miss… what is your last name?"

"Sullivan." Grace lifted a sweet smile.

"Hmm. Just like Hayes," she quipped, her tone inquiring.

Nadine was enjoying this too much. Hayes tried to use his perfectly starched white handkerchief to wipe the sticky sucker from Grace's hand and his. Without water, the cloth just stuck worse. He was so out of place. His handsome gray tweed business suit gave him that air of control but the little child next to him flustered his facade.

"We need to be on our way." They turned to the door. "You will watch her starting tomorrow, then?"

"Starting tomorrow." Nadine relished this small shift of power. Perhaps she should have asked him to leave her time at the Silver Holiday alone. She'd not seen the sheriff and prayed he was too busy to think about her. Yet, they were already out the door, and she didn't want to recollect that terrible day. So much had changed. With a dollar a week, she could pay the Wagners' rent and pay Nettie back for food and supplies.

Locking the front door and checking the wood stove, she blew out the downstairs oil lamps. *A dollar a week! Good heaven's—that was a lot.* She stopped and grabbed the little food basket Mrs. Kary had given her in trade for lessons for Frank.

She had no desire to do any kind of business with Hayes Sullivan—he was too candid and smart. Honestly, she'd never met anyone like him. But that little Grace pulled on her heart. Obviously, he was in a pinch with his grandmother's death.

Gracie Sullivan. Interesting, his grandmother's last name was Burden. Was she a niece of Hayes? He prided himself in honesty—maybe she would just ask him.

Freighter Nick was in town tonight. It was sweet of him to come by and offer an invitation to dinner. Nettie seemed to plan a meal for the back room of the Feed and Seed on these nights. She locked the front door and blew out the light on her desk.

Hayes looked cross when he walked in today. Maybe she should have introduced Nick. Did it look suspicious him coming through the back curtain? Oh, what did it matter?

She headed over to the back of the Feed and Seed. All propriety had literally gone out the window with Mr. Sullivan long ago.

"Edgar's closing up for me in an hour. I wanted to cook the beef and vegetable soup that Nick likes." Nettie looked up as Nadine entered.

"I brought the bread." Nadine put her basket on the table.

"Mrs. Kary?" Nettie frowned. "You'd think she doesn't know the country uses coin."

"It's all right. I got another child today, and it's a dollar a week."

"What!" Nettie stopped stirring. "Who could pay that?"

"It's for Hayes Sullivan." Nadine braced herself for a double word.

"That sweet little girl with the big eyes?" Nettie asked.

Nadine walked over to look in the pot. "You know her?"

"Just from today. Mr. Sullivan actually placed an order with me this afternoon."

"I told you I saw her at the funeral. I'm guessing he's not doing well with his grandmother's passing. But he also said that his family's coming out soon, and they may take her back with them."

"Well then, God will still provide." Nettie smiled. "Nadine, can I ask you a big favor?"

"Of course."

"Would you stay after supper? I found a game that the four of us could play. Usually, Nick and Edgar play checkers or cribbage. But this one needs four players, actually two teams."

"Nellie, I'm flattered. You would like me on your team?" Nadine watched Nettie's flat expression. "Or not..."

"I was wondering if you would ask Edgar to be on your team," Nettie whispered, looking down.

"Well... I can ask..."

"Oh, nells bells...forget I asked." Nettie swept around her and sat with a huff at the table. "I'm ridiculous. I just have such a hard time with..."

"You have feelings for Nick..." It suddenly hit Nadine as she sat next to her friend, resting her hand on her back. "I've been so busy with my new little business...oh, Nettie. I'm a poor excuse for a friend. I didn't think..."

Nettie looked more dejected. "I think he has eyes for you."

Nadine sucked in and covered her hand with her mouth.

"He knows you're a new widow. He would never be rude or...anything."

Nadine sat up straight. "How long have you known him?"

"Almost two years."

"He seems like an honorable man? Yes?" Nadine's fingers tapped quickly on the table.

"Yes." Nettie sighed. "He has always been kind, and he often stays on Saturday night to go to church with us."

"Perfect. Have you seen him talk about or court other women?"

"Not really, except he talks about you."

"Forget that. All I've asked him to do is to mail my parents my letter from another town."

"What? Nadine…why?"

"That's another story. What about you? What is your heart telling you?"

"That's easy." She huffed. "I'm too backward, awkward, duckward…nutward…"

"No. Miss Wagner, your heart," Nadine growled at her. "What are your feelings toward him?"

"Anyone can see he is strong and handsome."

Nadine had never thought that. But she wasn't looking for a man either. "That's a good start. So you are attracted to him?"

"Yes, but not just that. You should hear his story, Nadine. He's been on his own since he was fourteen. His pa was a drunk and kicked him out. He's such a hard worker. He helps everyone."

"Like someone *I* know." Nadine tilted her head.

"There's not a thing wrong with him, so that can only mean it's me."

"Hey! I'm going to sew those lips together." Nadine interrupted. "There *is* nothing wrong with you. Have you told him how you feel?"

"No. That's a bit farfetched, don't you think?"

"Maybe he doesn't think you would ever be interested in him."

"Nadine…" Nettie's shoulders dropped. "I only cook all his favorites and follow him around like a sick puppy. We talk, I laugh at all his funny stories…and then he turns to Edgar and plays checkers."

"He still could be lacking confidence. You just admitted he had a troubled youth. Maybe he's never seen a man in love with a woman."

Nadine caught herself sounding like an expert. She'd thought she was in love—she followed the freedom her heart craved and look at the price she was now paying. She wanted to amend the conversation. "All I'm saying is you are pretty and loving and smart and…it's only a man's loss who doesn't see that from a mile away."

"What's up, buttercups?" Nick entered the back kitchen.

Nadine jumped and rolled her eyes. Why, oh why hadn't she seen it before? They *were* perfect for each other.

12

The black coat was aired out, and Nadine reluctantly slipped her arms inside. The only reminder of anything Marcus ever did right by her; he purchased this coat after she ran away with him. She rubbed her temple, trying to wipe away her unforgivable stupidly.

The brisk afternoon air broke into her painful thoughts as she stepped outside. Still gripping the knob, she looked carefully both ways as she began her anxious walk. She wondered if Hayes would meet her to make sure Grace was accounted for.

The school, a two-story building with tan bricks, was just around the corner. It was one of the finer buildings in Carver, with short brown grass surrounding it. She saw her student Emiline first and asked her if she would mind bringing Grace with her to the little piano store. Nadine dreaded being out any more than she had to. Grace came down the steps to her, and the teacher smiled at Nadine.

"Grace, I'd like you to meet one of my best students Emiline. She comes for lessons and will walk you to my store from now on. So don't go anywhere unless she brings you."

"Okay," Grace replied, staring at the ground.

"Thank you, Emiline. I'll look for you tomorrow."

"Yes, Miss Von Keller." Emiline smiled and walked away.

Nadine watched her for a moment. "Miss Von Keller" was right. Miss Nadine Von Keller, the same young woman who fought to get away from home. Now in broad daylight, she doesn't even like to leave her little building.

On the northeast corner of First Street and a bit out of sight, Hayes leaned against the stone building, watching Nadine talking with the girls. Even though he felt confident she would not forget, his spying on her seemed justified.

From the first time he got a full look at Mrs. Von Keller, she seemed graceful, responsible and refined under her disheveled appearance. Today her hair was swept up in a simple bun. Longer wavy pieces of her deep brown hair framed her face. The black coat was back in place.

He stared, somehow curious about the mysterious defenseless young woman who needed him in the middle of the night. He missed their quiet moments, now feeling the loneliness she'd awakened. Unfortunately, with the loss of his grandmother, he felt like the hapless mess now.

He turned back to his office. Business thankfully was the one thing he still had control over. Home was not home anymore. Mrs. Fox agreed to continue with her daily housekeeping tasks, and she would bathe Grace, but the rest was up to him.

He had never dressed a child until two weeks ago. He didn't understand the layers underneath her little dresses. Mrs. Fox insisted she'd show him once and then it was his to do.

Letting out a heavy sigh, he walked back to his desk and his stack of invoices. How he dreaded bedtime. Surely his grandmother had spoiled her. A story, a favorite stuffed animal, another drink of water; and that was on a good night.

Usually, the tears started in as soon it was time to blow out the light. She 'wanted grandma' and would bawl over and over. Nothing he said seemed to comfort her.

Frankly, Grace was the most irrational child. Many nights he sat in the chair in her room, tormenting himself, *if she really was your child, you would know what to do.* Was that the reason he had no capacity to parent her? He would fall in bed exhausted and wake up to start the routine all over again.

He longed for one evening to get outside to do some shooting. He shook his head, trying to break the melancholy. Focus, he chided himself. He desperately needed to focus on work.

"Hello," Hayes called out to the empty store—only the grand piano seemed present.

"We're coming." Nadine peeked out from the upstairs door.

He waited and looked around. A small line of paper stood behind the keys, the notes all written out and placed above the appropriate spots. Some paper sat on the bench, a line of the capital G across the page, the corresponding note on the scale below it. He hit the G note and listened to the tone of the grand piano. At the top of the paper, it said Grace Sullivan in mostly large forward letters, though the As faced the wrong way. He looked up to them descending the stairs. He couldn't help notice Nadine was holding Grace's hand.

"It was cold today, so after our practice and school work, we made some hot cocoa."

Hayes felt slighted. Nadine had already won her heart, something he-

"She has cows," Grace piped up.

"Here in the store?" He smiled, curiously looking around.

"No…at home. A dairy has cows, and the cows give us milk."

"She is a very good listener." Nadine frowned. "And repeater of my words," she whispered, pulling her hand forward to hand off Grace.

"Where are her home and her dairy?" he asked, taking Grace's hand.

Grace shrugged.

"Here I thought I could get more straight talk from my five-year-old." He stopped, realizing he had called her *his* five-year-old.

Nadine walked past them up to the glass windows. "It is getting quite dark. A few weeks ago it was still light at this time." She smiled coyly and held her hand on the doorknob.

Hayes raised his brows and nodded. "Time to go. Thank you for doing this. I know how hard her care can be."

"It was no problem at all." She met his eyes as he walked close by. "And that *is* the truth."

The next week Nadine wanted to try something different. Nettie's four-person game was fun, but it didn't offer any time alone for Nettie and Nick. Edgar always stayed to eat when Nick was in town. She wondered if-

"Nick, what are you doing at my back door?" Certainly, he wasn't looking for her attention, she hoped.

"Nettie asked me to come by and make sure you are coming to dinner. I brought a deer roast, and she's had it cookin' most the day. It smells like it might melt in your mouth."

"Of course I can come. Would you be willing to do me a favor?"

"Oh sure, I told ya I'd mail any of those letters home."

"No, I have no mail. But…" Her mind was turning. "I want to do the dishes tonight, so I need you to take Nettie on a walk. You've brought the meat, she does all the cooking and she won't let me help. I need you to take her on a stroll. Maybe thirty minutes or so. That should give me time to do the cleanup." They entered the back kitchen where Nettie saw them, too soon for Nick to respond.

"Thank you for the invitation, Nettie." Nadine walked past Nick and began to set the table.

"Is little Grace gone for the day?" Nettie pulled out the steaming meat.

"Yes. She has become a delight of my afternoons. I am going to miss her if she moves back east."

"Who's moving?" Edgar walked in and washed his hands.

"Nadine. Mr. Sullivan has asked her to marry him and be a mother to little Grace." Nettie snickered.

"Nettie Wagner! You are awful!" Nadine swung a cloth napkin at her.

"How long do you have to wear that black dress?" Edgar interjected, bottom lip hanging out.

Nadine and Nettie looked at each other. What a strange question coming from him.

"It's customary to mourn for... a... year." Nadine, perplexed, turned to Nettie.

"Miss Wagner," she smiled, sitting up. "This dinner looks wonderful."

An hour later, even though Nick looked like he was about to have a tooth pulled, he asked Nettie to go on the walk as planned. Nadine would have enjoyed the quiet kitchen except for Edgar sitting like a sack of potatoes at the table. She wanted to shoo him out, but he looked so pitiful sitting with his head hung forward.

"Edgar, maybe you should have some cobbler and coffee now. Who knows how late they will be?

Edgar stayed unmoving. Nadine wondered if he'd fallen asleep. She finished drying the dishes and was putting things away when she turned and saw he'd poured two cups of coffee and two bowls of cobbler.

"Why Edgar, this was nice of you." She slid the bowl and cup away from him and to the other side of the table. Now she was the one who felt uncomfortable. "Was this for Nick or me?"

"You." His head shot up. "Sit down."

Nadine felt herself bristle at his command for her to sit down. He has no social graces, she reminded herself as she pulled out the chair. He often sounded abrupt whoever he talked to. Keeping her head down, she sipped her coffee and nibbled at the cobbler.

How did one act kind without giving the wrong impression? She hadn't been this uncomfortable since being left at the Silver Holiday. Oh Nettie and Nick, where are you? The silence in the backroom kitchen was hanging as thick as wool rugs. Nadine took a larger bite and tried to think of something else.

Tomorrow was Saturday, and she only had an hour appointment. She could clean her room, do her wash and work on her lessons for the upcoming week. *Oh, Nettie, you'd better be making the most of this time, because I can feel your brother staring at me.* She took another large gulp of coffee. *And his hand is inching closer to me...*

"Well...thank you, Edgar, for the coffee and cobbler. I should be going." She dropped her things in the cold water. "Please tell Nettie and Nick good night." She grabbed the back door knob and almost flew next door.

Turning the lock to her little store, she stopped to calm her erratic heartbeat. Edgar has always been different. It was just too uncomfortable to be alone with him. Nettie had always been the buffer. Never, never would she allow that again.

Nadine awoke to a pitch black upstairs room, heavy rain pounding on the roof. She turned over and grabbed her belly. It felt like someone had kicked her in the gut. The rain was somewhat a distraction, but something had gone terribly sour from dinner.

She gripped her side and roughly flipped off her covers. Opening up the front of the little stove, the warm firelight illuminated what she was looking for. For heaven's sake, she hadn't had to use a chamber pot in the middle of the night since she was a child. She paced back and forth around the bed as the pain wrapped around her back and stomach. She picked up the chamber pot and set it on the chair. Maybe she should just get down to the outhouse.

A wave of nausea hit, and she fell back into bed. Hot and cold shivers ran up and down her spine. She clutched the sheets and began to moan.

"What now?" All those little hands on the piano. What had she caught? Why did she think she could do this? This is why a woman can't live alone. *Oh mama, I would take your care now.*

Another hard shot of pain curled her up. It passed for a moment, then she reached far off the bed and pulled the chamber pot into bed. Before she could get her next breath, she vomited.

The beef and potatoes were cooked perfectly, she whimpered. What is this horrendous burning? Setting the pot on the floor, she grabbed her pillow and tried to wrap her shivering body around it. What had she possibly eaten that would cause this?

Rocking back and forth, she stilled for a moment, feeling the gush onto her nightgown. She flipped the pillow and sheets away to see blood soaking her bedding. "No… ohh….nooo," she cried out, holding her shivering legs. "Please God…no…no…no…"

Disoriented, Nadine tried to sit up in bed.

"Nadine, your two o'clock lesson is here," Nettie said through her door.

"Nettie." Her was voice raspy. "Please tell her how sorry I am. I caught a stomach ailment and have…been…in bed all day." Nadine bit on her finger as the tears rolled down her cheeks. So many lies. What's one more?

"Dear friend, I'm so sorry. I will get you some soup."

"No, Nettie…please…I just need to sleep. I couldn't possibly eat anything."

"But you sound terrible and so sad. Can I just come in and wipe your brow?"

Nadine struggled to find her voice. Dizzy she lay back down. "Maybe later."

"Okay then, you rest and I will be back to check on you."

When she heard Nettie close the back door, she turned into her pillow and sobbed, rocking back and forth.

Before the sun set and darkened her room, Nadine crawled from the bed. She slipped the heavy black coat on and buttoned it over her chemise and pantaloons. Her once soft, beautiful nightgown was now covered in blood and rolled into a ball with the stained sheet.

She tried to take a rag and water and clean the mattress, but it was no use. Hopefully, Nettie would never see it. What was left of the top sheet she had to tear and roll into pads.

Her cramping and bleeding had decreased but still continued. She sat on the edge of the bed, emotions locked in a new prison cell. Her baby was gone. The one thing she could love was gone. Her future, her one ray of hope, now faded to nothing. She thought her sin and shame might be forgivable; apparently not.

Without realizing the dark shadows had overtaken the room, Nettie's knock made her look up. The heavy coat tried to add weight to every weak step. Cracking the door she peaked out. "I'm doing better. Thank you for checking on me."

"Can I come in? Don't take this wrong, but you still sound like a train ran you over." Nettie held up the lantern, flashing a crooked smile.

"I'd rather not. I just want to sleep, and tomorrow too."

"Okay, but when you feel better, I want to tell you about the walk with Nick." Nettie raised her eyebrows.

"Of course." Nadine knew she should show some interest, but nothing in her would respond. "Good night."

13

Wet pelts hit the top of her head. The rain was felt but unseen in the pitch black of the night. But she didn't need to see. If she walked straight out from the back of the store, she would find the trees and underbrush, and then all she had to do was walk straight back.

She couldn't risk drawing the attention a lantern might bring. No one would see her bury her shame. Wobbling to pull the black coat free from the underbrush, she found the strength to move up the hill. If there was any way to dig a hole large enough for her, she would. The tiny little life now gone, wrapped in blood-soaked rags. They should have died together.

Looking back, she couldn't make out the buildings, rain soaking her hair down into her face. Just a bit further. This would be her own private cemetery. When her body began to shake from the exertion, she fell on her knees and dropped her bundle.

With only a large metal cooking spoon, she began to dig in the soft soil. The rain and dirt fell back into the hole, so she gave up and scooped the dirt out with her hands.

When it was finally big enough, she pulled the bundle over and put it in. Covering it back up, she found larger rocks to place on top.

Leaning back on her heels, she wondered if God would give her strength to even say a prayer. Was her judgment over, or just starting anew?

She reached up for a branch to steady her weary body. A large, dark, ominous object moved in between the brush. She jolted backward, using the small tree like some pitiful shield. She wiped the rain off her face, trying to see through the gritty mud smeared across her cheeks.

It moved again, and she screamed. As it weaved closer, she stumbled back on the hem of the coat, landing on her backside. She found another tree to slide behind before she realized it was only a large dog sniffing around.

Peering into the darkness, she didn't see anything else moving. Her heart was beating so erratically she barely remembered which way was back to her store. Down the small hill, one muddy step at a time, she gripped each thin tree for support, finally making sight of her back door.

Stepping in and locking the door, she dropped her wet coat and muddy shoes. Dizziness overwhelmed her as she tried to steady her reckless breathing. She dragged her cold and shivering body upstairs and found a blanket. Grabbing her pillow, she lay on the floor in front of the little stove. Every bone and muscle, from head to toe, ached. The hard floor matched her condition perfectly.

Pink curtains waved softly from the open window. She was home in her safe room. Even in her sleep she knew the hard floor was not her bed. Dark shadows replaced the light of her old room. "Remember me?" The dark form came out from behind a tree and loomed closer. Nadine felt like a cornered animal, terrified and panicked. She needed to awaken. *Please, back to my room, where is my bed and soft covers?*

"You were supposed to work for me, remember?" His tone was low and threatening.

More darkness and confusion loomed in. Blinking past the rain, she recognized the terrifying man, Clyde, from the hotel. *Mother, father, someone find me. Someone...help, she screamed, but no sound would come out.*

"Your man Marcus took off with two of my best gals and left me with a pregnant broad. I was even willing to wait, keep you hid away, 'cause with a face like yours... umm... umm. But you demanded, you would never, never..."

"Never." Nadine growled low.

"But now your little problem is gone, so you're coming with me. Your man didn't know who he was messing with." A swift blur of dark grabbed her arm. He jerked her so hard she shot past him, tumbling into a dark hole. Heavy, wet dirt and rocks hit her head...*I'd rather be buried alive*...a large rock fell swiftly toward her, a split second from crushing her skull.

Nadine woke up with a start. Her heart was pounding hard and she felt another wave of nausea. Nausea meant she must still be...she looked around quickly, the few early rays coming through the window. She'd slept on the hard floor, her sheets were gone, and her fingernails were caked with dirt. It wasn't all a dream. She closed her eyes. These last two days had been nothing but an unending nightmare.

Monday afternoon, Nadine slowly opened the door to receive Grace from Emiline.

"Thank you, Emiline. I'll see you tomorrow," she whispered, closing the door.

"Unfortunately, Miss Gracie, I've spent the last few days in bed with a tummy ache. Have you ever had a tummy ache?" Nadine took her hand and slowly walked up to the inside staircase.

"Yes, I have," Grace answered with those beautiful sweet eyes.

"Well then, I hope you will be all right if we skip piano today. I was wondering if we could maybe curl up and read books. Do you have some from school?"

"Yes. I can read to you, and you can rest." Grace followed Nadine up the stairs.

"Perfect, little goose; I would love that."

After work, Hayes walked his horse down to the front of Nadine's store. The sun was gone, and a chill was already in the air. He tied the horse up, wondering why everything looked so dark.

This past week, he'd gotten used to meeting Nadine at the door. He imagined she lingered near the windows, planning how to pass Grace over without letting him in. Only a few words of small talk about Grace and then she would nod goodbye. He turned the knob, surprised she wasn't in place poised to give him the nightly rushed dismissal.

"Hello," he called out to the large empty area. Probably having tea or cocoa, he pondered. He approached the stairs. "Hello," he called upward. He waited and heard nothing.

It was so strange, no warmth from the wood stove, no lights lit. He looked on top of the piano, no lessons lying around. The place seemed deserted, strangely empty.

His mouth went dry. What if something had happened to Nadine or Grace? What if someone had kidnapped them? What was he thinking to leave Gracie in the care of a woman who had obvious troubles? He started up the stairs and turned around quickly.

"Settle yourself, man." He exhaled the correction. They're probably just next door with Miss Wagner. He ran down the steps and stalked the five large strides to the front door, going out. Approaching the next door, he saw it was closed. He peered through the windows and saw no one about.

"This is ridiculous." Grunting, he went back into Nadine's store and called louder, "Nadine! Grace!" Taking the steps two at a time, he flung open the door to the up-stairs room.

The room was sparsely furnished with a few dark shad-ows across the floor and bed. He saw Nadine, who rose swiftly, bumping Grace from the crook of her arm.

"Oh, I'm so sorry…" She swung her feet off the barren mattress and stood quickly. "We must have fallen…asleep." She swung back, helping Grace stand.

Hayes' breathing had almost returned to normal when Nadine swayed forward, eyes rolling—trying to grasp thin air.

"Hang on." He gripped her waist as her body went limp against him. He pulled his arm across her back and pulled her legs up with his other arm. "Grace, do you know what's wrong with her?" He debated putting her back on the bed.

"She has a tummy ache," she mumbled, rubbing her eyes.

"Follow me, Grace." He turned and carried Nadine down the steps.

"Open the door."

Grace ran around and opened it and pulled it closed behind them. "Stay with me," he said, nodding to her as he marched across the street and down half the block.

Nadine pulled her head up from his shoulder. "What happened?" She looked around. He took the steps up toward the doctor's office.

"Hayes, please, just wait," She begged breathlessly. "I just fainted…I…just…got up…too fast…" She tried to push away from him, but he held her tight. "Can you put me down, give me a chance to show you. You don't need to see a doctor for fainting."

"Unless I say you do. Gracie, knock on the door."

"Gracie love, don't knock-"

Hayes moved in and pounded twice. "He's going to wonder about us…" Hayes raised his eyebrows, tongue rolling inside his cheek. "And I think you've gained weight." He lifted her up closer, smirking.

Nadine growled and failed again to push free from his arms.

The door swung open, and the doctor gave them a strange look. "Mrs. Von Keller. I can see you are conscious this time."

"I just fainted." she fumed, as Hayes walked her in and placed her on the examination bed in the first room. She sat stiffed backed with her arms folded across her chest. "Mr. Sullivan seems to have an agreement with you. Does he get two bits from every damsel he brings here?"

"Ha!" The doctor laughed. "What a grand idea. Since you are alive and breathing, I want to grab my supper before it turns black. But stay put, Mrs. Von Keller. You are very pale, and I want to hear what's going on."

Hayes took Grace by the shoulder and led her to a chair in the hallway.

He walked back in wondering if she would be forgiving or hateful.

"I don't need to be here. This is very embarrassing." She glared at him.

"How do you think I felt, coming to pick up Grace…no lights…no one anywhere?"

"I am sorry about that. We both fell asleep."

"Do you often sleep in the afternoon? Why don't you have any bedding?"

"No." She slumped her stiff back. "I'd been... sick... over the w...we...weekend."

"Obviously. As soon as you stood up, you fainted. Have you eaten at all?"

"Yes, Nettie has... been bringing me soup."

"Does this happen to you often?"

He could tell she resented his questions but leaned in any way. "Maybe you are expecting?"

Her eyes suddenly narrowed, and her nostrils flared. Somehow she seemed even paler—maybe she was about to faint again.

"Mr. Sullivan." Her voice was heavy and thick. "You are the m...most e...ego...egotistical, cond...condescending, impertinent..." She sucked in a breath and locked her jaw. "Man I have ever...met. I would like you to get out!" Her arm flew up, pointing to the door. "I don't care to ever see you again!"

Hayes took a steadying step back. What did he say? He was only asking a question that might explain her condition, wasn't he? This reaction was beyond-

"I have grown fond of Grace." Her chin quivered. "But I w...will n...n...no longer be able to h...hel...help with her care because it would mean see...seeing you. You'll have to..fi...find someone else."

"Nadine, I am sorry." He stepped forward, realizing to late he was out of line.

"Stop... don't. "She glared, shaking her head.

"I just want to be your friend," he continued firmly, wondering if it was even true.

"Listen to me, Hayes…" The air thickened the space between them. "You are the kind of friend I'll never want. Just get out."

14

Hayes held his pocket watch close to the flickering candle sitting on his bedside table. Three in the morning, and he'd yet to sleep. Rising, he stooped in front of his fireplace, pushing the embers around. The almost empty wine bottle stood on the table, reminding him of his futile attempt at drowning out his evening.

He pulled the pillow off the chair and threw it on the rug. Flopping on his back, he rested his head on the pillow, staring at the hot glow. Why did he ask her if she was pregnant? He'd rehearsed it over a hundred different ways.

For some reason, from the first moments he'd met her, he had trouble believing her. But what did it really matter? He said he didn't judge, yet her lack of cordiality towards him...hurt. Would he look at every beautiful woman and judge how soon she would reject him? He was impertinent and brash, but deep in his heart, he did want to be a friend.

He should have been respectful of her station as an alone, frightened widow. Didn't he read in the Bible true religion was taking care of orphans and widows? He rubbed his hands up and down his face. He was two for two. God had put an orphan and a widow in his life, and he'd failed miserably at helping both.

What would he do if his parents would not take Grace? Since she had spent after school time with Nadine, she was happy. She hadn't cried herself to sleep once. He arched his back off the hard floor.

"Why didn't I keep my mouth shut? Lord, I don't want to be resentful. Can you do anything with me?"

He sat up and wrapped his arms around his knees. *Please, Lord, I believe you've written many things to lead us to greater truth, peace.* In the shadows, he saw his Bible on his desk. Picking up the flickering candlestick, he set it down and looked to the page it was open to.

Philippians 2. Something in here was for his grand-mother's funeral…verse three…*Let nothing be done through selfish ambition or conceit, but in lowliness of mind.* Lowliness of mind. What an odd idea. He'd always challenged himself in using the mind for all its superior ways. Why would a brilliant God ask His creation to use lowliness of mind?

He read on; *let each esteem others better than himself.* He sat back in the chair and raked his hands through his hair. Coming back quickly, he placed his elbows on the desk. The paper and inkwell seemed to call to him. *Esteem others.* All right, Lord…I'll try.

Rolling over with only her pillow and one blanket to clutch, Nadine let out a long sigh. She needed to make a decision. Why hadn't she waited to mail that letter to her parents? Certainly, they had already received her pack of lies. Over and over she tried to form the words for the next letter.

She rose up and scanned her little upstairs home. It once held some kind of future for her and the baby. How stupid, she'd naively believed she could teach piano and raise her little one herself. Chewing on her bottom lip, she closed her eyes. Now she even lied to herself. This place did nothing but depress her more.

She looked over to her small nightstand. The doctor had sent her home with a bottle of blackstrap molasses. He prodded about her dizzy spells and pale coloring. He didn't seem to believe her tummy ache reasoning.

And then there was Hayes. Oh, if her stuttering weren't so bad, the other words she would have liked to call him. Frowning, she picked up the spoon and poured the thick dark molasses into it. Closing her eyes, she swallowed the elixir. Without his money coming in, she would have to save for a month for stage fare to Wisconsin.

She set the spoon down, already missing Grace. She was such sweet little thing. The way she curled up next to her yesterday was like a warm balm for her soul. Surely Mr. Sullivan never wanted to see her again either, she thought, pulling on her black dress.

He looked so despondent, so wounded. Probably a façade, she grunted, finishing her last button. It was time to see Nettie. Once again her kindness was sacrificial, and she hadn't even taken a moment to ask her about the stroll with Nick.

"He hardly said ten words." Nettie huffed. "And I tried to shut up. You would be proud of that."

Nadine sat at the table in the back room of the Feed and Seed. "Did you ask him questions, oh, I don't know, about his other stops or…" Nadine quit when she saw Nettie lower a crooked frown.

"I couldn't think of one good question. I'm doomed to be an old maid." Nettie plopped in the chair next to Nadine. "We did share a smile when we both stepped off the sidewalk at the same time. Our shoulders…touched." She slapped the top of her forehead. "That sounds pathetic."

"Nadine…Nadine?"

Nadine looked back at her, realizing she was somewhere else. "I'm sorry. I was listening, really…"

"I hope you don't have a busy day, friend. You still look so pale and drawn," Nettie said. "I prayed for you. Do you think it was something you ate?"

"Maybe." Nadine dropped her head to the side. "I had coffee and cobbler with Edgar."

"You did?"

"I think he was waiting for Nick to come back, so I was just trying to distract him, I guess. But hours after that…Oh…I can't speak of it…terrible; just terrible." Nadine rose. "Thank you for the biscuit. It helped." She waited until Nettie got up, then hugged her. "You are the dearest person I know." Nadine felt fresh tears trying to overflow. She released her quickly and headed to the back door. "We'll catch up later."

"Yes; come by as soon as Gracie leaves."

Nadine stood at the back door of her little store, hand on the rusty knob. She rolled her eyes but couldn't stop the tears from overflowing. Grace wasn't coming back...just like the tiny someone from her womb. She slowly looked back up the small hill of brush and trees.

She hadn't had the strength that night, but something in her wanted to now. She looked around the back side of the block of buildings. No one was about. Crossing the small gravel road used for deliveries, she walked up into her secret area. Some of the rocks had slid down from the rain, so she carefully placed them all back and stood over the grave.

Dear Lord, I have no hymn to sing, no words worth your time. But I pray you would forgive my sin... She clutched her hand over her mouth and smothered her sob. *Please... m... me... merciful Father, receive this wee one into your care. Amen.*

Taking a deep breath, Nadine walked back into her building and headed to her little desk across from the piano. She had Emiline's older sister at ten and then two students after school. She was thankful for Mrs. Thomason lending her the pages of sheet music. She needed some more challenging pieces for her older students.

Lighting the oil lamp and putting some wood in the stove, she came back to the piano and arranged her lessons. Nettie had asked her last week about having Thanksgiving with her family. Staring out her front windows, she knew she would be a terrible guest.

A dark gray cloud moved over the new day sun. Could she possibly make it through the winter here? Mr. Wagner had assured her any amount of business was better than no business. But their generosity seemed so extravagant.

Something white lay on the floor in front of her door. She walked over and picked up a letter. She flipped it back and forth, only to find "Mrs. Von Keller" written in beautiful script. Someone must have slid it under the door. Slowly she opened it and unfolded the pages. Who would this be from? Flipping to the other side of the paper she saw; "Respectfully, Hayes Sullivan" at the end.

Shaking her head, she dropped the paper onto the piano. Walking slowly around the large piano three, four times, she thought about throwing it into the wood stove. Were there any words to excuse his rudeness? Asking her if she was expecting after what she'd just gone through. It was an unforgivable vulgarity.

Nadine stopped and tapped her fingers rhythmically on the shiny black finish. She wanted to be forgiven for her folly; how interesting that she had no charity to give away. She chewed on her pinky fingernail. Nettie had such strong convictions that God forgives everything, and He even calls us a new creation.

She walked over to the steps to the upper room and sat down. Forgiveness was so incredibly difficult. If she was to forgive Hayes, would she have to forgive Marcus as well?

Closing her eyes, she dropped her head to her knees. *Lord, you know I can't do it. I have no earthy ability to just casually wave off these offenses. And yet, it is the very thing I want from You.* She squeezed her head with her hands and turned to look at the letter sitting atop the piano. Letting out a long sigh, she walked over, picked it up and sat on the piano bench.

Dearest Mrs. Von Keller,

Your first thoughts would be that I write this apology to see Grace reinstated into your care. This is not the motive of my words. I want to speak as a man humbled. Your words sent me to a deep place of self-evaluation. I believe I know why pride has taken hold of my good sense and I want to take responsibility for the change I know needs to take place. This letter is a first step I would like to take if you would be so gracious to hear me out.

According to the Hopi, Spider Woman sang the world into existence, a word at a time. In the New Testament Book of John, "In the beginning was the word." Ethiopians believe God created both the world and himself by saying his own name. The Egyptian god, Thoth, created the word through language. Indians, and Nada Brahma believe the same. Existence was by one song, one word, one note.

There is power in the spoken word. I do believe that. I choose to follow the God of the Bible. That's how I was raised. He has instructed me in the night hour by His Word and Spirit.

My words and familiarity were pernicious. They were and have been disrespectful; hurtful to your plight, your heart, your beauty. I have thought of myself over you. I have questioned you like you were on trial and lent no forbearance to your circumstances.

You are absolutely correct in saying that is a friend you will never need. I know there is little I can do to make recompense. But I am truly sorry. I feel sick within myself and have only myself to blame.

You are amazingly strong and resilient, and I likely felt threatened by the very gifts God has given you. And I will admit it now, though nebulous, that I think I have been envious of your connection with Grace. I feel this is something else God is challenging me with. I struggle in a dark place these hours before dawn. In humility, I do want your forgiveness, yet I truly understand if reconciliation is not warranted.

Respectfully, Hayes Sullivan

Nadine straightened her back and looked about the room. His words were truly touching. She glanced back at the form and excellence of his handwriting. He was an academic through and through, yet somewhat like a poet. How strange to hear this stirring eloquence from his heart.

It was the same extraordinary feeling she had when they talked in the middle of the night. A surprising familiarity existed between them. It made no sense, yet her heart had lifted to a new place. She placed her fingers lightly on the piano and played a soft chord. Humm, what to do? She played a few more chords and let the soft melody go where it wished.

That afternoon, out of the corner of his eye, Hayes saw Ralph and George rise from their desks, standing stiffly.

Like the parting of waters, Nadine timidly entered the railroad office, in full black dress and coat, ignoring their stares. She met his gaze and walked slowly to his open door. He blinked to make sure he hadn't fallen asleep at his desk. Expressionless, she waited. He finally rose and extended his hand. "Please come in."

She brought her hands around from her back and handed him a folded piece of paper. Her eyes held his, but she would give no hint to what he would read. He opened it and read the few lines.

'I accept your apology. As words can create, they can also hurt, and some have the power to heal. I would love to continue to watch Grace.'

He knew his mouth probably hung open and he glanced over her shoulder as the men turned quickly to act like they weren't watching this strange encounter.

"Thank you," he mumbled, folding the paper with heart pounding. "Can I walk you back to your piano...I mean your store?"

She smiled at his mishap. Not only did she appear forgiving, but she'd also walked bravely into his office, turning his stomach upside down.

"I think I will venture on to the Nickel Emporium, and then pick up Grace from school, if it's all right with you, of course."

"Of course." He swallowed hard, savoring her deep brown eyes. He'd started his day with little hope of ever talking to her again. Now they seemed back to sharing parental roles. Something between severe attraction and redemption warmed him through and through. He scratched the back of his head and gave her an awkward smile.

"I can't...thank you...enough."

15

Still glancing left to right, Nadine checked her surroundings before turning the corner. Nettie had told her the Nickel Emporium had a mixture of things the Carver Mercantile didn't carry. And it was down the street from the railroad office, farther away from the Silver Holiday. The crisp fall day seemed to breathe a bit of fresh new life in her. Either that or blackstrap molasses. She opened the door and heard the small tinkle of a little bell. The store smelled like beeswax and rosewater.

She had almost forgotten how much she enjoyed shopping. Her eyes were delighted to see racks and stands of little things everywhere. She turned to her right and saw various candles and soaps on a shelf. She took her time picking them up and enjoying each scent. Looking one last time at the street, she tried to settle her nerves and move down the aisle.

"Is there anything, in particular I can help you locate, Ma'am?" a young man with a thin mustache asked.

"No thank you. I'm just enjoying the luxury of looking." She smiled as he nodded and moved on.

On an old wooden table some leather pouches and bags caught her eye. She fingered the soft pieces and noticed some longs strips with some kind of printing on them. She picked up what looked like a bookmark of some kind. "I can do all things through Christ which strengtheneth me." This would be perfect for Nettie, she thought. Two for a penny, a little card said. She supposed this would be a needed word for her also. Even though she needed some new bedding, these were also a required purchase.

She walked on, thinking about the strength it had taken to walk into Hayes' office. The shock on his face reassured her he understood what a huge step it was. Before reading the letter, she could find no forgiveness for him. Yet something in his words—the sincerity, the repentance, was like nothing she'd ever heard before. He had every right to be angry with a caregiver asleep on the job, knowing full well she'd yet to explain why her life was a precarious mess. He could have shamed her for putting Grace at risk, but he didn't.

Nadine found a simple cloth to cover the old mattress in her room. Taking it and the bookmarkers to the counter, the clerk took her money and wrapped her purchases. She walked slowly to the door and front windows, looking across the street.

Some of the children were walking down the steps as school let out. Perfect timing. Little Grace was a gift. Nadine's own loss was so deep and personal and yet this little one also experienced loss; the loss of her grandmother, her caretaker.

Holding her hand forward, Nadine met Grace as she skipped across the empty street to meet her. Her big round eyes stared up with admiration toward any of the attention Nadine gave her. *God, you have seen my heart and given me strength.*

Pushing his hands through his short hair, Hayes approached Nadine's store and cleared his throat. The lights were on, and he looked over the checkered curtains to see Nadine sitting on the piano bench with Grace. He tried the door and found it locked. At the same time, she looked up and jumped to meet him at the door.

"It's getting so dark now." She looked at the ground. "Do you mind if I lock it when it's just the two of us here?"

He walked in. "No, no, I think that's smart."

She looked up and his eyes locked on hers.

Nadine pulled on the collar of the black dress. "We had a good afternoon." Her voice was broken and shaky as she moved away. He wanted to ask her how she was feeling, but didn't want to risk the familiarity. Though she did look tired, the way those brown eyes and long lashes met him, oh heaven help him, instead of more distance there seemed to be more awareness. He had a sudden urge to grab her, hold her and comfort her.

"So… Grace…" He patted her head. "Are you ready? Where is your coat?

Nadine pulled it off her desk chair and bent down to help Grace with the buttons. "Tomorrow we will work on the 'cat in the barn,' yes?"

Grace nodded. Nadine gave her a quick peck on the cheek and stood, frowning. "Sorry," she whispered.

Hayes realized she was referring to his letter. "It's okay." He smiled. "Really." How could he fault her kindness to Grace? He knew he stared to long, oh, how he wanted to touch those loose brown strands of hair. "We're off." He grabbed Grace by the shoulder and led her out.

"Nadine, I love it!" Nettie held up the leather bookmark as she stirred the beans. "This was so thoughtful, and I am so proud you ventured out. Speaking of that, my mother keeps asking about Thanksgiving. I really want you to come. I want to ask Nick too. It would be so much easier if it weren't just him sitting at my family table."

"I would love to, I just feel embarrassed by your wonderful family and their kindness toward me. I will never be able to pay them back."

Nettie walked over to the table and grabbed her zippered pouch. She took out a penny and handed it to Nadine. "I owe you this for the wonderful bookmark."

Nadine shook her head and marched away from Nettie's extended hand. "It was a gift." Watching Nettie plop the coin back in the pouch, she looked up quickly to her friend's dropped chin.

"Mmm hmm." Nettie grimaced. "How do you think we feel? God has blessed us, and we in turn love to bless others… unless the others don't feel worthy of His gifts?"

"Why are you running this store? You need a pulpit." Nadine announced, shaking her head. "Move over and let me help with the cornbread."

Nadine set the table and tried to push away Miss Nettie Nosey's words. Of course, she didn't feel worthy of any gifts. The other truth was the Wagner house was around the corner from the Silver Holiday. It had been a miracle to walk to the railroad office and the Nickel Emporium today, but to venture anywhere near the Silver Holiday?

She sucked in a deep breath. "Nettie, I would love to come if you don't mind walking to and from my store with me."

They looked up as Nick walked in. "I'd be happy to walk you. Where do you need to be?"

Nadine gave him a reluctant smile. "We were talking about Thanksgiving."

"Yes, Nick." Nettie cut in. "My family would love to have you for the meal."

"And I need Nettie as my escort because she's going to help me with…with making ah…a pie."

"Mmm, what kinda pie you gals cookin' up?

Nettie and Nadine looked at each other. "Apple." "Pumpkin." They said at the same time. "Whichever one moves us." Nadine fanned her hands out and smiled.

Boxie Roxie sauntered in and flopped down on the braided rug. "Has that cat gotten even wider?" Nadine asked.

"My guess is kittens are coming," Nick added as he bent down to scratch under Roxie's chin.

"Least someone has a boyfriend," Nettie mumbled over the stove. Nadine looked at her wide-eyed, pressing her lips together and fighting back a belly laugh.

"Oops. Did that come out...loud?" Nettie whispered, glancing at Nick as he played with the cat.

Nadine slowly nodded. Laughter spilled out as they quickly moved to get the meal on the table.

Edgar walked in and grabbed a bowl. "Everything's locked up," he told Nettie. They sat down together, like some upside down backwoods family, and passed the food. The men were scooping in the hot beans fast, and Nettie and Nadine shook their heads at each other.

Both young women could be home at their families' fine table, and yet this was their choice. So many things were unconventional, Nadine thought as she took a bite. But different isn't always bad.

"So Nick, can you join the Wagners for Thanksgiving?" Nadine asked.

Nick nodded. "I'd like that. Nettie, can you ask your pa if I can bring the turkey? I've spotted some nice ones on my route."

"Oh no, that's not...ow." Nettie quit when Nadine's foot kicked her shin under the table. They exchanged crossed eyes.

"I know that would be appreciated. I will tell my mother and Alma; she does most of the cooking." Nettie gave Nick a sweet but awkward smile.

"Why aren't you eating?" Edgar growled, looking up from his bowl at Nadine.

Nadine felt uncomfortable again by his abrupt tone.

"I am." She cut her cornbread in half. "But I enjoy conversation around the table." She looked at his pinched expression. He seemed strangely upset with her.

Nadine turned to Nettie. "What time does your family like to eat on Thanksgiving?"

"Let's say one. Maybe we could play the new game after the meal."

"Yes, a wonderful idea. Don't you think, Nick?"

He looked bright-eyed over his glass of milk.

"Cheekers tonight, Nick," Edgar piped in.

Nadine took a deep breath and picked at the warm meal. Nettie did have a problem. It was Edgar, her own brother. Sweet-hearted Nick was probably his only friend. Edgar didn't seem like the type to know when to share or smile or be kind or...much.

16

At Nettie's prodding, Nadine finally got up the nerve to attend church the following Sunday. She hadn't been back since the uncomfortable funeral. She listened to the wonderful message—many parts were truly inspiring, nothing she'd ever felt in her old church. But her one goal was to get out and get out fast. At the last Amen, she whispered thanks to Nettie and headed for the side door Mrs. Thomason had brought her through before. Her heavy black coat was threaded past her arms, with only a few steps to escape.

"Mrs. Von Keller, can I grab you for a moment?"

Nadine swung around to see Gracie's teacher. "Of course, how are you, Miss Pruett?"

"Very well, thanks." She nodded. "I should begin by telling you what a wonderful thing you are doing for Gracie. She has been smiling again and participating in class. We even did a little project about what's in our homes. She drew you inside at the piano and Mr. Sullivan outside with a shot gun in his hand."

Nadine felt her jaw drop open.

"I thought it was sweet, really. Some of the children had their barn animals inside too." She laughed.

Nadine cleared her throat. "I...I... I've never been to their home."

The teacher rattled on as Nadine prayed she'd grasped those last important words.

"But what I really wanted to ask you was if I could have your help for the children's Christmas program next month. I was wondering if you would want to help some of the children you teach learn a few Christmas songs for the program. I'm only in charge of the primary children. We invite the parents and do a little program here at the church. So they could practice with you and hopefully perform here." She glanced at the church piano Nadine had tried to ignore all morning.

"Yes, that would be fine." Nadine buttoned her coat. "Would you like to pick out the songs or..." Nadine reached for the door handle.

"No, no, I trust you know what the parents would like. So many parents have commented to me about how well the lessons are going. You are a wonderful asset to our little town."

"Oh well...thank you." Nadine opened the side door and was stepping out when she saw Mrs. Thomason cut in.

"Nadine! I was so delighted to see you today."

Grace's teacher nodded her goodbye. "I'll be in touch."

Mrs. Thomason had already wrapped her arm around her and stepped outside. "I never really had a chance, but I have wanted to apologize for my complete lack of consideration."

Nadine squinted at her—she could not imagine what she was talking about. "You have been nothing but helpful and kind."

"The funeral." Mrs. Thomason nodded toward the door they'd exited. "It was completely inconsiderate to ask a young woman so fresh with her own loss to play at a funeral. I am so sorry, dear. It was asking too much. I don't know what I was thinking."

"Oh, I never thought of…" Nadine could feel a few sprinkles falling, like her past coming to taunt her. "I never took it as a misstep from you. I never, really, all is…f…fine." She glanced at the crowd leaving the church, looking for an opening.

"Thank you, dear. I wondered if you stayed away because of my thoughtlessness." She sucked in a deep breath and smiled. "Could you join us soon for Sunday dinner? Or better yet, Thanksgiving?"

"That is so kind." Nadine took a few steps back. "The Wagners have invited me for Thanksgiving."

"Perfect." She nodded. "Do you need anything? We'd heard you were ill. My Wednesday morning prayer group has been praying."

"Thank you." Nadine's face flushed while a tremble went through her belly. "You of all people know God has been taking care of me."

Mrs. Thomason smiled and reached out to hug her. "He *is* a good God," she whispered in her ear.

Nadine returned the embrace. Her parents had never showed affection. This care was so... she looked up to see Grace running towards her.

Grace flung herself into the folds of Nadine's skirts. "Hellooo." She looked up with those happy blue eyes, fabric encompassing her.

"I feel some rain. I'd better leave you." Mrs. Thomason scurried off.

Nadine pulled Grace off her legs and fought the desire to sweep her up in her arms. She hadn't expected so much attention. People watch and talk. Maybe she could just make sight of Hayes and get Grace going. What happened to her plan to leave unnoticed?

"Mr. and Mrs. Sullivan are here," Grace squeaked.

Nadine bristled. Hayes' parents, here to take Grace to another family member or...she didn't ask. She looked down at Grace. "Are they enjoying their visit?"

Grace shrugged, "We did a talk at Grandma's grave. Mrs. Sullivan cried."

"I'm sorry. Did it make you sad?" Nadine brushed her fine reddish curls across her forehead.

"Yes." A little frown appeared.

"It's starting to sprinkle. I think you need to get back to the carriage." Nadine walked towards the front as Hayes came around the side of the church building.

He was shaking his head, giving Grace a stern look. "You were to only go to the carriage. You scared me, Grace." He stopped, hands on hips.

"Mrs. Von Keller." He nodded, formal demeanor in place.

"Mr. Sullivan." She nodded back, moving away from Grace. "Should I expect her tomorrow?"

"I…I…" He shook his head as Grace ran off. "I don't know." He turned after the child. "I will be in to talk to you," he called over his shoulder.

The next morning Nadine added wood to her store stove. Between Nick and Edgar, she never had to worry about wood or kindling. It was always stacked and at her disposal. She stood with her back to the stove enjoying the heat, her hands wrapped around a hot mug of coffee. Glancing towards the front door, she spied another white envelope. She set the mug on her desk and went to pick it up. The same well-crafted cursive writing made her smile.

She went to open it, but stopped and tapped it against her lip. What if Gracie was leaving? He probably didn't want to tell her in person. Would he explain where they were taking her? Did she have the right to know? What if they were taking her to an orphanage? Could that happen, being left alone without family or friend? Could Hayes endorse such a horrid idea? Flipping the pages open quickly, she determined she would beg for Grace if they had no suitable plan for her.

Dearest Mrs. Von Keller,

Two one-dollar bills slipped out, and Nadine set them on her desk.

I know I said I would speak with you, but I find writing to you in the middle of the night somehow rehabilitating. My parents are staying through the holiday, and though this trip for them was about paying their respects to my grandmother, they seem unwavering in their decision not to take Grace with them. Nadine looked up to the ceiling. "Thank you."

We were raised in a nine-bedroom home overlooking a beautiful vineyard. The children's house was left of the front driveway. All of my siblings stayed there with nannies until we could sit still at the formal table. We had governesses and tutors and servants all around us.

You can clearly see why it is so difficult for me to see to Grace's upbringing. Besides being a man with no nurturing instincts, I cannot manage her care and the running of the railroad office. Your help has been immeasurably valuable and needed. I have a new respect for many mothers who do the job alone day after day with no domestic help.

Unfortunately, my parents don't share in my distress. My housekeeper Mrs. Fox is as stubborn as they are. Nadine lowered the letter and bit her bottom lip. This was better than a novel. *I have to travel to Minneapolis in a few weeks, and yet they seem to think I can manage it all. It's extremely frustrating.*

None of this is your concern, but somehow getting it out on paper frees up the constriction in my lungs. Please never doubt my gratitude for your care and concern for her. I see the ease you have with her, the special attachment. I am jealous, not of the attachment with you—but between the two of you. The ink seemed to clog up his perfect script.

I've enclosed this week and next week's payment. "I would do it for free," Nadine whispered. *Our family will try to enjoy this holiday time together, and I wanted you to do the same.*

I've wanted to ask you if you would be traveling to family or friends to inquire if you will be alone. If that is the case, I would want to extend an invitation for you to join us. Grace talks about you with the family, unfortunately providing pretense that this is a workable solution. Poor Hayes. She pursed her lips, wishing she had some philosophy to quote back at him. Nadine giggled. "It works for me." *If you are free and could join us, please leave me a note at my office. If I don't hear from you, I'll assume you are otherwise engaged.* Like the Wagner's Thanksgiving wasn't difficult enough; the Sullivan meal would be excruciating.

With Care and Respect,
Hayes Sullivan

Care and respect? Is that how he signed his other letter? Nadine dug it out of her desk drawer. She'd read it over many times, but…no…she flipped the other letter over and held it up next to the new one. Respectfully. The other says, respectfully. *With care,* she bit her bottom lip trying to judge his motives. She would have signed it with distance and disengagement, Nadine Von Keller.

"Ha!" She laughed at her own vindictive humor. Setting the letters on the desk she looked slowly around the large room. She'd changed. Before coming here, she'd been self-centered and manipulating. Slowly her eyes fell down to her black dress—now she was just a liar and a fraud.

The slamming of her back door made her jump.

Nettie flew through the back curtain. "Oh blimey slimy…Nadine, I need you!"

17

Nadine had trouble keeping up with Nettie as she flew around the corner and into the back room of the Feed and Seed.

"I can't get her to get out." Nettie scurried to the dark back corner of the building. Pallets and full burlap feed bags lined the wall. "She's way back there." Nettie pointed for Nadine to look.

"I hope we are talking about Boxie Roxie." Nadine tried to peer in between the slats of wood. "Why get her out? She knows every nook and cranny of this store."

"She's having the kittens!" Nettie said wide-eyed.

"Oh." Nadine felt naïve. "Do you need to help her?"

"Not really. I just want to count them and know they aren't going to crawl off under something and get crushed."

"Ugh." Nadine scowled. "We use to have a veterinarian that would come out and take care of the cows. Do you have one here?"

"Yes, but I don't think he cares about store cats. I suppose I will put some food out in a trail to a box near the back kitchen. She should carry each one out. Oh, sweet sound!

Listen, Nadine." Nettie grabbed her arm and brought her to the opening in the pallets. Nadine clung to her and pretended she knew what they were doing. Soon she was rewarded with the tiniest mew she'd ever heard.

"I hear it," Nadine whispered, smiling.

"Boxie Roxie is a mama." Nettie exhaled and released Nadine. "Guess that makes me a granny." She frowned.

Nadine grabbed her brown calico dress and gave Nettie a playful shake. "Stop it. You will have your own little ones...one day." She hooked her arm and took her back to the kitchen. "Let's have a cup of tea to celebrate. Oh, and I just found out Gracie Sullivan is staying with Hayes."

"And you," Nettie added.

"I think so. I only agreed for these weeks until his family came. From reading his letter, he might just decide to hire a nanny or governess for her."

"He writes you letters?" Nettie filled the tea kettle and smirked over her shoulder.

Nadine rolled her head quickly. "Yes, nothing personal." She considered her own words. Somehow those letters became intensely personal to her. "He paid me for these weeks even though she has been with the family." She watched her friend nod and prepare the tea. The silence wasn't like Nettie.

"Tell me about Nick sitting with your family at church." Nadine took the hot cup and sat down at the table.

"Yes, it is something he always does." Nettie sighed.

Nadine badly wanted to give her tips on getting a man's attention, but all her own efforts just left a trail of pain. "Nettie, you are so much more strong and patient than anyone I've known." Nettie stirred her tea and shrugged. "I know God has something wonderful for you, I just know it. So…what are you wearing for Thanksgiving?"

Nettie's face shot up. "I hadn't thought about it. Why?"

"You looked special at church. Was that a new dress?"

"No, it's the same one I wear every week."

Nadine reached over and squeezed her arm. "Then let's make those pies, find a box for Roxie and get to some shopping."

"One more pin." Nadine held Nettie's hot ironed curls in place as she secured them behind her head.

Nettie held the mirror up, trying to see. "This is so much fuss for turkey and potatoes."

"Oh, oh, my dear…" Nadine imitated a British accident. "This is so much more than a meal. That new white puffy blouse and the blue vest are stunning on you. This is not the feed store Nettie Wagner; this is the strong, lovely, single, available Miss Wagner."

"I appreciate your time and effort, but I could never keep all this up."

Nadine spun her to face her. "And why not?"

"Because it's so much work." Nettie smirked.

"And I've seen how hard you work at the Feed and Seed. What if you took another half an hour for yourself in the morning? You could call it Nettie's... Necessity." They smiled at each other. "It's necessary that Nettie take time for her skin and hair and...I don't know...yourself. Don't do it to turn a man's head. Do it for you."

Nettie seemed to like the idea. Nadine could see her thinking about it. "And you are free to take any days off you want."

"Thank you for your confidence, Nadine."

Nadine nodded, "And thank you for your goodness." She patted Nettie's back and pulled in a deep breath.

Confidence was the very thing she was lacking. Knowing they might ask her personal questions over the meal made her stomach clench. But they couldn't hide in Nettie's room all day. She straighten her back. "I suppose we should go downstairs."

Dabbing the corner of her mouth with her napkin, Nadine wanted to smile. Nettie's grandmother from St. Paul had arrived this week. What Nadine hadn't known was that she never stopped talking. She monopolized the entire meal. No one could get a word in edgewise. Mr. Wagner couldn't wait to clear his plate and excuse himself. Mrs. Wagner got in a few 'ohs' and 'is that sos,' but soon everyone gave up and just tried to enjoy the food.

With the meal winding down, Nettie asked if anyone wanted to play her new game. Nick and Edgar quickly walked into the parlor. Nadine helped clear the table as she watched Nick and Nettie talk. Edgar hovered near, and

Nadine glanced back at the table. "Edgar, would you be so kind as to help with the heavy dishes?"

He walked over expressionless and grabbed the dishes. Nadine thought by Nettie's smiles it was going well. They just needed some moments to themselves.

Alma served the young people pie at the parlor table, and soon after losing two games and drinking a second cup of coffee, Nadine was ready to leave.

"Nettie, have you shown Nick Roxie's new kittens? Maybe he could walk back with us and check on them." She leaned into Nettie's ear. "And I can get home. He can walk you back."

Edgar rose and pulled his jacket off the hall tree. Fiddlesticks, Nadine grumbled. Nick and Nadine gave their thanks to the Wagners and walked out the door. The girls fell into walking ahead, the guys behind.

Nettie pulled her arm around Nadine's elbow. "Sorry my grandmother wouldn't stop talking."

"It was fine with me. I just didn't think Edgar would trail along this time." She frowned. "It is rather cold since you don't have your gloves. You could certainly thread your arm in with Nick's."

Nettie's eyes widened. "You think? Why would Nick walk me back when Edgar is here?"

"Because you are going to ask him. Pretend Edgar isn't…following." Nadine looked back, shaking her head. "And tell him your hands are cold and just do what we are doing."

The group turned off the sidewalk to the back alley. Nettie pulled out her key and unlocked the back of the Feed and Seed. Nick lit the lamp, and the girls fell on their knees with delight. Roxie had moved her little kittens to the box with the old towel. "There they are," Nettie beamed. "One, two...goodness, I count five. That's a lively litter, Roxie." Roxie briefly raised her head, as if acknowledging the appreciation.

"Aren't they precious?" Nadine looked up. Both Edgar and Nick looked dismayed.

"I guess you can always use more cats for mousing." Nick shrugged.

Nadine raised up and brushed off her black dress. "Maybe when they are weaned I could have one for the little store. Gracie Sullivan would love to play with a kitten."

"And let's let her pick one out and name it." Nettie smiled.

"Can we go?" Edgar looked at Nadine.

"If you mean will you hold the light while I unlock my door, that would be kind, Edgar." Nadine looked at Nettie and made a movement like walking fingers.

"Oh, ahh, okay...Nick, would you mind walking me back?"

"Okay, sure." Nick opened the door, and they all filed out.

Edgar followed Nadine, holding the lantern up. She looked past him to see Nick and Nettie at the end of the ally. She smiled to herself. She pulled her key from her pocket, and Edgar quickly grabbed it out of her hand.

"Edgar! I can do it myself." She swiped at his hand as he pulled it out of reach. Suddenly he bent his head forward, and Nadine swerved to avoid knocking heads with him. He pulled back, his face turning red.

"Give me my key, Edgar!" Her heart pounded as it dawned on her. He was trying to kiss her.

He turned on his heel. Stepping away, he threw her key against the brick building, stomping off with the only light.

Nadine bent quickly and searched the cold ground where she thought the key had fallen. Hands shaking, she found it and hurried to get it in the keyhole. She saw him turn at the alley and quickly opened her back door and locked it behind her. She leaned against the door, her throat constricting. "Oh Lord…"

18

Shuffling the beginner Christmas music around, Nadine wondered if the Coon children could do a duet for *Oh Holy Night*. It was a bit difficult for Sadie, but if she reworked it maybe she could simplify the notes.

Her front door opened and she could feel the cold air blow in. "Hello, Miss Von Keller." Emiline smiled, pulling Gracie in and closing the door.

"Hello, ladies." Nadine bent down to help Grace with her thick gray jacket.

"Can I see the kitten?" Grace asked before her arms were free from the sleeves.

"Of course. She has been waiting for you." Nadine smiled. Grace flung her freed arms around Nadine, almost knocking her over.

"I love you," her little voice whispered in Nadine's ear as she quickly released her and ran to the back of the store.

"Tell Mittens hello for me." Emiline hollered after her.

Nadine rose, bemused. "Oh, that little bug." She shook her head feeling the warmth of her words down to her toes.

"Okay, Miss. Let's see how far you got on your Chopin."

Hayes wrapped a wooly scarf around his neck as he pulled his horse down to the front of the familiar yellow-checkered covered windows. He knew he was taking a great risk tonight—he could almost hear her rebuttal. Suddenly he was too warm. He pulled the scarf back off.

He paced a few extra times around his horse, rehearsing his speech. He shook his head at his indecisiveness. Maybe he should have just written it all out in a letter.

He knocked and watched as Nadine saw him at the door. His gut flipped. How ridiculous that she had this kind of influence on him.

"Come in." She motioned with her hand. "Gracie has a hard time saying goodbye to Mittens." She turned toward the back. "Gracie, please come. Mr. Sullivan's waiting."

"I have a question I've needed to ask you."

Thankfully she turned and didn't look too put off. "Sure. What is it?"

"I have to be in Minneapolis Thursday and Friday. It's required for my job."

She nodded, seeing him through those long thick lashes. He sucked in a quick breath. "I was hoping you might agree to stay with Grace while I'm gone. At my home. Mrs. Fox will be there. She will cook and see to anything you need. She just won't do her job and watch Grace." His tone stiffened. "So I need someone to watch Grace."

Nadine stepped back and pulled her hand over the shiny black piano. "Could I possibly watch her here?" Hayes looked up the stairs and frowned. "I'm not comfortable with that." He shifted foot to foot, prepared for her to show him the door.

"And when I am there, you won't… be there?" she asked softly.

"Certainly not," he responded, "and I will compensate you for your extra time."

"I don't care…" She tilted her head to the side. Somehow that last part seemed to upset her. "I am just quite busy with the Christmas program at the school."

"I could ask George or Ralph to pick you both up in the morning, bring you to the piano store and get you back to my home when you were ready."

Grace came around the piano, Mittens dangling from her grip. "Look, Hayes." He reached out and held the squirming kitten. "Look at these big black paws."

He touched the soft fur. "Great name you picked, Gracie. She told me you let her pick." He glanced up at Nadine, as her eyes seem to relax.

Nadine chewed her bottom lip. "I suppose I could help."

"Thank you, you are and have been a great help." He put Mittens in her arms. "We'd better go." He turned to grab Grace's coat. Thankfully, Grace had heartstrings ties with Nadine. The evident bonds are the only reason she agreed. "I'll see you tomorrow." He reached for the door and led them out before she could change her mind.

Since the humiliating disaster with Edgar, Nadine had begged off the recent dinnertimes when Nick was in town. She didn't want to tell Nettie what had happened and she didn't want to sit across from Edgar acting like it was nothing.

Later in the week, she saw Edgar going by with a delivery, so walked over to see Nettie. The warm back room greeted her as soon as she walked in, the other kittens bouncing around with each other.

"Hello, stranger." Nettie walked in, setting a clipboard down. "We have missed you."

Nadine poured herself some hot tea. "I know. I wanted to come over and catch up."

"I was thinking you were maybe trying to be out of sight for my benefit with Nick. Which I should tell you is a bit more interesting, though he does ask if you are sick."

"A bit *more* interesting? So please tell." Nadine smiled, lifting her eyebrows.

"Well, I've been taking more time on myself as you suggested, and he notices things. Like when I curl my hair or wear a new sweater."

Nadine tapped the tips of her fingers together. "This is good."

"And the days I know he's not in town, I wake up, and I feel like doing all that work anyway."

"Wonderful!" Nadine scooped up one of the kittens circling her ankle.

"And there is this other boy...I mean young man that works on Alden's ranch. He seems to come in and spend extra time in the store. He's always asking me questions, smiling a lot. It's so strange…"

"Are you hearing this?" Nadine held up the kitten, talking to it. "Our Nettie is turning not one, but two heads now."

"I am not." Nettie swatted her hand in the air. "I just said it was strange."

"Humph." Nadine squinted at her. "If this other gentleman…what is his name?"

"Ike," Nettie said quickly.

"If he were to ask you to, say, supper after church or a buggy ride, what would you say?"

Nettie sat stoic, staring. Her head began to shake a bit. "I don't know!" She dropped her face into her hands, but came up quickly. "What would you do, Nadine?"

"Oh no." Nadine rose and put the kitten on the rug. "I am the last person to ask." She began to scratch the side of her neck. "In fact…I'm doing something a bit unorthodox. I'll be…staying…" Nadine rolled her eyes shut and spit it out. "With Gracie at the Sullivan home."

"What?" Nettie stood.

"Just for a few days, while he's gone on business. He won't be there." Nadine rattled. "Nope, won't be there… at all."

"Would you be helping him if he wasn't so handsome?" Nettie asked.

"Of course I would. It's about Grace. I…I…" Nadine felt a wave of exhaustion at the contradiction between truth and her past deceit. "You know I was just going to be here until I could make arrangements to go home to Wisconsin."

She took in a deep breath, speaking slowly. "I just wanted… deep in me somewhere…to make my own way. I love my family. I just don't want to go back to live with them."

Her head tilted to the ground. "I've always felt like the problem daughter." She looked up. Nettie frowned sympathetically. "And you gave me the opportunity to try to make it here. I am not romantically interested in Hayes Sullivan. But I am interested in seeing if I can make it here."

Nadine pressed her lips. "I suppose people will talk. It will look bad." She dropped her head to the side.

"Who cares what people might say? I see your heart, Nadine. And that's all God sees too. Just be free to be you here in Carver." Nettie laughed. "Now I sound like you!"

Nadine laughed as she grabbed and squeezed Nettie's hands. "Let's do Bible time tonight. I've missed your preaching."

19

It was only a few miles outside of Carver, but the wind, rain, and sleet made the trip miserable. George pulled the reins taunt and set the brake in front of a large two-story Victorian. He ran around to the other side of the carriage and helped Nadine and Grace out. They ran up the front stairs, finding shelter under the large covered porch.

Nadine looked out to the rain-soaked property. "Thank you, Mr. George. This is quite the storm."

"If this turns into snow later, we might be looking at a few feet." He drained the water off his derby.

"Let's skip picking us up tomorrow," Nadine conceded. "My schedule is clear, and missing one day of school won't hurt Grace."

"Thank you, Ma'am." He plopped his hat back on. "I think that is wise. You might not see Mr. Sullivan until Saturday, maybe Sunday."

"Oh." Nadine frowned.

"I'll be going. Stay dry." He smiled as he ran down the stairs and into the carriage.

Nadine was pondering the storm keeping Hayes away when the door opened quickly.

"Well, get on in here." The short, gray-haired woman glared at them.

"Thank you," Nadine and Grace filed in, the smell of sauerkraut hitting her. "I know you are Mrs. Fox. We haven't met, but I remember you from Mrs. Burden's funeral."

Nadine extended her hand in greeting, which Mrs. Fox ignored.

"Your coat is dripping."

"Oh, yes." Nadine pulled the heavy black coat off her shoulders. Mrs. Fox was already pulling Grace's boots off.

"This hem is wet, little girl. Get upstairs and change." She gave Grace a little shove forward.

Nadine bristled. "I would be happy to help you," she called after Grace as she bounced up the stairs.

"I'm here to assist." She smiled at Mrs. Fox. "I don't want to be any extra work."

"That's good." Mrs. Fox didn't look convinced.

Nadine wiped her shoes two extra times on the mat and walked up the large oak steps. She ran her fingers up the polished banister. It reminded her of the lustrous grand piano. The walls had a beautiful green flocked wallpaper, with two large countryside paintings surrounded by thick golden frames. The staircase circled to the left and at the top landing was a deep red carpet. The doors were large with dark brown moldings—nothing like the upstairs in her childhood home.

For the Von Kellers, their modest home contained a music and schoolroom, front and center. Margaret's room was on the left with Nadine and Minna's on the right. Their hardwood floors banged with running shoes and echoing girl banter. The back staircase led to the kitchen—the infamous escape route for all her foolish ways.

"I'm in here." Grace's head popped out of a doorway.

"Coming." Nadine walked in to see a simple pink and white room. "It's just how I pictured...sweet, like you." Nadine walked past the iron footboard to the wardrobe. She opened it to find Grace's beautifully tailored dresses all hanging in order, her little shoes and boots below.

"How about the blue dress for tonight?" Nadine pulled it from the hanger and helped Grace change into it. "And who is this special friend?" She tapped the little stuffed rabbit on Grace's bed.

"Pippy. Grandma gave him to me when I was little."

"Take her to the brown room," Mrs. Fox announced from the bottom of the stairs.

"Mrs. Fox doesn't like to climb the stairs," Grace said, pulling her little fluffy slippers from under her bed. She grabbed Nadine's hand and pulled her back to the hallway. "Over here is Hayes' room."

Nadine looked in. His desk across from the fireplace stood out, where papers and books were piled here and there. His feather quill stood erect. Her eye landed only a moment on his bed, and something squeezed her chest.

She barely had time to shake it off when Grace pulled her into the brown room. It was dark, so Nadine went over to the large brocade curtains and pulled them back. The gray light illuminated a large burl wood bed frame with thick brown coverings.

"This was my grandma's room." Grace put her foot on the frame and jumped up on the bed.

Nadine stared out the window mesmerized, the grand home encompassing her in this dark storm. Hayes had called her *his* grandmother, yet that was what Grace called her. Confused, Nadine turned to watch Grace pluck at Pippy's fur.

"I wish she didn't have to die," Grace professed.

Nadine came and sat beside her on the bed. "I know you miss her."

Grace crawled toward the nightstand and pulled open the drawer. She grabbed a little glass jar and brought it back to Nadine. "My grandma had these big bumps on her hands. At night, I put this on and rubbed her hands for her." Grace stuck her finger in the oil, dotted Nadine's palm with it, and began to rub her fingers back and forth. The smell of fish oil filled the room. "Sometimes I just like the smell."

"It reminds you of her?" Nadine inquired gently, bending down to her see her eyes.

Grace barely nodded. Nadine took the little jar and set in on the nightstand. She swiftly pulled Grace onto her lap and cradled her. She held a long kiss on her soft cinnamon hair. "It's hard to lose the ones we love," Nadine murmured. Gently rocking her back and forth for a few minutes, she rested her cheek on her head and looked out to the empty hallway.

A baby without a mother, and she, a woman without a baby. Interestingly, her own pain and loss centered on the miscarriage. No grief haunted her over losing Marcus. She closed her eyes. She'd thought she loved him. Feeling the soft oil around her fingers, her hands melted from a child's massage. Marcus' words, actions, his touch, whatever those were…they were not love.

20

Grace led Nadine by the hand into the large dining room. "This is the table where we eat dinner." She let go and skipped around it. "Hayes sits here." She tapped the chair at the head of the table. Why, of course, Nadine thought. "I sit here." Grace skipped by tapping another chair. "Grandma used to sit here." She tapped again, but quit skipping. "And where do you want to sit?" Her big eyes watched Nadine.

"By you, of course."

After finishing the tour of the parlor and library, which seemed like just one long room, Mrs. Fox called them to the table. Nadine pulled out the large chair and helped Grace scoot under. She pulled out her chair next to her. Looking at the fine dishes and linens, Nadine felt like she was in another life. Mrs. Fox came in with the sauerkraut, sausage and a large basket of bread. The smells were familiar, yet everything was so far from her old life at home.

"Hayes asked Mrs. Fox to cook this for you."

Nadine was taken aback by Grace's words, realizing she was staring at his empty seat. Looking over to see Grace watching her with folded hands, Nadine remembered. "Oh yes." Nadine folded her hands. "You pray, love."

"Dear God, Your many blessings are...great...and for this food...we are *internally* thankful."

Nadine couldn't help but smile. Internally still worked. "Very nice, Grace." Nadine smiled at Mrs. Fox's droopy frown. "This looks wonderful. Would you join us?" Mrs. Fox shook her head and walked back to the kitchen.

"Oops. What did I say?" Nadine wondered, taking her first bite.

Grace shrugged. "I think Hayes is always asking for her to sit down."

"Oh," Nadine pondered, looking around the formal room. Hayes had said he was from the East Coast. The house dripped of stately furnishings and art. Yet, a five-year-old calling him by his first name? Certainly, if he was her uncle, she should address him as Uncle Hayes or Cousin Hayes. Grace and he both dressed in fine clothing, surely nothing purchased in Carver. The night he pulled her from the Silver Holiday, however, he was dressed in old flannel and denim. He'd raised his blood soaked arm over his head, unconsciously revealing his bare skin...belly button. Where were his under-

Grace tapped her arm.

"Ahh, yes, little one?"

"I don't like this white stuff. Why is your face red?"

Nadine quickly covered her flushed cheeks. "I was just thinking about you and me... and... curling up in that lovely settee in front of the big fireplace."

That evening, Nadine slowly closed the heavy door to Mrs. Burden's room. After watching Grace fall asleep, she contemplated sleeping next to her. A familiar fear of Hayes walking in struck her.

He didn't seem to embrace the attachment she shared with Grace, implying in so many words he was jealous of it. She shook her head as she dropped her black dress on the floor. Quickly pulling her nightgown over her head, she glanced out the window. A light snow was falling. How could he be jealous? Grace was the sweetest child. Hayes could have her loyalty and affection any minute of the day.

She walked to the bed and pulled the heavy layers back. Tucking herself under the covers, she sighed. The bed was pure heaven. The quiet of the snow and the warmth of the bed brought a mixture of comfort and melancholy.

Lord, what am I doing here? She rubbed her tired eyes. *This town, teaching piano, helping Hayes with Grace. I still feel so lost. I've wanted to be forever angry at You.* She rolled to her other side. *But here I am in this safe home, full on a meal handpicked just for me. Oh, this lovely child, does she know I need her as badly as she needs me? I want to trust in Your providence, but what do I know of You? Are you angry? Do you despise my sin?* Remembering sitting with Nettie, reading the Bible, pulled on her heart. *The woman who washed Jesus's feet with her hair, You received her with forbearance.* She wrapped her arms around her pillow. *I want that to be true for me…*

"Snow!" Grace came crashing on top of Nadine the next morning.

"Maybe a knock first?" Nadine sat up, trying to push the child and the hair out of her face. "And Grace?" Nadine held her arms out, trying to catch her. "I can't do this much bouncing before breakfast."

Grace flew off the bed and landed with a thud. "Can we build a snowman later?" She ran back to Nadine, bright with excitement.

"I...I...think we ...can." Nadine knew Mrs. Fox didn't like wet hems. "Let's start with clothes and food first."

Nadine was able to curb Grace through the morning and even get a few piano lessons in, but they finally put on her gloves and scarf and headed out to the fresh snow. The sun was still behind the heavy clouds, but the white power was fresh and fluffy. Grace ran back and forth in the front yard making trails.

Nadine looked up the soggy roads. Certainly a buggy could make it, she thought, wondering if Hayes would be back on time. She stood back and looked at the home of Hayes Sullivan. It suited him, so tall and stately, the gables and trim ornate but serious.

A flurry of snow flew by her face. She turned wide-eyed to see Grace laughing.

"Oh, you little stink bug." Nadine bent down and scooped up a ball of snow. They ran and chased each other until Nadine thought she might fall over, her lungs burning from the cold air.

"Really, I mean it, Grace. We are soaked; we are going in." Nadine looked up to the front door and wondered about Mrs. Fox. "Let's go in the back door." She looked back over her shoulder as they walked around the house. "We can hope for a bit more snow. I think we need it to cover our muddy tracks."

The kitchen felt like an oven as they entered and dropped their coats. "I already expected this mess." Mrs. Fox walked in, hands on her hips. "Missy, I've got a hot bath waiting for you." Mrs. Fox pointed Grace to the hallway on the right. Nadine gritted her teeth. Should she ask for one after Grace? It had to be bigger than the tub at the feed store.

"You have something else to wear?" Mrs. Fox asked Nadine, walking Grace out of the kitchen.

"I'll make do." Nadine pulled off her wet shoes and stockings. Stopping for a moment to warm her hands over the stove, she walked through to the front and up the stairs. Her dress was too wet to wear.

Stopping at Hayes' door, she looked hesitantly over her shoulder. Could she walk in? Just for a peek at his desk? Lightly walking up to his personal things, she touched his Bible, then picked up another old book, Voltaire, something her teachers didn't ask the Von Keller girls to read. She opened another title, *Influences from Enlightenment,* to the first chapter. Reading the first paragraph once and then again, she couldn't grasp what the book was about. So many big words. She shrugged and put it down.

Fingering a stack of paper, she smiled. It was the paper he'd written her on. He was a strange paradox, smart and refined; yet his words were sincere and almost sappy. Was he an academic or a romantic?

She noticed an envelope under the mess. Maybe another letter for her? She grabbed it and noticed it was addressed to a Molly O'Leary. She tapped it on the stack of books. How gullible to think she was the only woman he was writing his thoughts and feelings to. Maybe Molly lived in Minneapolis. Perhaps this trip he was on was business and pleasure. The first night she met him, he had confessed he was at the Silver Holiday looking for a woman. It didn't matter—she shoved the letter back where she had found it. She shouldn't be in here.

Nadine was rewarded with a glorious soak after Grace finished. It took a bit of convincing, but she finally was able to talk Mrs. Fox into taking the night off. Now Grace and Nadine could stay in their fuzzy robes and slippers and not dress for dinner.

They started with popcorn and hot cocoa in front of the fire, then borrowed two of Hayes' white papers and made paper dolls. They played and sang at the piano, and when Grace began to yawn more than sing, Nadine carried her upstairs to bed.

"No one has ever carried me up the stairs before." Grace snuggled down as Nadine tucked her in.

"You were probably asleep." Nadine kissed her forehead.

She shook her head with a crooked smile and started picking at Pippy's fuzz again.

"Poor Pippy! Are you going to pluck him like a chicken?"

"Mrs. Von Keller…" Grace whispered.

"Yes, *Miss Sullivan.*" She smiled, pulling a piece of soft copper hair behind her ear.

"Could you ask Hayes if you could live here with us? He said you don't have a husband or children." Her eyes were pleading. "This is a nice house; you can have the brown room."

Nadine froze. She tried to muster a small smile, but her chin began to quiver. It was too much. Just too much. This was all Hayes' fault. Why didn't this lonely child have a mother or father?

She quickly swiped a forming tear. "I…I…wo…wo…" Her stuttering returned and she stood from the bed. "I wo… wouldn't be able to do that." She swallowed the lump in her throat. "I…you…" She almost wished her sweet dreams. This poor child. "Good night now." She grabbed the candle off the nightstand and walked into the brown room.

Closing the door, she felt her anger rising. It had been the most delightful day Nadine had experienced in so long. The snow, the warm fire, the singing carols; she almost felt like a child again. How lovely to have a few moments of carefree time. But no, this house was haunted, this family haunted. This child so sad for the loss of the only one that loved her. No wonder she clung to Nadine. Why hadn't

Hayes made more effort to reach her? She dropped her robe and blew out the candle. *It isn't that hard.* Throwing back the covers, Nadine crawled in and tried to sleep.

Awakening with a gasp, Nadine dreamt Mrs. Fox was beating Grace with the rug beater. She sat up and swung her feet to the floor. *It was just a stupid dream,* she sighed, rubbing her forehead.

She struck a match and lit the candle. *This house is not haunted; forgive me, Lord.* She stood and poured some water from the pitcher. *Just one peek at Grace would help her sleep.* She swallowed the water and walked into the hallway, peering into the pink and white room. Grace was snuggled down deep in her covers.

She turned with a sigh. *How could she make Hayes understand?* Her own father was not perfect, but as a child, she never lacked anything. She looked back to his room—maybe it was time for a heart to heart letter *to him.* Walking in, she held the candle towards his desk and reached out for the paper, noticing the room was unusually warm. *Had elderly Mrs. Fox braved the stairs to stoke the-*

"What are you doing?" A cross voice broke the stillness.

Nadine jumped, dropping the candle to the floor. "Oh Lord." She inhaled, clutching her chest. The room dropped into darkness, and she realized the voice matched Hayes.

"What are *you* doing here?" She bent down to find the candle. When she stood up, he was already standing next to her.

"Well, this is my room. My bed...I-"

"Stop it," she snapped, breathless. "I know that."

He lit a match and held it towards the candle in her hand. Her hand was trembling, and the flame had trouble meeting the wick. He put his free hand around hers, instantly connecting more warmth than the room already gave, letting go when the candle caught. He stood only inches away in nothing but his drawers.

"Do you mind?" she growled.

He looked wide-eyed, almost innocent, pulling his hand down his bare chest. "It *is* my room. Don't you think you should tell me why you are in here going through my personal things?"

"I wasn't going through *your* things." She stepped back, angry. "I needed a piece of paper."

"In the middle of the night?" he protested.

"Why are you home? This terrible weather-"

"Oh no..." He stepped back up to her, his eyes intent. "You are not going to change the subject. Sit down." He reached around her and pulled out his desk chair.

"I am not sitting down."

He turned toward his fireplace and turned around on his heel. He brought his arms up and clutched his fingers behind his head. "You are so stubborn."

She swallowed hard, the mixture of his bare muscular arms squeezing his head and his bare feet making it hard to concentrate. His body was perfect...by candlelight anyway. But he couldn't tell her to sit down. She needed to run and run far, now forgetting why this letter was so important. "I...I wanted to write you a letter about Grace." She forced her breathing to calm down.

"Okay." His tone was skeptical. "Why don't you tell me now? I'm right here." He dropped his hands, now gripping his waist.

Nadine flushed inside and out. Here they were again. This small room, dim light, the familiarity overwhelming her. "I...I... ca... can't...think with you standing..." She twirled her finger in the air at him.

"I'll stay right here," he said.

"Why is it so warm in here?" She looked down, seeing his clothes all over the floor.

"I tried to get home in time to see you home. I knew you wouldn't like this." He leaned over and scooped up his clothes. "But the roads were bad." He tossed everything on the bed. "I rode into the night, and I about froze to death. So I needed it warm just to thaw out."

Nadine felt her indignation fade. "You should have found an inn or something."

"I know it wasn't right to be in the house with you here. I'm sorry. I just thought I'd get a couple hours of sleep and face your wrath in the morning. I promise to have you home as soon as you can be ready."

He was trying to avoid her wrath? Biting back a grin, she looked to the floor. Riding into the night, almost chivalrous, not to mention the planning of German food. The silence in the room seemed to magnify her rapid heartbeat.

"So, what about Grace? Did something happen?"

"No," Nadine whispered, looking up. She needed to leave. She refused to develop romantic feelings for this man. "We can talk in the morning."

"I can take you home at sunrise if you want." He stepped forward.

"No. After breakfast is fine," she added, stepping backward, thinking of Grace.

He nodded, a lazy smile covering his face.

"What?" She smiled back.

"I've never seen you in anything but black."

Nadine sucked in a quick breath and realized she didn't even have her robe on.

"This white nightgown is much better." He held her gaze. "Chances are I won't ever see it again, but I think I will remember you, your loose hair, your bare feet, your flushed cheeks, standing in my room, as long as I live."

Nadine felt her jaw drop then clamped it shut as she hurried back to her room.

21

The smell of bacon made Hayes roll up on his elbow. Looking around the sunlit room, he felt like he'd slept only a few minutes. Did he dream Nadine was here in his room? He rubbed his eyes back and forth. It seemed too outlandish to be real. Glancing at his other pillow and bed covered in clothes, it didn't look like she'd spent the night with him. Certainly, he would remember that.

He flopped his head back onto his pillow, arm over his face. Of course, she wasn't in his bed. She could barely tolerate him. He needed to give up this madness. There was no doubt he was attracted to her. Who wouldn't want to get lost in those long lashes and soft skin? Of course, he didn't know if her skin was soft, but just seeing her outside of those heavy black layers made him sure there had to be soft touchable skin underneath.

Standing up, he shook his head. Every weekend he dawned his favorite flannels and denim. But now he had a lady in the house. Should he dress for breakfast and the short ride to Carver? Sighing, he opened the wardrobe.

Why was this so difficult? She was probably already at the front door waiting for her ride. Thinking it a compromise, he pulled on his denims and a starched white shirt.

Coming down the stairs, he could hear Grace giggling. Turning into the dining room, they both looked up from the table and sat straighter.

"Please don't stop on my account." Sitting in his seat, he wondered why Grace now had a sour expression. Meeting Nadine's eyes quickly, he thanked Mrs. Fox as she set his breakfast before him.

"We would have waited for you. But I knew you came in late and…" Hayes watched Nadine's face drop. "I mean…" She covered her hand over her mouth. "Forget that."

He stabbed his eggs and looked up, smiling. The black dress and proper bun were all back in place, but the color of red in her cheeks was delightful.

"How did you like the house, Mrs. Von Keller?"

"It's beautiful, inside and out. Did your family build it?"

Hayes wondered where she was going with this. "No, I bought it when I came to work for the railroad."

"The furniture, decorations. We're these all your things from back east?"

"No," he said casually. "My grandmother's."

"What prompted your grandmother to leave and come to Minnesota with you?

"She had to take care of me," Grace piped in.

Hayes saw Nadine watching him, her meddlesome eyes begging for more. She turned to pull a curl behind Grace's ear.

"Would you go get your paper dolls? I'd like to show Hayes what an artist you are." Grace pushed back from the table and ran toward the stairs.

"Who is Grace's mother?" she challenged.

Hayes leaned back and rubbed his chin. At least he'd gotten most of his breakfast eaten before the interrogation.

"Do you know it's crucial for a child to know who they belong to?" Nadine stood and looked back to the hallway. "Trust me, Hayes, I know all about family secrets, and maybe your grandmother didn't want anyone in Carver to know your personal..." she waved her hand in the air, "business. But Mrs. Burden is gone and this little..." they both turned as Grace ran back into the room. "needs to know."

"Look, Hayes. This is Charles Dickenson." Grace placed the cutouts on the table.

He lifted his eyes, curious.

"Charles Dickens, love." Nadine patted her back. "I told her the five-year-old version of A Christmas Carol."

"These are wonderful. Is this Mrs. Dickens?" He lifted the paper.

"No, it's the Christmas Ghost." Grace giggled.

"All right then." Hayes nodded, standing up and carefully putting his chair under the table. "We need to take Mrs. Von Keller home."

"Noooooo...." Grace slumped to the floor. "I don't want her to go!" She began to bawl. Hayes felt his jaw lock. How long had she expressed these fits after his grandmother passed?

"Grace, get up." He bent over and lifted her to her feet. "Go upstairs." She took two steps forward and fell to the floor again. Curling up in a ball, she tucked her arms in and wailed louder. "I don't want her to gooooo! Please let her stay….*Please!*"

"Grace, this is enough. She doesn't live here. She has her own life." He raked his hand through his hair. "You can see her on Monday." He looked at Nadine, shaking his head.

Nadine bent down and touched her. "Grace, if you stop crying and get your coat on, you can go with us in the carriage to take me home. If you stay on the floor and cry, we will leave without you."

Grace got up slowly and wiped her face, slumping toward the kitchen.

Nadine swung around. "Where is her mother, Hayes?" she commanded.

Hayes let out an exhausted breath, "I don't know."

"Or you just don't want to tell me?" Nadine stared at him.

"Humph." His eyes narrowed. "With the tables turned I should tell you, it's a philosophical term called karma, Mrs. Von Keller." He stared back at her. "How do you like it?"

Nadine stood on the porch, looking darker than her black coat, clutching an unwanted bowl of sauerkraut. Hayes went to take it from her and help her into the carriage, but she pulled away from his assistance.

He shouldn't have said those last words. For someone whose philosophy of life is to allow all things to broaden him and stay out of judgment, he'd just received a failing mark. Grace sat somberly in between them. As he hit the reins to drive the horse forward, the ruts of ice and slush bumped the carriage side to side, and Nadine gasped.

"Sorry. It's going to be rough. The rain washed out the roads, and then they froze unevenly." Never looking his way, she clutched her small bag and bowl tighter.

They rode in silence until he pulled the reins back at a small low bridge. He'd never seen the runoff so fast. It wasn't a deep creek—he just didn't want the horse spooked.

"What are you doing?" Nadine asked as he jumped down.

"I'm just going to lead the horse by the bridle."

"You're going to get wet. The water is rushing over the bridge." Nadine broke her apparent vow to be silent.

"I'll be fine. I just want to keep him steady." He moved the horse forward and turned to watch as Grace jumped up to look over the side.

He was just about to tell her to sit down when Nadine went to pull her back. He looked down for only a moment to gauge the fast flowing water, but the moment he looked up he saw the bowl of sauerkraut flip out of Nadine's hands.

Grace, trying to catch it as the horse jerked forward, went to grab the side of the carriage but missed and fell head first into the fast flowing water. He heard Nadine scream and watched in shock as she jumped in after Grace.

The horse jerked forward again, knocking him back, the swift water covering him. He struggled to avoid the horse's hooves while crawling back to get out from under. He pulled up the horse's leg to see Grace tumbling in the swiftest water. Nadine was limping far behind, struggling to stand up.

"Stand up!" he yelled." It's not deep!" He tried to pull the horse forward.

She pulled on the heavy fabric and struggled to stand, only to fall again. He watched her jerk on the buttons of her coat and peel the heavy-soaked coat off, the rushing water taking it away. Throwing her skirt layers over her arm, she slogged to the shallows.

Dropping the reins, he ran into the other side of the swift creek and grabbed Grace, who was struggling to stand in the shallow water. He didn't realize how icy cold the water was till he saw her pale face and purple lips. Lifting her quickly, he drew his jacket around her and trudged through the water to see Nadine coming up on the other side.

He met her at the bank of the creek and reached out his free arm. She grabbed a hold of his coat and Grace with so much force his knees gave way, and they all fell backward onto the icey bank.

He couldn't move with these two wet, shivering bodies on top of him. "Is everyone okay?" He panted, arms still tight around them.

Nadine's head hovered over his chest. "I don't think… the…sauerkraut made it," she said, fighting for breath.

He released a short laugh and kissed her forehead. Pulling Grace up higher, he kissed her cheek. "You...you did a few somersaults." He closed his eyes, feeling the elation they were both all right. "I haven't been that scared in a long time."

He tried to sit up as they moved off him. Nadine and Grace were shaking head to toe as he helped them stand up. "Let's get home and get warm. Nadine," he panted, putting his arm around her, "Your coat. I know how important it is to you."

"I...hope...I hope...it floats to hell," he thought she said through chattering teeth.

22

The parlor fire snapped and crackled as Nadine sat on the rug, trying to comb out Grace's wet hair. "You were so brave. But next time you want to swim in the creek, let's wait until summer." Nadine looked around to see Grace's face. She still looked pale and scared. Her body trembled and Nadine wrapped her closer in her lap. "You're safe now, little bug." She looked at Hayes sitting on the footstool in his dry clothes. He leaned his elbows on his knees, watching them.

"Let me get you another blanket." He jumped up and pulled one from the stack Mrs. Fox had brought. He came down on one knee and pulled it over their robe-covered legs, looking at Grace and back to Nadine with a worried expression.

"I think our hot cocoa's about ready," Nadine said, still trying to get her attention. "Do you want a cup?"

"No," Grace whispered, pulling the blanket close. She snuggled down over Nadine's crossed legs. Nadine stroked her hair as her head rested on her leg.

"Do you think she's sick? Should we take her to the doctor?" Hayes fretted, chewing on his bottom lip.

"I think she's in shock," Nadine said, looking down to the child's closed eyes, "...and tired."

"I couldn't believe my eyes when you jumped in after her," Hayes raked his fingers through his damp hair.

Nadine shook her head and shrugged. "It was my gut reaction. I didn't plan on the weight of the water holding me down."

Hayes came off the footstool and sat on the floor. "Your black coat might be halfway down the Minnesota River, but I would be happy to go look for it."

They both looked up as Mrs. Fox handed Hayes a tray of hot cocoa. He set it on the floor and handed Nadine a cup. She took a few sips, closing her eyes to the warmth. "Please don't. I can buy another."

"Why did you mention you hoped it would go to hell? When I first met you, you gripped that coat like it was your very life."

Nadine exhaled. "Can you think of something worse than hate? Because I really hate that coat." She stared at the crackling flames and looked back at him intently, "*Please* tell me about her mother." Nadine looked down to make sure Grace was sound asleep. "Who does this child belong to?"

Hayes stood and walked to the window. "I have nothing to hide. But you're right about family secrets." He stared out the window. "I believe when we remove the lies and secrecy we have more chances to unlock doors; doors that might even reveal our secret dreams." He was pensive, but looked at her for permission of some kind.

"Possibly." She lifted one shoulder. Was he going to ask her to reveal her secrets, her lies? Was it fair to ask him to disclose these locked things? In her vulnerability, would she be willing to do the same?

He walked back around the footstool and sat. Leaning forward, he gripped his head. When he looked up, Nadine remembered this tasseled hair from the night in his room. His eyes seemed pained but contrite. Without a sleeping child in her lap, she might have risen to touch that troubled face.

"My family wanted me to go into law. I was teased mercifully by my siblings about my face being in a book, so it would only make sense. My indecisiveness became my addiction, and I got two degrees from Brown University, neither in law." He sucked in a deep breath. "About this time, a young woman who worked in our home caught my eye." He sat back and looked at the fire. "She was amazing, funny, kind, fiery."

As soon as he said those words, Nadine touched Grace's soft brownish-copper hair.

"She acted like she loved to hear me read, though I'm not so sure about that now. She complained she'd had to leave primary school at age eleven to go to work." He glanced at Nadine and then to the floor. "So, she didn't understand philosophy, but it didn't matter because she was the first person I felt understood me."

He stopped, contemplating. "I believed she loved me and I…in turn…loved her." He cleared his throat. "I did confide in one of my older brothers, even though I knew my family would never approve of our marriage." He stood again and walked back to the window. "I wanted to find a solution where they would accept her and…us. I took a little too long I guess, because she quit her job at my parents' estate and left me a note. She was moving back to Ireland."

Molly O'Leary. Nadine had known it.

"I was devastated. It was my first real heartbreak," he said somberly, glancing at her. "But just when the crushing of my chest was starting to lessen, there was a mad commotion at the house one weekend. Someone had left an infant on the doorstep. Who would do that? The babe somehow got shuffled off to the staff quarters. After a few days my parents called me in."

He placed his hand on the mantel and leaned on it. "My grandmother was there. Supposedly this was Molly's child. Presumably my child." He turned quickly. "They'd given her the money themselves to go back to Ireland. You can imagine how that felt. They argued they had done all they could for her to start over and now she only blackmailed them for more."

He stopped and shook his head. "What was I to think? This sounded nothing like the young woman I knew. Was it all a lie?" He stretched his back, gripping his head. "I was at a loss; my parents decided she would go to the orphanage."

He sat back down on the stool. "I ran back to college, hid in my books and didn't come home for a long time. You can imagine my shock when I came back for the holidays to see my grandmother holding Grace." He nodded down at the sleeping child.

"How did your grandmother override your parents' wishes?"

"I think they thought Molly would come forth and take her. Or probably some hogwash about teaching me a lesson. You would have loved my grandmother. She always had the last word."

Nadine opened her mouth, but her rebuttal wouldn't come out.

"So, Grace *is* your child? You and Molly?"

His silence was exasperating, and Nadine gently slipped Grace onto the rug. Standing, she tied her robe tighter.

She couldn't determine if anger or just disappointment flooded her mind. Why had she asked? Why couldn't she just mind her own business?

"I saw a letter on your desk to Molly. Does she not want her? Has your family forbidden her?"

"I don't know."

"Why, Hayes? Why doesn't she know you are her father?"

"Because I don't know that I am," he responded quickly, putting another log on the fire.

Nadine softened her words. "Could you be?"

"Yes. Because of one time, I could be." He shook his head, walking in circles. "But maybe she had other beaus.

How do I know? That's the very question I would ask her if I ever locate her."

"And for the needs of this little one, what would it matter?" Nadine stood in the path of his circling.

"It would matter a lot to me." He glared, moving around her. "I doubt you have known the depths of this kind of betrayal."

Nadine stepped back, stunned at the irony of his words. "So as long as you don't ever claim her as yours, you and she can live as strangers in the same house. An orphan without a chance of ever having a family. That sounds just lovely... just lovely."

"Something happened today," he said softly.

Nadine looked up, shocked at his calmness.

"When I saw her head go under in the creek, her little hands and feet fighting, looking for air; I've never experienced such fright. For a split second, I thought I was going to die. Not physically, but I...I don't know how to explain it." Something tender and unaware lingered in his voice.

"That's how I felt too." Nadine sensed herself tearing up. "I've never been a parent." She dropped her head to the side. "But that's just the kind of love it takes. Wither you are blood or not, I don't think it matters. She just needs someone to call Daddy. Can you be that, Hayes? Can you?"

He looked down, nodding his head. "I can. To be honest, I didn't know what it would look like or where I would begin. I even asked God to help me. I would say He has. You are so natural with her. I watch the two of you. I think I'm too serious with her."

Nadine's eye brows rose, her lips pinched. "Mmm hum."

His charming crooked smile reached her, and she couldn't help but smile back.

He shook his head. "The night I found you at the Silver Holiday, I had heard there was a gal named Molly working there. I had this ridiculous notion she wanted to find me. Of course, it wasn't her." He turned away then turned back to face her. "It was something about finding you and now knowing you. You're right." He rubbed his fingers back and forth over his forehead. "My need to know the truth has locked me in the worst place. I wasn't even embracing what I have."

Nadine realized too late he'd stepped in front of her and held her arms in his hands. He waited, the air thick with confession and desire, searching for her approval. Trying to find her breath, she couldn't take her eyes off him. Move away, something yelled in her head.

"Hayes." She rested her hand on his shirt, willing distance to reappear. His eyes turned a dark gray, and he gently leaned forward, pressing his lips against hers. He didn't try to pull on her, just hovered, breath mingling, forehead barely touching, waiting. Another small tender kiss made her knees go weak. Just when she wanted to kiss him back, he stepped back, grasping one of her arms.

"I want you to tell me why you are in Carver… and who's after you." His tone was serious. "Nadine…" He squeezed her arm. The taste of his lips still lingered as she tried to get her heart to stop pounding.

"…you can trust me."

23

"I need to get dressed." Nadine rushed from the parlor and up the oak staircase.

"Nadine wait," Hayes called, following her. "I'm sorry. I know you said you are a widow. If you are…"

She stopped at the top landing and glared at him. "How dare you? If I am..?" She turned and approached the brown room. "I just need to go."

Hayes hung onto the door frame as she tried to close it. "Just talk to me, please. I truly care about you."

"I need to change. Please move." Her voice held a tremor. "Hayes please, I can't talk when I'm this frazzled and upset. I..I..ju…ju…" She dropped her head back, frustrated.

"I know you stutter when you're upset." He was touching her arm again. "I just want…"

She pulled her arm free from his hold. "No. I…I… just *wanted* to see Grace have a chance." At that last word the tears unleashed. "She's the…sw..sw…sweetest little thing, and I…just want her to be l…lo…loved. Okay…please… that…that's all….I want her to live…" Nadine realized too late, those last words rose up from her own pain and loss.

She groaned and pushed the heavy door closed, grab-bing a pillow off the bed and curling up on the floor. She wept, rocking back and forth. Her deceit was so deep. Why hadn't she left Carver when she had the chance?

Slush and ice broke off the steep roof and dropped in front of the brown room window. She waited all afternoon in the room and had an idea about pulling on the damp black dress. Hayes and Grace had both knocked on the door earlier. She told them she just wanted to rest.

Staring out the window, she breathed in the strength to leave this place. Hayes had said he would be Grace's fa-ther—her work was done. Pulling on the thick damp dress, she needed to get back to her little cave. It was only a few miles. If she started now, she could make it before dark.

Looking at the door, she reminded herself she was the master of sneaking out. Wincing as the door sounded a low creak, she leaned out and looked around. The house smelled like onions. Mrs. Fox was probably in the kitchen. Carefully coming down the stairs, she peered over the rails, looking both ways. Hayes wasn't in front of the parlor fire. Grace was nowhere that she could see.

Very carefully she opened the front door and stepped out. The frigid air struck her, and she pulled her hands under her armpits as she headed out. If she could keep up a brisk walk, she might not freeze to death. With each step, she vowed not to look back. Making sight of the low bridge, she was thankful to see the swift water no longer ran over it.

Her teeth began to chatter uncontrollably as she crossed over, her feet stinging in the damp cold leather. One more turn around the muddy slush and she could make sight of Carver. Her lungs began to ache, but she didn't want to slow down. She gritted her teeth. Even now, half frozen, she was glad never to have to see her black coat again.

Her mind wandered to the details of Hayes' story. The irony was inconceivable. Likely getting a young woman pregnant out of wedlock. Allowing his grandmother to raise the child, then the family shuffling the scandal off to Minnesota.

The outskirts of town were just ahead. Thankfully, not many were out in this forsaken cold. Coming in at the end of the main street, she fought for air as she leaned against the back of Hayes' building. Shivering so hard, she was shocked her legs had cooperated. Breathing into her hands, she covered her ears, the throbbing pain inside them excruciating.

Glancing down the length of the ally, she pushed off his building. At least there was no one back here. Only a few blocks and she would be home. Dodging a stream of water, she realized water was running down the hill. As she got closer, she stopped in shock and horror.

A large path of water came from her secret place—the only place that was supposed to be safe and hidden looked to be running freely right into the back alley.

"Oh Dear God, nooo…." She ran up into the mud and water, unbelievable fortitude surging her forward. It was so dark that night. Maybe not sure, even in the daylight, if this looked right. She wandered the area with panic. Is this where she had buried the baby? Or here? Tears and gasps for air resounded from her as she trudged left to right. Was it farther up? Had she passed it? It was so cold that her mind wouldn't focus. Ankle deep in mud, she pulled and pulled on her feet. "Nooooo," she wailed.

Something grabbed her from behind and pulled her up from the mud. She screamed before she heard Hayes in her ear. "Stop, Nadine. It's me," he panted. "I'm here."

"My baby!" she cried as she fought to get free of him. "I have to find my baby!"

Hayes lifted her into his arms and held her tight. He struggled to take her down the small slick slope. She wiggled and kicked but could not get free of his muscular hold.

Crying for her baby was racking him in confusion. Was she talking about Grace? Did she have her own baby? He set her on her feet at her back door, pushing his hands into her dress pocket, finding the key. Her eyes began to roll into the back of her head as her knees buckled. He held her with one arm and unlocked the door with the other.

Stepping inside, still supporting her, he blew out an icy breath. The old building felt as cold as outside. He lifted her and carried her upstairs to her room. Laying her on the bed, he saw the stack of wood and started a fire in the small cook stove.

Turning quickly, he untied her boots and pulled off her stockings. Everything was wet. "Nadine...please..." He tried to rub her frozen feet and legs. "Wake up….please…." He saw her thin blanket and tried to cover her. The black dress was stiff with the cold, and he knew what he needed to do.

"Nadine, wake up and swing at me…go ahead." He quickly unbuttoned the line of black buttons down the front of her dress. He yanked it open and shook his head. Her white nightgown was on underneath. The same gown she'd worn in his room. She must have thought it would keep her warm. He pulled the heavy dress free and began to rub her hands and arms.

The little stove produced a bit of heat, and he took off his jacket and wrapped her in it. Her lips began to move. "My baby, oh my baby," he thought she mumbled. Kicking off his muddy boots he climbed onto the bed and pulled her shivering body against his chest. Clutching her frozen hands, he opened his flannel shirt and drew them in against his skin. "

What baby?" he whispered next to her ear, gently keeping his cheek next to her cold face. She melted into his body.

"My baby…" her eyes opened and closed slowly. "Oh Hayes…" she whimpered softly, slow tears rolling down, meshing with his chest. Pulling his fingers through her loose hair, he kissed her temple. "You can tell me…" He inhaled the same sweet scent he'd come to know was only hers.

"I hate myself. I'm so soiled," she moaned.

How many times had he wondered if she was a cast off from the Silver Holiday? He'd rehearsed the possibilities of her situation. None of them were good. He desperately wanted to be able to trust her but as long as she-

"I came here with a man named Marcus." Her voice was low and lifeless. "I had snuck out of my home and from all that was right. Even ran from my wedding day to another, t…to…one who was going to stand by me." Her body went slack. He held her tighter keeping the warmth they shared. "Because I was pregnant."

He let the words sink in as she smothered her face against his chest. "It's so humiliating." She clutched the collar of her nightgown. "I was so s…stupid. Marcus said we were going to be married. When we got to the Silver Holiday, he wanted me to help him—I don't know—recruit some of the ladies to join us." Hayes still held her as her body shuddered. "He planned to open a saloon in Helena. S…supposedly, his father, had given him the m…money. I refused, and we fought…ohh…" she groaned. "When I woke up in the morning, he was gone. Left me…" She covered her mouth.

"Before I could even think of what I was going to do, Clyde was in my room, yelling and cursing. Marcus had left with two of his working ladies. He threatened me, insisting I would take their place. I told him I was pregnant." She finally stopped rambling, tears running everywhere. "I…I…didn't know…I…I've never been so scared…except maybe when Grace fell in the water." She sucked in a gulp. "He locked me in that room… said I wasn't coming out until…"

Hayes wrapped his coat tight around her and sat up. Nadine wiped her face and moved back against the rusty metal headboard. Sitting on the edge of her bed, gripping his knees, he shook his head and stood. He paced back and forth and added more wood to the fire. "So you've never been married?"

Nadine curled her knees close and squeezed them. "No."

"So you are not a widow."

"Oh God." She dropped her head and buried her face. "No, but I am a dirty liar and a deceitful woman. I'm so glad you know. I've hated the lies. So many, I lost count. Mrs. Thomason, Nettie, you—all the people I care about, I've lied continually to."

Hayes watched her sob into her knees. He wanted to feel empathy, but he felt nothing. "What happened to the baby?"

She looked up, her face wet and pale. "I was violently ill one night." She stared at the wall. "Then the cramps start-ed…" Her eyes were void of emotion. "I buried the bed-ding up above the incline, behind the building, where you found me today. But I couldn't remember…the rain and water." She was talking slowly, like she was drifting away. "I was still so weak, that I didn't hear you come for Grace."

He blinked, confused, then remembered. "The day you fainted and I took you to the doctor?"

She nodded, still staring with empty eyes.

"Did you tell him?"

She barely shook her head no.

"And I gave you that remark about being pregnant?"

She closed her eyes and sighed. "It doesn't matter," she whispered, the silence enveloping the room.

"How are you feeling?" He sat on the corner of her bed.

"Better. You can… go." She still didn't look at him.

He scanned the small room and saw the kettle on top of the stove. "Let me make you something." He stood and found the water was already heated from the fire he'd built. "Tea or coffee?" He stepped to her small cupboard and opened it. His hand jerked back like a snake had bitten him.

Hanging by a noose was a dead kitten.

24

"What are you doing?" she questioned. Hayes wrapped something in a towel, her only hand towel. "The tea canister is right there." She leaned back against the rusty bed frame, completely exhausted. "Hayes, what?"

His eyes skimmed around the room. "Mittens is in the towel. Dead."

Nadine sat forward. "What? Are you sure?" She threaded her arms through his jacket and stood on unsteady legs.

He pulled back a corner of the towel. Nadine gasped. "I left her at Nettie's. Edgar saw me."

Hayes chewed the corner of his lip. "The cat had a noose around its neck. It was hanging from your cupboard. Someone did this to harass you."

Nadine turned away, pressing her hands to her head. "I need to leave here. Everything gets hurt here. I need to crawl back to my family. I thought I could have a new start." She pulled on her knotted hair and shook her head. "Poor Mittens. This will crush Grace." She looked away as he laid the towel down.

"Nothing would hurt her more than losing you." He grabbed the front of his jacket and pulled her close. "I don't want you staying here. I don't think it is safe." His eyes flashed more gray than blue. "Get whatever you need. You're coming home with me."

She pulled his hands from his coat and walked away. "Really? Just come home with you?" Her eyes narrowed. "And what, move into your room? Now that you've heard the depravity of my poor choices, surely I would become… what…" She shrugged. "Your mistress?"

His face twisted. "I never even…"

"If Molly could have no part of your family," she snapped, "I certainly would not be welcome."

"All right then, I'm taking you down to the boarding house. I don't care where, just not here Nadine. Get your things." He bent over and picked up her black dress. "This is still damp. Where is the other dress you had on under the black coat? Tomorrow we go to the sheriff. Attempted murder is a crime here in Carver."

She slowly took the black dress from his hands. "I appreciate all that you have done for me." Her eyes narrowed. "But just because I was weak enough to tell you the truth doesn't mean I'm going to tell anyone else." She draped the dress over the chair. "I'm ready for you to go."

"Nadine." He let out a long breath. "You're being stubborn."

"I was stubborn because I wouldn't tell you everything you wanted to know. Now my shame is out, and you still call me stubborn?"

He dropped his head back and looked at the ceiling. "Please." He met her eyes. "Don't shut me out. Please…I'm not Marcus."

Nadine winced like a child who just got the switch.

"I hope your endeavors to find Molly come to pass soon." She walked to her door, opened it and handed him his coat. "Goodbye."

Hayes' intense stare locked on her and then he pulled money from his pocket. Stepping over to the bed, he threw the bills on it. "That's for Grace's care these last days, and nothing more." A vein in his neck bulged. "Unless you are smart and use it to get yourself out of Carver… for good."

Nettie knocked on the back door and walked in through her back curtain the next morning. "Hey friend, would you like to ride to church with us?"

Nadine looked up from her desk. "I think I will skip this morning." Somehow she knew Hayes would not attend. But her heart was so heavy, it was better to stay in. "Is Nick attending with you?" She tried to muster a smile.

"Yes…" Nettie dragged out the word. "Like…he…*always*…does…" She leaned her hip into the brick. "How did things go at the Sullivan place?"

Nadine shook her head lightly. "Fine, except Grace fell from the carriage into a swift creek yesterday morning and I jumped in after her."

"Great goosebumps!" Was everyone all right?"

"Yes, just cold and wet. That's why I was late getting home. I didn't have a spare dress."

"Did you get to snoop around?"

"Nettie! How inappropriate."

"Well?"

Nadine lacked the energy to explain her complex weekend. "Grace and I had a wonderful time in the snow playing and just everything with her...except watching her tumble down the creek."

Nettie shook her head. "I'm glad she's all right. When the pastor asks about baptisms this spring, you can tell him you were already dunked." She laughed, patting her on the back. "See you later."

Nadine raised her hand to say goodbye, but Nettie was already gone.

Baptized? What a funny remark to make. Nadine reached for the little Bible Nettie had given her. Something about baptism for the remission of sin. Is that just something she'd heard somewhere? Maybe Matthew? She thumbed through and saw something in Mark 1, verse 4. John preached the baptism of repentance for the remission of sin. Maybe she should ask Mrs. Thomason about it?

Certainly thinking that black coat had washed away felt like a load off. She could suddenly move like a woman set free. What had overtaken her to plow into Hayes and Grace, knocking them all over? Relief, that's all it was. She couldn't get to Grace fast enough, but Hayes, of course, reached out.

Nadine moaned and dropped her head in her hand. Everything must have spoken more than friendship to him. Sitting in front of the fire of his home, telling dark secrets.

She could see the desire in his eyes. How long, she wondered, until he tried to kiss her? It wasn't even passionate; it was just caring and serious, like Hayes.

How could he know anything could be more disgusting to her, reminding her of Marcus? Truly, it was the kindling flame in her that made her run into his arms. She had shamelessly pursued Marcus. Her goal of avoiding Hayes wasn't working either. It almost made him more attractive. They talked, argued, made up.

Oh, how could he hurt her so deeply—telling her he wasn't Marcus. He'd no business being so blunt. From the moment he'd met her, he watched her too closely. He noticed everything. He picked out every discrepancy in everything she said. But now he knew the truth. He knew it all.

She wanted to tell him it was Edgar who killed Mittens. He was so inept, his malicious way of retaliating. She rubbed her temples back and forth and finally stood. Walking around the grand piano, she pulled out the bench. Her hands felt like lead weights. She didn't have the strength to sit up straight. One of the simple songs for the Christmas program came to her. Her hands gently touched the chords, once through, twice, more dramatic notes flowed, and the piano began to swell under the swift movement of her hands. Something deep in her began to sing.

O holy night! The stars are brightly shining. It is the night of our dear Savior's birth. Long lay the world in sin and error pining, till He appear'd and the soul felt its worth. A

thrill of hope, the weary world rejoices, for yonder breaks a
new and glorious morn.
Fall on your knees! O hear the angel voices!
O night divine, O night when Christ was born;
O night divine, O night, O night Divine.

She stopped singing and played the beautiful notes through again. *A soul can feel its worth.* Nettie and her silly comment about baptism, the remission of sin. She'd asked God to forgive her; maybe she needed to believe there was a new and glorious morn. Jesus was born and died to free sinners. What more was she waiting for? Maybe she just needed to believe it in her heart. Even confessing everything to Hayes was somehow liberating. She knew he would react, being so repulsed by her and all the pretenses. Maybe he wasn't asking her to be his mistress. Realizing her sin could be washed away was a long time in coming. Realizing others are not judging her might be just as long a journey.

25

The trunk of costume dresses sounded like a good distraction. Nadine had done so much fretting that Monday—how would she tell Grace about Mittens? Would Grace even come? Should she talk to Nettie about Edgar?

Her stomach twisted. The Christmas program was next week. She let out a long sigh and held the first dress up. Maybe she would leave town after the Christmas program. If she was going to leave, which dress could she redo? The cream one was pretty. She held it up, but there was a dark stain under the bodice.

Maybe she would take the train to Chicago and see her sister. The weather had turned cold and blustery. More likely, she should find a new coat and quit playing dressmaker.

She pulled on the bright red lace surrounding the red dress. Without this, she thought, it might be presentable. *The train and Commissioner Hayes Sullivan,* she sighed. *Oh, Hayes, would you help me escape this life? Do you know the train schedule for that?* She tossed the dresses on the bed. The red one was the gaudiest; it deserved the scissors.

That afternoon, two lacy red bows sat atop the black grand piano. She'd walked to the store window ten times looking for Emiline and Grace. Maybe the new bows would soften the loss of the kitten. She moved them around on the piano and looked up to see movement at the door. Just as she was feeling the joy of seeing the girls walking in, Edgar entered. She felt her nostrils flare and had a strong instinct to hurt him. She came back behind the piano. "What do you want?" she demanded.

"Why don't you come eat dinner tonight, in the back room?" He gestured toward the back of the store.

"No thank you." She stiffened.

"Why not?" His mouth hung open.

"Because." She glanced over at her front window again. "I'm not partial to the company."

He shut his mouth with an odd frown. "But I want you to."

"And I want you to leave me alone. I will not walk or eat or talk with you. I know what you did to Mittens. It was cruel and inhumane. I pay rent for this place. You have no right to ever enter it. I will go to your parents and then on to the sheriff!" Her heart was beating so hard, the words spewed out of her mouth. "Please leave. This is the end of our conversation."

His eyes narrowed. "I brought this piano in. I can take it out."

"Leave, Edgar." She pointed to the door just as she saw the girls walk up. She hurried to the door wishing he would just disappear. He stalked by her and slammed his fist into the piano. The strings reverberated a tangled sound as sheet music slipped to the floor.

Nadine found her voice and welcomed the girls in. The back door to her store slammed shut. The girls looked up at the same time.

"How are you doing today, ladies?" She tried to steady her voice.

"A bit sad." Emiline was helping pull off Grace's scarf and hat. "Grace told me Mittens had run away over the weekend."

Nadine opened her mouth and shut it quickly.

"Hayes, I mean Papa, said that Mittens likes to play behind the store and probably ran off with some friends."

Nadine rubbed behind her ear, her pinky finger resting across her lips. "Umm Hmm." He, of all people, should know lying is not good. But he'd also saved her from being the one to bring pain to this sweet child. And Grace called him Papa, which was a wonderful thing.

An hour later, Emiline's brother came to pick her up, and Nadine's nerves were as tight as could be. She was still jostled by Edgar and now wondered if Hayes would want to talk. She showed Grace the little hairpins that would hold the bows in place. Hayes knocked on the door and she walked there, key in hand. She wanted to gauge his expression, but he was looking down the street. He politely nodded as she let him in.

"Hayes." She nodded back. His eyes seemed softer, almost contrite.

"How is everything...here?" He looked around.

"We checked outside and still *nooo* Mittens." Grace pulled her coat off the chair, frowning.

Nadine was sure he could see her heart pounding through her dress. She loved his dark gray tweed suit, he looked so confident. But now she knew what was under all those layers. Her own hands had touched his skin.

"Hayes, I mean Papa." Grace chuckled. "Mrs. Von Keller made me these red bows." She held her hand out. "Can I wear them to the Christmas program?"

Their eyes finally met and Nadine felt like the air had left the room. It was a powerful connection, just like the first night they'd talked in the shadows of the doctor's office. Such a pulling combined with the fierce unknown. His eyes wouldn't let her go, and she didn't want to be anywhere but back in his arms.

"Papa." Grace tugged on his jacket. "Can I?"

"Yes, of course." He nodded slowly, never looking at them. "They are…beautiful."

"I'm ready." Grace had her coat and hat on crooked.

Nadine bent down and straightened her out. She wrapped the scarf around her neck and kissed her cheek. "See you tomorrow." She slowly stood, already missing them. Hayes took Grace's hand and reached into his coat pocket with the other. Biting his bottom lip, he took out a white envelope and tapped it on the piano. He looked long at her and finally released it and walked to the door.

"Good night."

Nadine locked the door behind them. Another letter. She tried to push her emotions in as she pressed her hands to her cheeks. Was it wonderful? Was it painful? He did have the right to speak to her dishonesty. "Oh, this man," she breathed out as she checked the fire. She tried to tidy her desk but kept looking back at the piano.

It was too much. Grabbing the lantern and the letter, she headed up the stairs. The undone red dress was laying on the bed, and she quickly swept it onto the floor. Setting the lamp on the side table, she pulled off her boots and curled under her blanket. What was his expression? It wasn't dark, and it wasn't angry. But he had every right to be angry. Holding the parchment to her chest, she could picture him sitting at his desk, quill in hand.

She rolled her eyes. Since when did she become a silly school girl?

Taking a slow deep breath, she broke the seal on the envelope-

"Nadine!"

She jumped at the sound of Nettie's voice and quickly hid the letter under her blanket.

26

"Oh, Nettie...what?" Nadine pleaded, meeting her tear soaked friend on the stairs.

"It's...it's Edgar." Nettie clutched her arms, head hanging.

"Oh, dear Lord." A chill ran up Nadine's spine. "What happened?" They both walked down the stairs clinging to one another. The street lamp poured a yellow shadow into the store and over them.

"I...I'm...just sick." Nettie swiped her face.

"Here, let's sit." Nadine pulled her down on the last step, her own legs shaking.

Nettie dropped her face in her hands. "I guess only an hour or so ago, Edgar went to the Silver Holiday and... hurt one of the women who work there."

"Why would he do that?" Nadine knew the answer in the pit of her gut.

"I guess he goes there all the time," she whimpered. "I had no idea." She threw her hands up and slapped her legs. "They said they told him to come back later, but he broke the door down, and when the gal tried to grab his arms, he threw her back so hard she was knocked out." Nettie grabbed her skirt and covered her face. "They have him in jail."

Nadine wrapped her arms around her distraught friend. She looked out to the blackened street, her heartbeat slowing. *Time to tell the truth,* she heard somewhere inside of her.

"Nettie?" She stroked her arm back and forth. "Recently...Edgar has been...unkind to me."

Nettie's face shot up. "What?"

"I was stupid and so focused on myself I...I didn't add two plus two." Nadine felt like she was giving an excuse. "I think it started around the time you and I tried to get...Nick's attention." She shook her head. "All those little dinners and card games. He must have gained some affection for me. I never saw it...because he always has been...different." She dropped her head to the side. Nettie seemed to be listening. "Thanksgiving night, all I was thinking about was you and Nick walking home...but Edgar grabbed my keys out of my hand and tried to kiss me."

"He did?" Nettie moaned.

"When I moved away from him and demanded my keys, he threw them against the building." Nadine rubbed her forehead back and forth. "I just wanted to let it go. But Saturday when I got home from the Sullivans'..." She brought her hands together and squeezed them. "Mittens was hanging from a noose in my cupboard."

"No!" Nettie gasped.

"Unless it was you or Nick who killed..."

"No—never in a thousand years." Nettie rattled.

"I believe it was Edgar. Who else would have keys to this building?"

"Ohhh," Nettie groaned, clutching her knees, rocking back and forth.

"And then today, he asked if I would come to dinner. I'm so sorry Nettie. I told him I knew he killed Mittens. I was so angry—I told him I would never eat or walk or talk to him again." She tried to pull on Nettie's arm. "I'm so sorry. I made him angry. It was me. I know how furious he was. He pounded his fist on the piano."

Nettie moaned and dropped her head on Nadine's shoulder. "You are not to blame," she murmured. "Mean kids at school would call him the village idiot, and Edgar attacked them. That's when my parents pulled him from school. He is big and strong...I'm so sorry, Nadine. You should have told me."

"He's your brother. I'm sure he has done as well as he has because of your love and care." Nadine rubbed her back.

Nettie sniffed in a ragged breath. "My parents are sending him to my grandmother's, if and when he gets out of jail."

"The woman at the Silver Holiday?" Nadine asked.

"She's all right, from what I understand." Nettie shook her head. "Maybe Edgar thought she was his girlfriend? I just can't believe he's been going there. You should have seen the look on my parents' faces."

Nadine slowly released her and stood up. She gritted her teeth and closed her eyes. "Nettie." She swallowed hard.

"It's not fair to burden you on a night like this, but I feel like my chest is about to burst if I don't tell you the truth."

"About Edgar?"

"No, about me."

Nadine turned around and had trouble looking her in the face. She didn't know where to begin with Nettie, so sweet and pure. "Do you remember when Mrs. Thomason brought me into the Feed and Seed?"

Nettie nodded.

"I thought I would just wait to get the wire from home and then leave." Nadine dropped her chin. "So many times I have kicked myself for not just leaving." She breathed deep. "Do you remember I was wrapped in that long heavy black coat? Well, underneath that was my wedding dress. I'd run a week earlier from my own wedding. A young man named Ben Graham was going to marry me. The Grahams had been friends of my parents when we were children and lived in Michigan. I had liked him, and I knew his feelings were stronger for me, but I was also seeing someone else. I had this ridiculous infatuation with the manager of the saloon in town. It was something my parents would never approve of." She rolled her head, ashamed. "I was stupid, craving independence...I believed everything he said-"

"You're not a widow?" Nettie broke in.

Nadine stilled and slowly shook her head. "I've never been married."

Nettie stood and walked next to the piano. Nadine hated that she couldn't read her expression in the dark.

"Did Mrs. Thomason say you were? I can't remember."

"It was Hayes at the doctor's office. He saw the coat and said I was too young to be a widow. It never even occurred to me to make up a lie like that. I...I...didn't know...I would be so accepted. I lied to everyone who cared about me. I was hidden behind the black fabric, and it's kept me alive in some queer sense. I've had the money for at least a month to go home. But it always feels like I have to jump off a cliff or climb back up the same steep mountain. I can't seem to move."

"I thought you must have had a mean husband. You never talked about him, never wanted to give me man advice. I figured it was a bad experience." Nettie rubbed her forehead.

"The man I left home with and brought me here was a bad experience." Nadine looked out the window. "He said we were going to marry, but now I believe he just wanted my help with recruiting woman, like the ones Edgar visits."

"Oh my lord..." Nettie dropped her head on the piano.

Nadine walked over to her friend. "I am so sorry, Nettie. You are the most accepting, loving friend I've ever known. Truly the last person that should have been heartlessly lied to." The minutes of cold silence felt deserved. Her heart sinking down into the ever familiar darkness.

"I just wish you would've told me the truth from the beginning." Nettie looked up. "I know I am older than you, but seem much younger." Nettie frowned. "In the beginning, you didn't want to stay in Carver and I pushed you to stay. Oh Nadine, I can't lose you and my brother in the same day." She met Nadine's eyes. "I forgive you. Desperation makes us all do crazy things." Nettie opened her arms, and Nadine felt the air surge her lungs. They embraced in the tightest squeeze, and as the tears fell, unspoken comfort surrounded them.

"Dear Lord," Nettie prayed, still hugging Nadine. "Grant us Your grace in this moment and upcoming days. Amen"

27

At the sound of the first rooster, Nadine jumped up. She hurried through dressing and saw the unopened letter from Hayes. In all her exhaustion last night, she'd forgotten about it. She stuffed it in her pocket. If Nettie was late this morning, she would have time to read it.

The frozen air hit her as she hurried from her back door to that of the Feed and Seed. The one day her friend needed some help was certainly today. Unlocking the door, she felt the back room holding the warmth of the large stove. Nadine hurried to add wood and build it back up. She lit the lamps and started the coffee then found some bacon in the icebox and pulled out yesterday's milk.

Looking around the back room, the round table, warm braided rug; she realized she had missed it. It had been a refuge for her at one time. She stared at the table, remembering the feeling when she opened the package from the Wagners. They'd been so good to her, and now she could return the favor. As Nadine flipped the crisp bacon, Nettie walked in the back door.

"Nell's Bells, Nadine." Nettie pulled off her coat. "I could smell the bacon from the alley and wondered who was cooking in the kitchen. I knew Nick wasn't supposed to be in town."

"This is yours." Nadine set the hot coffee on the table. "Breakfast is almost ready. I had some ideas last night I think we should discuss." Nadine turned from the stove and set two plates down. "I know this is your store and your parents will advise you, but I want to help out. I can arrange my lessons on certain dates and times. Then you can count on me to help at the Feed and Seed. I can do the books and ordering. You know all your customers, so…" Nadine watched as Nettie chewed on her eggs. "What if we worked together? *And…*" She said wide-eyed, "you asked Nick to work here? All the lifting, deliveries…"

Nettie dragged in a breath. "I appreciate your offer of help, but Nick wouldn't want to work for me."

"Why not?" Her voice rose.

"Because he's a man. He has his own business. He obviously doesn't like to be tied down." She frowned.

"Hmm." Nadine tapped her lip with her folk. "What if your father asked him? Maybe just a trial run until your family can find someone."

Nettie shrugged. "Maybe." She took another bite and looked at Nadine. "You have the children's program coming up. That's a big deal."

"It is?" Nadine looked up from her plate.

"Certainly. Everyone gets all dressed up, and after the program, they have a social time at the grange hall two doors down. Food and music."

"No one told me that." She shook her head quickly. "It doesn't matter. I'm doing my small part. I have time to help. I really do."

"Since you are trying to help me," Nettie said, dropping her chin, "why don't you get rid of that black dress? It's a wonder it isn't threadbare."

"Another confession." Nadine let out a sigh. "I am an appearance fussbudget. I used to spend hours with my dresses or in catalogs of dresses, my hair-"

"Oh, I remember trying to get your hair right." Nettie laughed. "We could have found someone fancy to do it right."

"You know..." Nadine loved this honesty. "I feel like that part of me; I guess the frivolous part, is gone. The old Nadine would have died a thousand deaths to wear the same dress day after day. This time I've spent in Carver has changed me, more than anything I could have imagined."

"I wish you didn't have to go through so much suffering. Carver, for the most part, is fairly sleepy." Nettie rose and poured them another cup.

Nadine wondered if she should continue on with the truth of the pregnancy and miscarriage. Nettie's shoulders still slumped. Enough was enough for now.

"I did attack those dresses in the trunk."

"Good. They were going to the moths anyway."

Nadine helped Nettie clean and straighten the store until she needed to go back and get ready for students. She reached for her hankie and felt the letter from Hayes. Her heart thumped as she sat on the piano bench. A warmth encompassed body and soul, almost a lightness she didn't realize she could have.

She wasn't sure what to expect from his words. The other letters had touched her so deeply. What if this one was critical? She played the four gloomy chords from Beethoven's Fifth and smiled at her attempt to make light of the looming mood. She flipped open the letter.

Oh Beloved,

Sleep and peace would come if only I could convince you how to feel and think. Hazardous, I know-

To be truly mortal, I believe all of us must escape our human limits. I have, and you have. There is no logic to suffice; there is no remedy that will right every wrong. But once those limits and barriers are broken, then we are free to live justly.

Oh, the God of our hearts, to stretch His image over such a wanton will for freedom. We, so untrustworthy, unimportant, what kind of risk he took in the perfect garden. Without our mistakes how could He show Himself faithful? Without the law how would we know the work of grace? Our errors were guiding us, like the glimmer of orange and rust pointing to the west – magic water bidding us to draw near. Take my hand at twilight, beloved, look down, use the water as your mirror. You are whole and alive. You are beauty and hope. The firefly drops in and tries to blur your image, but hold steady; it will return. Deeper and richer,

*your soul will soon remember that all you are, in this very
moment, is sanctioned for glory.*

    Hayes

Nadine felt her lungs swell as she held the letter close.
This poet, this philosopher, honoring her with his written
thoughts of acceptance and forbearance. Closing her eyes,
she felt the tears forming. She wasn't sure what swooning
was, but something was happening to her. Why was she fearful of him? He knew the worst of her every sin and still offered her this letter of mercy. The opening to her heart was
so thin. How had this man found the only minuscule crack?

She thought of his second letter. The power of words–
spoken with contempt, they bring immeasurable damage.
The only thing that healed was speaking love and acceptance into the dark places. He was so eloquent at it.

She breathed in a ragged breath. Could she ever really
open her heart? On days like this, it seemed possible. Maybe
she could fall in love again, believe there were honest, caring men out there. It was so much safer to fend for herself.
But watching him carry Grace through the raging creek
and that slow whisper of a kiss, she longed for the safety of
his arms. She glanced down at the opening. *Beloved…*

"Oh, my…oh my…oh my…" She sighed.

28

Expecting Hayes any minute, Nadine felt her heart racing. Grace had helped her cut some gray trim to add to the red dress. With Nettie's suggestion, she wondered about wearing it to the Christmas program. It seemed a bit brash, but the only two people that mattered in Carver knew why she should not be wearing black. The black coat, she could only hope, had sunk to the bottom of Lake Michigan. The next step would be to… Nadine jumped, startled by the knock at the front door.

"Oh, it's Mr. George," Nadine said to Grace. "Is he your ride tonight?" She unlocked the door and let him in.

"Hello, ladies," he said, tipping his derby. "Hayes had a problem out on the line today, so he will be gone."

Nadine finally felt her heart slow down. "How long? Does he need me to keep Grace?" She hoped she didn't sound too eager.

"Ahh, well… I'm not sure. He just asked me to do the pickup and drop offs to the house."

"Of course." Nadine reached for Grace's coat and school papers. "Mrs. Fox is there. Sooooo, I will see you tomorrow, little bug?" She forced a smile at George as he led Grace out the door.

Chewing her bottom lip, she turned the lock and heard it snap in place. What had she planned to say to Hayes anyway? Would it have been awkward silence or her fragile emotions exposed from mooning over his letters?

The entire day had been wonderful. Why did she feel like a rock had been dropped on her foot? She glanced at her attempts to remake the trim for the red dress. Suddenly it lost all its appeal. She gathered all the items on the piano and took them back upstairs.

Slowly sitting on her bed, her emotions churned. He didn't tend to his work to ignore her. She got up and added a few more sticks to her little stove. To think he'd been in here, sitting on her bed, wrapping her in his arms. He'd come up the day she had fallen asleep with Grace. Certainly, he'd seen how plain and bleak her room was. A brash suggestion, his offer to take her home. Glancing around her lonely surroundings, maybe she should have taken it.

She slapped her cheeks quickly. That was the long gone innocent Nadine, giving away her honor for a wagon of promises turned lies.

"So, are you ready for tonight?" Nettie asked over their morning coffee.

Nadine blew out a held breath. "Yes and no. The children are ready. Who would not love to see the little ones? Their teachers have given all the non-musical children a little speaking part. You should have seen them practicing yesterday after school. So many wiggles and confusion, but it was darling. I just feel for…" she tipped her head, "you know, Hayes, being away all week with this railroad problem."

"How is Gracie handling it? Will she be crushed if he's not there tonight?"

Nadine looked away. "She seems fine."

"Because she has you," Nettie piped in. "You are the mother she always wished for."

Nadine didn't know what to say.

"I know months ago, I didn't like Mr. Sullivan." Nettie bit her lip. "He didn't seem to care enough about how we ran things here before the railroad came. But I have to be honest, we've been fine. Our customers and his are two different groups. I probably judged him. He seemed so sure of himself. He's kind of intimidating, I guess. And I know you like him. I trust your ability to see people."

"You wouldn't have said that about me a year ago." Nadine felt her stomach roll. "I want to ask you a favor before you open the doors, but first, how did it go with Nick this week?"

Nettie scratched her head. "Fine, I guess. I did have my father do the talking. It works for Nick to skip a stop to help us here. I guess he was sleeping in a cold barn, trying not to be a burden to us. So he can work here Tuesday, Wednesday, and Thursday. He'll do his route Friday and Saturday."

Nadine sat up. "So, that sounds good…*right?*"

"Mmm hum." She stood and went toward the stove.

"Nettie Wagner, get back here and sit down."

Nettie turned, tears pooling in her eyes. Nadine stood quickly and wrapped her arms around her. "What, dear friend? What's wrong?"

Nettie moved back and dabbed her face with her apron. "I've been wondering if Nick comes here to be a friend to Edgar." She sniffed hard. "I used to think it was to get to know you. Ahhh." She groaned. "I just have to accept the fact that he will just be a friend. I've prayed about it, and I feel I just need to let all this silliness go."

"Your feelings are not silliness!" Nadine grabbed her elbows. "It's never been about me, I promise you. But you... you've' blossomed and grown so much. Even if it means accepting something that will never be, don't stop being Nettie. I love your spunk and smile; you are an original. God is so delighted with you."

Nettie cracked a smile. "What else did you want?"

Nadine wanted to forget it. "Only if you have time. I wanted your opinion on something."

Even though she didn't mean to, Nadine swooshed into the back room kitchen.

"Oh my marvel!" Nettie boomed. "That is gorgeous!"

"Is it too much? I feel like black to red might be overdoing it." Nadine pressed her hands down the silky fabric.

"Absolutely not. People get all gussyed up for tonight." Nettie looked long. "Is this really that old dress from the trunk? It brings out your chestnut eyes, just enough arm and shoulder showing, the way you added the gray piping and bow. You should wear your hair up." Nettie nodded. "Oh, radiant in red you are."

"Okay here's sappy me," Nadine sighed. "You know I hate going out. Can you close a little early today so we can do hair and get you looking holiday-themed yourself?"

"I guess so. Not many chances to dress up in Carver." Nettie nodded. "I'm willing."

Late in the afternoon, they both looked up to see a young man coming through the front door of the Feed and Seed.

"Excuse me. I have a delivery for the store next door, but I don't see anyone around."

"I work there," Nadine offered, "but this young woman owns the building."

"Well." He looked down at the thin square box. "It says it is for Miss Nadine Von Keller."

"That would be me." Nadine walked forward and received it. "Who is it from?" The use of miss made her nervous.

"Sorry, I just do deliveries." He smiled, scrunched his shoulders and walked out.

Nadine walked it over to the counter where Nettie was working. "The paper is pretty." She untied the small ribbon and lifted the lid. Both women looked with wide eyes.

"Chocolates," they said in unison, dazzled.

"I wish I knew who they were from, but it won't stop me from trying one." She picked one up, smiled and took a bite, pushing the box to Nettie.

"Maybe they are from Hayes." Nettie batted her eyelashes, taking one.

"Oh stop." Nadine chewed slowly. "These are heaven." She closed her eyes. "If we don't finish this box today, I'll save it for my Christmas."

"Better than a fruitcake." Nettie laughed.

An hour later, they'd pinned every hair and donned their holiday outfits. Nettie offered a soft black sweater to wear over Nadine's dress.

"This is perfect, Nettie." Nadine slipped it on. "I don't want to look like I'm coming out into society."

They locked the doors and stepped out onto the sidewalk. They could see the lamp lit carriages bringing the families to the church. Nadine tried to look through the dark. Would Mr. George be bringing Grace? Maybe she could meet them and get her settled with the other children.

As they entered the church, decorated with bows of evergreens and candles, she had to stop and take it all in. It smelled and looked beautiful. Watching the first rows of children, she thought she saw Gracie's soft copper curls.

"Let's grab a seat." Nettie pulled her down a side pew. Nadine was smiling inside and out. The noise of families and children filled the church. The tall, thin principal got the crowd to settle down and find their seats. He thanked everyone for coming and introduced the teacher.

Nadine had to regulate her breathing as each of the children presented their little Christmas songs or verses. Grace sweetly banged out *Good King Wenceslas*, while Nadine felt her fingers twitch like she was on display with her. Grace finished, and Nadine fought the urge to stand and clap.

All the children did amazing, and every parent must feel so proud, Nadine thought. The teacher ended the program and thanked the decorating committee. She gave out special thanks to Carver's own Mrs. Von Keller for helping with all the piano pieces. Nettie bumped Nadine's arm, and her face went flush. Thankfully the principal rose and invited everyone to the grange hall for food and dancing.

"It turned out so well." Nadine rose and held her hands over her cheeks.

"My favorite part was when the little blonde girl went to curtsy and popped her dress up," Nettie quipped. They looked at each other and covered their snickers. "At least she had her bloomers starched."

They moved slowly through the exiting crowd, Nadine rising on her tippy toes to see Grace. "Can you see Grace anywhere, Nettie? I've lost sight of her."

"No. So many children running around. Hopefully, she will be at the grange."

Nettie waited as Nadine stopped and received the appreciation of her piano students' parents. Finally, she noticed Nettie walk out with the Thomasons. Miss Pruett kept Nadine a few minutes, asking if she could introduce her to the principal.

"May I stay and help with the cleanup?" Nadine asked once the crowd had thinned out. They thanked her for the offer but told her to go enjoy the music.

Nadine walked out with a huge sense of relief. Not one person said anything about her dress. She'd worked on it all week, debating if she should wear it, a frivolous distraction from Hayes' absence. She saw a group of children running in and out of the hall and wondered if she should just go home.

Wanting to see Grace and let Nettie know, she approached the large back deck and open double doors. She stopped and hid behind the door opening. It was just a delight to see the large hall decorated with a tree in the corner, sconces on the walls brazing with light. A small orchestra was playing *Silent Night* as a few couples danced.

A chill ran up her spine. Someone was standing close, and their warm breath touched her bare neck.

29

"The man that hath no music in himself..." Hayes' calm voice caused a tremor to riddle her body. "...nor is moved not with concord of sweet sounds..." She fought to breathe and keep her eyes forward. "...is fit for treasons, strategies, and spoils. The motions of his spirit are as dull as night. And his affections dark as Erebus. Let no such man be trusted." He carefully reached under her black sweater and touched her waist. Her lungs froze, but as she tried to breathe, all she could smell was his fresh, clean scent. "Dance with me," he whispered into her bare neck.

She was swooning again. Nadine took a deep breath and turned around slowly. She was so happy he was here, now easily forgiving him for shocking her.

"Only if we can dance out here." The quaver in her voice matched the feeling in her belly.

"With that dress, Nadine, I should not want to share you with anyone else."

She smiled and reached to unbutton the warm sweater. He watched her every move.

"You know this is painful, don't you?" His eyes deepened as she set the sweater on the wood deck.

Nadine didn't try to hear the beat of the music. Holding her hand out, his warm hand soon encompassed hers. They both moved in perfect step in a waltz. She never doubted he would be a superb dancer. He held her with ease and strength, each step never taking the roguish grin from his face.

"Music is the balm," he said, a flicker of deep understanding covering his expression.

"Then what is dancing?" She smiled as they turned.

He squinted, thinking. "Dancing is for the captive set free." He led her to touch the corner of the deck and then turned quickly.

"Your letter." She struggled to find the words. "Was it a passage from one of your famous philosophers?" Her feet moved in unison with his.

"Once again, you honor my senses." He pushed her away, holding on with firm fingers. His eyes roved over her quickly and then twirled her under his arm and held her against his chest. "Those were my words, from my heart to yours."

"Thank you." She whispered, hating that her eyes were pooling up. She pulled from his body and hands. "I'm so winded...I...I...d...d...don't dance much." Walking away, she tried to smoothe the loose hairs that had come free. She dabbed her eyes and walked back to her spot behind the large open doors.

"I came with Nettie." She looked in to see Nettie dancing with a tall young man. Watching them, she looked to see Hayes was leaning against the other side of the large doors, watching the dancers.

"Doesn't look like she is missing you." He winked.

"Where is Grace?"

"With George and his wife."

"Do they have children?"

"No."

"Does his wife help you with Grace?" Nadine realized she really didn't know enough about Hayes.

"No." Hayes found something amusing as he smiled at her.

"Why not?" A group of giggling girls walked through their conversation.

Hayes watched them and the other people inside the hall. He looked back and forth and walked over to her. "Because I'm not interested in George's wife."

Nadine gripped the rough wood, heat rising over her. He walked past her and picked up the black sweater.

"You don't have to go in with me. I understand. But you shouldn't be hiding out here. The dress, your hair…you're the beauty that teaches the children piano. You belong here. You have nothing to hide from."

Looking into the full room of people and back over her shoulder, sincerity shone in his eyes. She slowly reached for the sweater, but he held it tight. The little tugs back and forth brought a grin to her face.

"I'm just cold." She chuckled as he finally let go and held it out for her to slip her arms in. He took more bold liberties, bringing his hands slowly down her covered arms, finally grasping her right hand between his hands. He rubbed them all together, bringing warmth.

"Miss Von Keller-"

"Chocolates! Did you send the chocolates?" Her body gave a little jump, but he still grasped her hand.

"I did. I think…you liked them?" He dropped her right hand and began to warm the other one.

"We did," She bit her bottom lip, hiding her smile. "We ate the whole box."

His grin and eyes widened.

"It was a rough week."

"Speaking of week…Miss Von Keller, would you be free to go to dinner with me Wednesday evening?"

"Oh, just you and I or with Grace or…"

"I was hoping just you and me."

Nadine swallowed hard. Her mind was flashing. She'd never been asked to formally step out with a man before.

"I don't know. I…I…maybe should think about it."

"It's just dinner, Nadine. You can tell me about your rough week and I can tell you about mine. And we enjoy some food."

"All right. Yes." Heat flushed her face. "What time?"

"I will get Grace home and be back for you by six thirty."

She nodded.

He raised her hand to his lips and kissed it lightly. "I'm glad you wore that dress. I know how hard it is come out into the light. But you deserve all the music and dancing your heart desires."

"Thank you for saying that," she whispered, savoring the moment.

His eyes studied her face, and she slowly smiled.

"I'll walk in with you," he offered.

It would make a statement to walk in with him. She shook her head. "Thank you though. Will you tell Grace I saw how wonderfully she did tonight?"

"I will." He waited.

"Really, I'm fine." She smiled. Between watching the sweet children, his letter, the dance and the look in his eyes right now, this evening had far surpassed anything her imagination could have hoped for.

He bowed quickly, released her hand and walked into the hall.

30

Nettie linked arms with Nadine and practically skipped back to the storefronts. "Did you see my mother scowl? Two young women having an overnight get-together." She imitated her mother's nippy words. "She just didn't like that we were staying at your place." She shook her head. "Like we are going to sneak out and go to the Silver Holiday." Nettie slowed to a stop. "Oh Pittle Pattle, I didn't mean to say that."

"I hate that place, so your mother shouldn't worry. We are young, but smart." Nadine pulled her key from her pocket.

"I just want to hear why you stayed outside with Hayes Sullivan all night. I want the real story."

"All night?" She gave Nettie a little push. "A dance and a conversation doesn't constitute all night. I need details on who you were dancing with." The door seemed to open before she could get the key to turn.

"When we left, I'd locked the door? Right?"

"I'm sure you must have. Why?"

"It just opened so easy. I probably just…" They walked in.

Nettie sniffed. "The question is if you left the flue closed on your little stove. It smells like smoke in here."

Nadine lit the lantern and held it high, looking around. Everything seemed to be in place. They began to climb the stairs, and Nadine felt her heart begin to pound. They opened the door slowly as the light illuminated the upper room. Nadine gripped Nettie's hand as she moved forward. "Nettie." She squeezed harder. "Be careful."

They both stepped carefully to the bed, where they saw a black hole in the bedding. Nettie looked up to the ceiling. "What did you do? Did you leave a candle burning on the bed?" She looked around, trying to make sense of it. "What could have happened? Nadine?" Nettie tried to pull her hand free. "Nadine?"

She heard her name but could not make her mind unlock. "I…i…is…" Nadine gritted her teeth, willing the words to come out. "Is…Ed…Edgar…gone?

"Yes. My father took him to Minneapolis."

"Are you sure?" Nadine's throat constricted. "Maybe he came b…b…back."

"No… no." Nettie shook her head and turned to Nadine. "My father said the sheriff threatened to put him back in jail if he came back early and bothered anyone."

Nadine didn't hear her. "I think the front door was unlocked. Who else would do that?"

"But Nadine." Nettie grabbed her elbows and gave her a shake. "Why would anyone burn a hole in your bed?"

"Oh, friend." Nadine dropped her head to the side. "I…I…hate how…I should have left…a long time ago…"

"Nadine," Nettie said sternly. "Tell me…"

Nadine turned away. "The night Hayes found me at the Silver Holiday, someone had started the fire. Some hot coals were left in the center of the bed in the room I was in. I really don't remember, but if I did fight to get out, it didn't work. The door and the window were nailed shut."

"What?" Nettie cried out.

"Hayes broke the door down I guess and found me. I woke up later that night in the doctor's office." Her voice trailed off.

"You think Edgar nailed you in that room?"

"I…I…don't…really, he didn't even know me. The only person who did was the owner. He was angry about Marcus." She almost choked on his name. "The man I ran off with. He had left with two of Clyde's working girls. Clyde told me I would have to work off the debt. Of course, I refused. Maybe if it weren't for Hayes, I would still be locked in that room." Nadine closed her eyes and pulled the pins out of her hair. "Or dead."

"No wonder you looked so lost and dazed the first time Mrs. Thomason brought you in." Nettie wrapped an arm around her shoulders.

"This," Nadine flicked her hand at the bed, "is just reminding me. He wants money or restitution of some kind. He hasn't forgotten about me. He knows where I am." Nadine turned quickly and grabbed Nettie's arms. "What if it wasn't Edgar who killed Mittens? What if I wrongly accused him?"

"It doesn't matter." Nettie shook her head. "You weren't the one who pushed that girl down, knocking her out." She pulled on the burnt bedding. "This is all ruined. The mattress has a hole clean through. I'm glad this happened," Nettie said bluntly.

Nadine stepped back.

"You have to come home with me." Nettie insisted. "You can't stay here."

Nadine shook her head. "I don't want your parents to know…"

"It doesn't matter," Nettie cut in. "My mother wanted us to stay there tonight anyway." She sighed. "Surely our girl night is ruined, but we can still talk about what to do. Don't look so sad." She shook Nadine's arm. "We'll figure this out."

Nadine couldn't help but enjoy the wide feather bed she and Nettie shared. It was dark and cold, but she felt the security of the house and company surrounding her. Even in Hayes's grandmother's bed, she was alone.

"I told you I have an older sister?"

"Mmm hum." Nettie drowsed.

"We used to be close as girls. After our mother put us to bed, we'd sneak into each other's rooms." She chuckled. It seemed like another life. "We would tell stories and laugh until my mother would come in scolding, wagging her finger."

She wondered if Nettie was still awake. "But things changed. I resented my sister for wanting to go off to college. Really, I just resented being stuck at home. We weren't allowed to go to school and Margaret was my closest friend. My mother's harping always seemed directed at me.

"I blamed Margaret for not being the buffer anymore. Margaret tried to befriend me again, but I never let her reconnect. Even the dreadful day I said I would marry Ben, she was upset, but kind. She was good to me, and I certainly didn't deserve it."

Nettie flipped over to her side. "Why don't you write and then visit her?"

"Probably because I'm falling in love with Hayes." Nadine sighed.

"What? You mean with Grace?" Nettie flipped back, rubbing her face.

"Well, of course. Her too." Nadine dropped her arm over her eyes. "But nothing ever works out right, not for me, anyway."

"Or for me." Nettie let out a long sigh.

"What about the young man you were dancing with?"

"He's not Nick."

"Hmm…I understand." Nadine pulled the blanket closer to her chin and closed her eyes.

"We are just two sad sacks." Nettie snuggled down in the soft bed.

"Sad…sacks…that's a good one, Nettie. Good night to you, friend."

"Good night, and good riddance to this day," Nettie whispered.

31

Hayes kept his pocket watch out on his desk. He didn't want the other men in the office watching him clip it open and closed every ten minutes. The afternoon was dragging on, and he could hardly focus.

Tonight was the first step in a proper courtship—or was it? No parents to meet, no community group to be seen in. He was a father with a child. She was a single woman living and working in town on her own. What were the rules? Certainly, her sleeping in his home had crossed some suitable line.

Thinking he could ignore propriety and have Molly had been a hard lesson. He looked at his watch again. He needed to do this right. He was not a smooth-cheeked young man anymore. He wanted things different this time.

Darkness had fallen, and he bid the other gentlemen goodnight. He took a deep breath and locked up the railroad office. Each evening this week she had had the chance to change her mind, but she just smiled and handed Grace over like they'd done a hundred times. Whatever she was feeling, she'd a magnificent way of keeping her cards close. Blast it. It just made her all the more desirable.

Small flakes of snow glistened in the street lamps. They might get a white Christmas after all. He knocked on the door, and she approached smiling. Grace was already getting her coat on as he entered. Standing inside the door, he wondered if he should just be the coward and cancel.

"A bit of snow, I see." She handed him Grace's school books.

He cleared his throat, not wanting any small talk. "Are you still …interested in dinner tonight?"

"I think I am." She turned away and stacked some papers on the large black piano. "Unless you want to make it another time."

He brought his hand down his face. "No, tonight is fine." *Because I'll pull my hair out if you turn me down.* He shook his head, glad he hadn't said that aloud. "I have a table for us at Mrs. Poole's. I can be back in thirty minutes."

She finally faced him. Thankfully, her face, eyes and lips all looked soft and willing.

"I will see you then." She nodded.

He flung the third shirt on the bed and stalked around it. He wasn't going to change his clothes—he didn't smell bad, and the gray tweed was one of his nicer suits. So why was he putting himself through this? He was just wasting time. He grabbed his jacket back off the bed and slid it on. Denim and flannel were his preferred attire. Why couldn't he just wear that? He'd never seen her in anything but black.

No, he remembered, as he pounded down the stairs. The white robe had initiated their first kiss, and that red dress could stop a train. He checked in with Mrs. Fox and kissed Grace good night. They both wished him well. It must have been clear how badly he needed it.

Back in front of the piano store window, he knocked, noticing she'd changed into a gray cape coving a deep navy blue dress.

"Are you ready?" he asked as she opened the door.

"I hope so." Her eyes widened.

Perfect, he thought. She seems nervous too. He offered her his elbow. "Do you mind if we walk? I have the carriage if you prefer."

She looked back and forth at the empty walkways. "The walk would be nice." She locked the door before lightly threading her arm through his.

"This outfit, is it new?" He covered her bare hand with his glove.

"No." She shrugged lightly. "Just sharing Nettie's wardrobe."

He smiled and looked down at his hand over hers. *Gloves. Buy her gloves for Christmas.* He would try to remember. They stepped off the end of the first block and back up the walkway. The silence seemed to increase with each step.

"What kept you away last week?" she asked as they passed the railroad office.

"Union problems. We are so close to finishing the line that the unions sweep in and try to get the workers to walk. They know we are under the gun with deadlines and financing."

She nodded slowly. "And you sway them with your skills; at least as a master negotiator."

He smiled, knowing she was teasing. "My best skills I try to save for you."

"Really? I've seen the best?" She dropped her chin, her eyes mischievous.

He stopped walking and turned her to face him. "When the time is right, you'll see them all."

Her face flushed and she tried to move back. "I...I.. didn't mean to imply..." She walked on, her arm slipping from under his.

He didn't like that she'd dropped her arm, but he loved their banter. Opening the door for her, they stepped into Mrs. Poole's quaint dining establishment. A young woman smiled at them and showed them to a little table by a large window. He carefully took her cape from her shoulders and held the chair out. He watched the way she smoothed her hand down her backside before she sat. He knew all woman did this, but on a night like tonight, it seemed alluring. Sitting down across from her, he watched as she stared out the frosty window.

"You told Grace you are from Wisconsin. Did you get much snow in your area?"

"Some winters." Her brown eyes locked with his.

He fought the urge to tell her how beautiful she was. They looked up as the young woman approached with some hot coffee. "We have turkey and fixings or corn chowder tonight."

"I'd like the turkey," he said to the waitress.

"Yes. That sounds good to me, too." They watched as the woman walked away.

"Hayes?"

The pleasing way she said his name stirred his insides. "Yes…"

"I don't think I ever thanked you for asking Mrs. Fox to cook German food for me."

He nodded and took a sip of his coffee.

"I grew up on nothing but German meals. I like all American food, I just rarely ate it."

"Can you cook?" He wondered if that sounded too forward.

"A little," she said warily.

"Tell me about your family." Hayes asked, watching her rock in her chair and watch out the window.

"Ahh well, my parents came from Germany as children. They met and married in New York but wanted an adventure, I guess." She shook her head. "So they moved to Michigan. My sister Margaret was already born, then my brother and then me. I also have a younger sister, Minna, who still lives at home. The winters were very harsh in Ready Springs, and we lost my brother to influenza." She sucked in a rattled breath. "My mother was very unhappy, and her family had sent my parents some money. That's how they were able to buy the dairy in Elbert County, where I grew up."

"I'm sorry to hear about your brother." They both looked up as their hot plates were set before them. Hayes felt at a loss of what to do next. Nadine put her napkin in her lap and looked at him.

"Do you want me to pray?" he asked.

"If you would like." She held his gaze, and he almost forgot what he asked.

"Father in Heaven, we thank you for this evening, this food, the way you made the snowflakes. Your care and concern for us is a blessing we cannot fathom. But we thank you anyway-Amen."

He reached to butter his bread. "I wanted to tell you that you did a wonderful job with the children. The program was lovely."

"You were there?" She lifted her fork with a small amount of creamy potatoes.

"I was standing in the back, on the other side from you and Nettie." He cut into his turkey. "Grace sits at the piano at home and plays the songs over and over."

She looked pleased as she took a bite. "You can help her with the piano as well as her dance steps."

"So you thought I was a good dancer? Is that what you're saying?" He raised his eyebrows, waiting.

"Let's see, Hayes." She held her coffee cup in front of her "What aren't you good at?"

Getting you to trust me, he wanted to say, but he kept chewing instead.

"Getting the carriage through the overflow of water." He scowled.

"That wasn't because of you. That was an act of nature."

His mind ticked through that crazy day. "How have things been at the store?" He regretted how serious his tone sounded.

She stirred her corn around with her fork. "Good. I've been helping Nettie more at the Feed and Seed." She starred out the window.

"I meant with any other strange things." He took another bite of turkey.

She wiggled again in her seat. The silence and starring out the window spoke volumes.

"I know you are about to change the subject. I can feel it." He grabbed her hand, and she finally looked at him. Her chin rose slightly.

"You will be happy to know I have been staying at the Wagners' this week."

"*Why* are you staying at the Wagners' this week?" He could feel the vein in his jaw pulsing. He set his fork down, suddenly losing his appetite.

32

Nadine watched the red start in Hayes' neck and slowly rise to invade his face. They were having such a nice time, sharing about her childhood, and now this. Why couldn't she just have a nice dinner with a nice man? Isn't this what other couples do? Normal people? It felt like he was suddenly angry at her.

"Why do you need to stay at the Wagners', Nadine?" he repeated.

"Because..." Nadine tried to square her shoulders. "Someone was in my room the night of the Christmas program."

"What? When you got home?" He leaned forward.

"No, bu...b....bu...but who...who...ever..." She closed her eyes and tried to breathe. This lovely dinner was a sinking ship. "Was...i...in...there burnt my bed." She exhaled. "But I...I...I am staying with Nettie. She was with me... when...we...saw it."

Sitting back quickly, he rolled his lips tight, looking everywhere but at her. "Just like at the Silver Holiday?" He turned, eyes boring into hers. "Yes?"

Feeling like a child who kept getting her skirt muddy, somehow negligent or just stupid, she whispered, "Yes."

His fingers kept pressing back and forth across his chin. "It has to be Clyde… or one of his thugs."

"I was sure it was Edgar," she murmured.

"Edgar?" He squinted. "Why?"

Nadine stared out the window again. The snow had stopped. She didn't anticipate being honest would be so difficult. But what did it matter? This would cause the distance that would keep her safe and alone.

"Edgar had wanted to pursue me in his own strange way. But he doesn't know how." She rolled her eyes. "So I thought I could just ignore him until he got the hint. But all my dismissals just made him madder. I confronted him on killing Mittens, and he became angry. But I had to make it loud and clear—I probably handled it wrong." She sighed, tilting her head to the side. "He went to the Silver Holiday and roughed up one the girls there. The sheriff came, and the Wagners agreed to send him away."

"Are they sure he stayed away?"

"I have no way of knowing. Trust me; it makes it a little difficult to find refuge in their home." She looked him in the eyes. "But I have Nettie…"

"Ohhh…" He held his hands up, mocking. "That makes me feel so much better, I-"

"Don't, Hayes," she quipped, her eyes intense. "That young woman found out who I really am and still offered me friendship. She took me in and cared for me. She never judges or asks for… anything… in return."

Hayes jerked back slightly. "I...I take that remark was aimed at me." He frowned, jaw tight. "I...do...not...judge... you. I told you about my mistakes with Molly. I have no desire to and never will cast the first stone." He paused, taking in a deep breath. "And you judged me corrupt that night in your room. Obviously still do." His voice trailed off.

The young woman came and filled their cups with coffee. Perfect timing. Nadine tried to tell herself to calm down. He didn't deny that he did want something from her. Her affections could be set aside. She would control her life and her choices, not his. A long silence hung in the air.

"I don't want to upset you...and I feel like I always do." Her voice was calmer. "It was so kind of you to invite me out and the fact that you have allowed me to care for Grace after school, and..."

"Stop," he whispered, shaking his head. "Tell me, straight up. What do you want? What do you want to do?"

Chewing on her bottom lip, fighting the emotion his question brought, she let out a huff. "I thought I wanted love and a family. But I already had that, and I ran from it. Then I cried myself to sleep..." her throat constricted and she swallowed hard, "for some feeling of redemption. But I believe God has been giving me that little by little." She clamped her mouth shut and looked around the small dining room.

"Freedom. I want freedom." She faced him. "I am the only one who can prove to myself that I can survive. I know you want to rescue me. I see it in your eyes. And many, many times, I have wanted to cling to your armor and hide behind your strength. You are smart and good and handsome. Any woman would be lucky to have you in her life."

Eyes narrowing, he sat up a little straighter. "You've been playing games with my heart since the first moment I saw you."

"I'm so sorry." Her voice was contrite. "I never-"

He held up his hand. "Don't take that wrong. I don't think it was intentional." He shook his head, the little dining room now empty. "My feelings for you are real. They are more real than any I've ever had. I wish I could convince you that I am different. I believe women should do as they wish. If it's home and family, fine. If it's running a business or running for mayor, I have no qualms. Women should have the vote and the same opportunities as men."

"Now you're being ridiculous." She dropped her head to the side.

"Maybe in Gracie's lifetime." He shrugged. "Freedom's a wonderful thing to have, but I don't want to feel like I'm selling you something." A peacefulness returned to the air. "When do you feel free now?" he asked, eyes deepening.

She pursed her lips together, thinking, then looked up. "When I'm sitting at the grand piano. My fingers begin to play the notes without reservation, the magnificent sounds bouncing from wall to wall. It starts outside of me and then begins to flood my soul. In those moments I can believe that life is good and right. I begin to float on hopefulness, my old sin and fear drowning out by crescendos of freedom." She smiled lightly. "Freedom in my fingers. Probably doesn't make much sense." Her voice trailed off.

"I'm making the music happen." She shrugged, grinning. "I know it's silly."

"*You* are the rich philosopher." He smiled.

"Your letters have certainly influenced me." Nadine stared at him, seeing that familiarity that they shared. He was the man with a bloody flannel shirt sitting across from her in the dark doctor's office. The same eyes, sitting on the stool in front of the fire after the tumble down the icy creek; the same deep, forceful, encompassing look when he held her shivering in her room.

"We'd better let them close up." He stood and grabbed her cape. "I am walking you to Nettie's, then?"

"Yes, please." Her voice matched the disappointment in her heart.

He paid the young woman and held the door open. They walked in the cold darkness, his face stoic. They approached Nettie's block, the Silver Holiday looming at the end.

"Did you know I enjoy sharpshooting?" he said as they slowed in front of the Wagner house.

"No." She sighed. "I'm sorry that all we seem to do is talk about me."

"The day you snuck from the house without saying goodbye…"

She averted his eyes.

"I found you by looking through the scope."

She tipped her head, confused.

"Freedom is something men go to war for. It should be every human's right. Unless…" His eyes flashed gray.

"Unless someone's going to harm another. You're never going to know freedom with someone after you. But you're a smart woman, and you have the freedom to figure out what to do." He took her hand in his and quickly kissed it. "Good night."

Her mouth hung open with a reply, but he had already turned and walked away. Waiting, she watched him, the cold making her ears ache. She finally climbed the large steps to the Wagner home and looked back over her shoulder. Was he being complimentary or terminating his interest in her?

33

66 I appreciate your help, Mrs. Fox." Hayes followed her, carrying the dishes into the kitchen the next evening.

"I don't understand why you don't have the piano teacher take her." She filled a kettle with water and placed it on the hot stove.

"It's complicated, and I wanted to ask you first. I will pay you extra, or if you want to have it in time off, I'd like to help you take a month this spring, to go back East and see your family."

"Well, that sounds like a fair deal. But we sit down and have a talk with that busy little bee. The piano teacher did nothing but play with her all day. Outside building snowmen in the ice and cutting up paper and on and on. I'm too old for all that. I've got enough to do."

Hayes remembered the glow on Grace's face. She had changed so much with Nadine's care. He almost hesitated, but what was best for Grace was his highest concern. "I'll try to break away early. I can do some activities with her." He could almost hear Nadine chide him about piano and dancing.

"All right then." Mrs. Fox started the dishes.

Walking back into the parlor, he looked out the window. It was too dark for any shooting, and it was almost impossible to get away by himself without thinking about her. She wanted her freedom, and he didn't begrudge her. But it was too hard to see her every day.

Seeing her gave him the intense relief that she was okay. But she made it abundantly clear that she didn't want his interference. She wanted her freedom. To want something so badly that wasn't his to have—he would not live in that prison again.

Cordial. He turned, rubbing his neck. He could go back to being cordial. But blast it, it had always felt personal with her. The Christmas holiday started this Friday, and with Grace at home, it would be a much-needed break. He would close the office at noon on Christmas eve. He could do this.

"Grace..." he called for her. "Let's hear your Christmas songs before bed."

Later in the week, Nadine checked on her cold and empty store. Nothing had changed since the day before. With the other students on Christmas holiday, she'd hoped to at least have Grace for company. Shocked and speechless were the only words to describe her reaction to Hayes' plan to keep Grace at home.

She wanted to be angry at him when he stopped in to tell her. But he was trying to be a father and actually make decisions for his daughter. She had nodded appropriately, but there were no warm smiles or long stares. Something had closed between them. Her freedom speech may have sounded brave at the time, but spending the holidays alone was crushing her heart.

Lost in her thoughts, she stepped out her back door, not seeing Nick until she ran into him.

"Oh, I'm so sorry." She saw the heavy gear in his hands. "Can I help?"

"You can grab the yellow horse blanket under my arm. The saddles I've got."

She grabbed the blanket and ran around him to open the back door to the Feed and Seed's little rooms.

He nodded to the first room. "You can throw it on the floor in there. I've been keeping my tack in here." He dropped the heavy saddles on top of the blanket and brushed the horse hair off his worn shirt. For a moment she stood and watched him. He cleared his throat and walked around her and out the door. She followed, wondering why she'd just been standing there like a gaping fish out of water.

He headed to the back room of the Feed and Seed and turned quickly. "I don't know if it's proper to say, but I think it must make a body happy to be out of mourning. I'm glad to see it." He nodded, walked on and turned again. "For you, I mean." He blinked fast and walked into the warm back room. Nadine followed.

"I haven't had the chance to tell you." She waited while he reached for a cup. "It is wonderfully honorable for you to change your route to help Nettie here at the Feed and Seed."

"The winters can get a mite bit harsh, and this gives me more time to sleep with a real roof over my head." He took a sip of coffee and checked the clipboard Nettie left with him with the orders. "I'm sure Edgar will be back soon." He flipped the pages, never looking up.

She gasped. "Why do you say that?"

He looked up, his eyes searching. "I realize this is temporary. When Edgar gets back, he will do this job."

Nadine clutched the collar on her new brown dress, then began chewing on her fingernail. "Did someone say when Edgar would be back?"

"I assume when he's done helping his grandma. Maybe the first of the year?" He shrugged.

Nadine's mind raced. Would Nettie tell her about the family's plan? Why would they? Who was she? Just a renter paying a meager rent. Edgar was family. Of course they were invested in him. Of course they would help him.

"Don't look so worried. Have you been running out of wood? I can go now and chop a stack for you."

"Oh...I...think its fine. I have no students right now, and I've been staying with Nettie this week."

Nick offered a quick nod before he walked into the store.

Nadine walked around the side of the stove and found Roxie stretched out.

"Hey there." She bent down to scratch her behind the ear. "What do you think I should do? Freedom is good, options are nice...but what if you're not good at choosing?

And when you do, they usually go bad?" Roxie began to purr. "I'm glad you can purr again."

For the first time, Nadine had an overwhelming sadness for what her mother must be going through. Christmas was her family's favorite time. The presents, the sweet cakes, singing and playing piano with her sisters. Why hadn't she thought of going home?

She stood up. Because she thought she would have Grace. Her eyes drooped closed. Was staying in Carver really freedom? Maybe it was just an excuse not to go home. She had come so far here. Nettie knew most of the truth, and Hayes knew it all. The Wagners were very kind, but she felt out of place in their home.

Looking at the store door, she swung on her heel. Time to go shopping. *Buy some new things for my little room, and hopefully, Christmas presents for Nettie and Grace.*

Nadine had enjoyed the leisurely afternoon shopping at the Nickel Emporium. Her packages were tied and tucked under her arm. She looked both ways, preparing to cross to the opposite side of the street to avoid the railroad office. But before she stepped off, she saw Hayes walking towards her.

He had a tight-lipped smile and nodded at her. "Nice to see you."

She swung her foot back to the sidewalk and grimaced.

"Like that side of Carver better?" He raised his eyebrows.

"I like your brown tweed." She smiled, twirling her finger at his suit. "It's one of my favorites."

"Nadine…Nadine…Oh, Nadine…" He shook his head, biting his bottom lip from smiling.

"Yes, of course, I like that side of Carver. How is Grace?"

"Grace is well."

They both moved to the side as a mother and son walked by.

"I have something for her for Christmas. I wondered how to get it to her." She closed her eyes with a tiny head shake. That sounded like she was fishing for an invite.

"Bring it to church. Or you can bring it by my office."

"Yes, yes…good idea. Well, I'd better be on my way." She scurried to get past him, but he reached out and grabbed her arm. Looking up, that grin she loved tipped up one side of his mouth.

"I really like that you are… you." He winked and released her quickly.

34

"Good morning, ladies." Mr. Wagner walked into the kitchen and grabbed a piece of bacon off the plate. "What a pleasure to have two hard-working young women in my kitchen this morning."

"This one works like two, doing circles around me," Nadine said, nodding at Nettie.

"Oh, Mrs. Von Keller, your new mattress arrived at the general store. I'll have some help bring it over today." He dropped his chin, giving them a fatherly look. "Let's keep the lantern off the bed, girls. I would think that you two are a bit old for jumping on the bed."

Nadine saw Nettie look away and grab her coat. "Nadine, are you ready?"

"Yes." She nodded to Mr. Wagner. "Thank you for the mattress. I so appreciate your hospitality these last several days."

"It was our pleasure. And Nettie, you know that your friends are welcome for Christmas dinner."

Nettie nodded back, but as they walked down to the Feed and Seed, she seemed usually quiet.

"What is it, Nettie? I know you told a story to your parents, but I was going to try to replace the mattress myself. I didn't want your family-"

"It's not that." She unlocked the back door and started a fire in the back room stove. "I didn't want you to feel torn over Christmas. I knew you would want to spend it with Hayes and Grace. I understand, I do. I just don't know if I can sit through a meal with Nick. For some reason, when I hadn't declared my feelings for him, I could get along. But now it feels so…oh, I don't know…"

"Painful," Nadine added.

"Pitifully painful." Nettie sighed.

"I haven't had a chance to tell you, but my dinner with Hayes didn't go that wonderfully. I am fairly sure I won't spend Christmas with that family."

Nettie squinted. "I wondered why Grace wasn't here."

Nadine let out a long breath and rubbed her hands over the warm stove. "You struggle when Nick shows no interest. I'm even worse. Hayes shows kindness, and I push him away, and then I find him even more attractive."

Nettie let out a squeak. "Are you okay to go back to the little room? You're welcome to stay with me as long as you want."

Nadine shook her head. "I gave Hayes a speech about wanting my freedom. Humph. I'm so naïve. I thought if I could just get away from my parents' house, I could finally breathe and be my own person. I had no idea it would be so hard. So thank you for the offer, but I want to get through the holiday and back to my little routine." She grabbed the large broom. "I'll start the sweeping if you want to unlock."

Nick came in the back door, shaking from the afternoon cold. "Mmm. Soup." He leaned over where Nadine was cutting some bread.

"Got time for a bowl?" Nadine asked.

"Yes, Ma'am. Have you and Nettie already eaten?"

"We were just about to, but Nettie had some customers walk in." She served Nick a full bowl and a slice of buttered bread.

He took in a deep breath and closed his eyes. He was a praying man, Nadine observed. Nettie loves the Bible. Why hadn't he ever pursued her?

"Say, Nick." Nadine glanced back to make sure Nettie was busy. "Do you think you and Nettie could ever be more than friends?"

His body stiffened, and he swallowed hard.

Nadine knew she had just dropped him into a hot kettle.

"I...I..." He held his bowl up to drink his soup.

"Do you have someone special somewhere else?"

"No, no..." He wiped his face with the back of his arm.

"Do you think she's attractive?"

He began to squirm in his seat, eyes wider. "Well...yes..."

Nadine took one last look to be sure Nettie was still busy, then leaned her hands on the table. "Then *what* is it? You can tell me. I would never do anything to hurt her."

"She...she...is Nettie. Nettie Wagner."

"Yes, that we both know good and well." Nadine leaned a bit lower to watch his face twist.

"I am a nobody. I have no family. The Wagners are the closest to family I've ever had."

"Yes and...sooo..."

"So they would never approve of me." He jumped up so fast that he had to catch the back of his chair before it hit the ground. "I'm sure...they...they want some upstanding gentlemen to court her." He looked left to right, trying to find the fastest way out. Nadine cut him off as he headed for the back door.

"Nick." She tried to soften her voice as she touched his arm. "We are talking about Nettie, our Nettie. If you have true feelings, don't let that stop you. It wouldn't be a problem, because they just want her to be happy."

"Exactly," he said leaning in. "What can I offer that would make her happy? I don't even live in a house." He grabbed her by the waist and scooted her over. Nadine felt the cold air fly up her neck, as he opened and quickly closed the door behind him. Frustrated, she shook her head and looked up to see Nettie standing in the kitchen.

"Did you hear that?" Nadine let out a long breath, seeing Nettie's face turn red.

"No, but I saw enough. I always thought he'd taken a fancy to you. How easy it was for him to put his hands on you? How many beaus did you have in your hometown—two that wanted to marry you? Then you turn Mr. Sullivan's head, then Edgar and now Nick. Holy hen walk, Nadine, *all* the roosters want you! But you can't be had. The gorgeous young woman who pulls the men around by a string."

Nadine felt her heart beating out of her chest. "Nettie..y...you..."

They both looked up as two young men came in the back room carrying a mattress. "Where does this go?" one of them asked.

"Follow her," Nettie barked, eyes glistening with tears. "But be careful—don't get too close."

Nadine stood in shock. Her feet wouldn't move. This dreadfulness could not go on a minute longer. "Nettie... please...listen!"

Nettie had already turned and walked away.

35

Nadine bent forward, tucking her new sheet under the new mattress. At least her nose and eyes could drip onto the bedding. She'd filled her only two hankies and wasn't close to finding relief. She threw the new blanket over the sheet and grabbed her pillow. Everything in her ached. Falling onto the bed, she buried her face in the pillow and sobbed harder.

Truly, she was an obvious trollop. Nettie had pointed out her list of mistakes so succinctly. Even though she had misunderstood the encounter with Nick, Nettie was right. Like a black spider hiding in the woodpile, she caught men in the sticky web for her purposes, just like Marcus had used her for his own purpose. She felt the darkness deep into her gut. Nettie had left out the lying and deceitfulness that poured from her jagged mouth. Nadine curled around her pillow and rocked back and forth. She'd wanted to believe in redemption for one so soiled, but she was wrong to think it could apply to her.

She couldn't sleep for the shivering in her body. Bending down over her little pot belly stove, she lit a match to the thin wood. The small flames crackled to life as she sat cross-legged on the floor. As hard as the heat tried to invade her skin, her soul was frozen.

Nettie was all that was good and right in this world. She was the constant Nadine relied on her faith, her hope, her acceptance. Nadine pressed her hand against her mouth. She could still hear Nettie's voice. It was so cold, so hurt. She sucked in another sob. How sweet and simple was Nettie's life before she came? Why did she have to press Nick? He clearly didn't want to talk. Nobody had asked her to intervene.

She cried out to the ceiling. "O…o…kay, o…o…o kay. I…I…I g…ge…get it!" Her stuttering competed with her sobs. "I'm l…leaving, I…m… leaving…" She wept into her hands. "Be…be…fore I d…do m…more d…da… damage."

Sunday, Christmas Eve and now Christmas had all come and gone. The silence and darkness of her little room were all she required. Even tea and bread were hard to swallow. If there was a moment her gut wasn't twisting, she pictured how she might say goodbye to Grace.

She'd separated her few things; she would leave the red dress back in the trunk. It was never really hers—just another costume covering who she really was. She looked down at her few bills and coin. Most of the money she had to buy a ticket home was from Hayes. How ironic. He had rescued her from that smoke-filled room and now was the one to pay for her ticket out. So, so overdue.

Chewing on her bottom lip, she wondered if she could give away all the piano music she had penned for the children. That would mean staying until she could meet with each of them. She closed her eyes, knowing she didn't have the strength to endure their questions.

She set aside the money for January's rent for the Wagners. If they only knew the details of Edgar's explosive day, they would realize how imperative it was that she leave Carver. Now he could return to work with the family, and she wouldn't have to look over her shoulder wondering if he was dangerous.

And then there was her delusional desire for freedom. Hayes had clearly pointed out she would never know that. It made sense then and even more so at this moment. She could never make a life in Carver. Another thing Marcus had ruined in this town. She dropped her face into her hands.

Facing her parents might be more painful than leaving here. Both felt excruciating. What was the story Nettie had read her? Something about the son running home after destroying his life. Nettie said the father was the picture of God running toward us with open arms. She tried to picture her vater, her own father, running towards her. It was a little too farfetched.

She looked up when she heard a sound downstairs. Someone was calling her name. Quickly putting her things back in her bag, she began to panic. It sounded like Nettie. Oh, dear Lord no—she looked around, wondering how she could-

"Nadine!" Nettie sounded like she was crying. "Please… please…come out. I have to see you…pleaessee Nadine…I am soooo sorry for what I said."

"I…I…" Nadine dropped her head, trying to clear the stuttering. "It…its…a…all…all…right Net…Net…Nettie."

"Please, open the door. I won't leave until you talk to me."

Nadine turned the handle, hoping to get the conversation over with. Nettie bound through the door, throwing her arms around Nadine.

"I'm so sorry for what I said." She squeezed her. "I didn't know." She pulled back, looking Nadine in the eyes. "I didn't know…that it wasn't what I saw. Please." Nettie gave her a little shake. "I can't breathe until you forgive me."

Nadine tried to speak but the words would not form. She pulled on her collar "I…i…it…it's …o…o…okay."

Nettie grabbed her in a tight embrace. "I can hear how badly I have upset you. I don't know if I can forgive myself."

Nadine found herself rubbing her friend's back as Nettie cried on her shoulder. Nadine knew Nettie would blame herself for her decision to leave. How could she leave Nettie without hurting her more?

"It's just unforgivable." Nettie pulled back her tear soaked face.

Nadine wiped her hand gently across Nettie's face, her smile trying to communicate she wasn't angry.

"Nick came for Christmas. Poor guy." Nettie chuckled. "I couldn't even look him in the eye. He didn't know I was upset. Well, I guess he figured it out." Her eyes widened.

"I just blurted everything out." She spun in a circle, hands waving. "It actually turned out to be one of the best conversations I've ever had with him." She nodded at Nadine, trying to convince her. "Really."

Nettie's face dropped. "Oh, Nadine, you look so pale."

"I...I..." Nadine swallowed hard, her words refusing to form. "a...am...f...fi...fine."

"Are you cold?" Nettie rubbed her hands up and down Nadine's arms. "I've made some sausage and beans. They're warm on the stove." Nettie grabbed her hands. "These are like ice. Please come sit with me." She tugged lightly.

Nadine tried to respond, but her throat would constrict each time she tried to speak. Nettie clutched her hand as they went down the stairs. Nadine pulled back and held up her hand for Nettie to wait. She walked back up the stairs and grabbed the gift off her nightstand. Coming back to where Nettie was waiting, she held it out.

"Oh friend, you are going to make me cry again." Nettie pulled on the little ribbon, opening the tissue paper. She sucked in a breath. "Oh Nadine, it's so beautiful." She pressed on the round silver compact's side until it popped open, holding it up to her face. "I love it." She hugged her again.

Nettie sat a steaming bowl of beans in front of Nadine. "Nick's been helping in the front of the store today, but because of the ice storm, there are not many people in town."

Nadine took a small spoonful. She still didn't have any appetite.

"So, there we were, Christmas night. My parents tried to carry the conversation as long as they could." Nettie stared toward the front of the feed store. Nadine felt her stomach clench. It was the same thing she had done days ago, watching to be sure Nettie didn't overhear. "Nick gave me a little box, but I was so mad I barely looked at it. It was a sweet little pin, a circle of holly." She glanced over her shoulder again. "I asked him what he got you."

She clamped her hand over her mouth. "I say the meanest things...I'm so sorry." She squeezed Nadine's shoulder. "He was oblivious of course, until I asked him what you two were talking about in the back room. His face turned red, and I knew I'd caught him. But then he told me..."

She threw her head back and covered her face. "I have never been *sooo* wrong in my life. I should have been thanking you. He told me he never believed my parents would allow him to court me. Something about being community business people and him a lowly freighter." She blurted. "Like we are uptown snobs or something." She let out a long huff. "So then-" Nettie stopped. "I need to shut up. You look so sad, and it's my fault."

Nadine tried to shake her head. "N...no...I...I'm...n...no...not s...s...sad." She dropped her head. "I...a...am f...f...frus...t...ra...rated." She pulled the clipboard and turned over a piece of paper, grabbing the little pencil. *Sometimes my stuttering gets this bad,* she scribbled. *It's not your fault. I forgive you. I'm so happy you and Nick talked.* Nadine pushed the paper in front of her and forced a smile.

"Well, this is going to seem funny, my buddy." Nettie grabbed a package off the shelf and brought it to Nadine. Nadine dropped her head to the side to see a flat box with a Christmas ribbon on it. She hated that her hands were trembling as she opened it. Inside were cream colored parchment paper and a stack of envelopes. Lifting them up, she saw a beautiful N and V scripted on the corners. "O..oh...N..Net...Nettie." Her eyes filled with tears.

"For all that letter writing... with a certain someone." Nettie lifted her eyebrows mischievously. "And your parents, of course. Or when your stuttering gets bad."

Nadine couldn't have conveyed her emotions if she'd wanted to. The tears flowed over her cheeks as she rose and hugged her friend.

36

The thin wool cape did nothing against the bitter Minnesota cold. Nadine stepped up the few stairs to the small house the Thomasons lived in next to the church. She rose her hand to knock, but hesitated. Mrs. Thomason had a large family, and might be too busy to break away.

Looking down, she saw a little blond boy move the lacey curtains aside. "Grammie, a lady is here," she heard faintly through the glass. As Nadine tried to breathe in a steady breath, Mrs. Thomason opened the door.

"Oh, Nadine, I didn't hear you knock."

"I...I...d...di..." Mrs. Thomason pulled her in and closed the door before she could finish.

"Ca...ca...can...y...y..." She dropped her chin and willed her tongue to cooperate. "T...ta...talk?"

"Yes, yes, you poor thing. You must be frozen solid." Mrs. Thomason pointed to a small parlor. She pulled the pocket doors together. "Let me get you something warm to drink first."

"No, ple...please, j...ju...just a m...mo...moment of your t...ti...time."

"Yes, please. Let's sit."

Nadine tried to sit tall and allow the warmth of this home into her being. "My," she took another deep breath, "stu...stut...tering, has g...go..got..ten wor...worse...than ...ever." She tried to offer a quick smile.

Mrs. Thomason lightly touched her fingers to her lips. "I'm so sorry, dear."

Nadine realized she was repeatedly twisting the button on her cape and dropped her hands quickly. "I will be l... le..leaving Ca...Car...Carver. I wa...wan..wanted to say...t.. tha..." Nadine squeezed her eyes shut. The tears forming were just making this worse. "...tha...thank you." She tried to keep the large lump in her throat down.

"You're leaving us?" Mrs. Thomason sounded uncertain. "You've become a delightful part of our little community. Look how far you've come from the moment I met you." Her face radiated motherly concern.

Nadine swiped back the slow falling tears. "I...o...owe it to you," she whispered.

Mrs. Thomason moved from her chair and sat next to Nadine on the settee. "Maybe it's just me being noisy." She grabbed her hands. "But maybe it's the Holy Spirit telling me to pray. So can we do that?"

Nadine nodded.

"Our dear Father, I ask for your child Nadine. Would you please come and be her peace? Fill her with Your grace and love today." Mrs. Thomason released one of her hands and began to rub Nadine's back. It was like someone was rubbing warm oil into her cold skin. Nadine brought her hand gently

across her wet cheek, the heat from her fingers surprising her. *"And for this fear to be released, this tongue to speak. Your wisdom Father, for this lovely one. And for our hearts to recover as we would painfully have to say goodbye. Amen and Amen."*

Nadine held her eyes closed. All she could feel was her heart beating. The relentless ache in her neck and back were gone. She felt peaceful, like she was wrapped in clouds. "Thank you," she whispered, not wanting to move from this moment.

"Can I share one of my favorite verses?" Mrs. Thomason asked. "It's from 2 Corinthians 12:9. My grace is sufficient for thee; for my strength is made perfect in weakness. Most gladly therefore will I rather glory in my infirmities, that the power of Christ may rest upon me."

Mrs. Thomason paused, and the silence felt holy. "As a young woman completely on your own, you have found strength. I wish I could say it just appears for us, but we only grow by going through the hard things." She patted Nadine's knee. "If there's something I can do or talk to someone for you or help…"

"No." Nadine shook her head, thinking. "It's just time."

Nadine walked slowly back to the Feed and Seed. She needed to tell Nettie, but with her stuttering so bad, it was painful to communicate. She wondered about the strange feeling she'd had praying with Mrs. Thomason—the complete opposite of how'd she felt when she walked in. Had God really touched her? Is that what it felt like? She watched the white air float from her exhaled breath. Time to find out. She opened the back door to the Feed and Seed and walked in.

"Nadine. How was tea with Mrs. Thomason?"

Nadine smiled. It felt like she was back to the first day she had met Nettie Wagner. "No tea. Just some prayer." Nadine was relieved that her words cooperated.

"Well, that's always a good thing." Nettie smiled.

Nadine looked around to make sure the store was empty. "I n...needed the prayer... be...because I have d...de...cided to g...go...home."

"For a visit?" Nettie's eyes were like saucers.

"For g...good." Nadine glanced at the floor, willing her tears to stay at bay.

"Please." Nettie almost fell forward. "I have hurt you beyond repair. Please...don't do this..."

Nadine reached out and squeezed her hands. "I would do anything if you would not blame y...y...yourself. You know what happened to me." She gave her a little shake. "I should have gone home months ago. I thought I could run from my past, but-"

"God has forgiveness for all of us, Nadine." Nettie begged. "Where sin does abound, grace much more does abound." Nettie sighed, letting go of their hands and squeezed her head. "I didn't mean to say you alone abound in sin—we all do. So sorry!"

Nadine smiled. "I love you, Nettie. You are the only real friend I've ever had. I don't have enough days to convince you that I'm not leaving because we had a falling out. I'm leaving because it's the right thing to do."

Nettie stood still, a blank look covering her. "You are the best friend I've ever had." Her face began to crumble, as a loud moan rushed out. Throwing her arms around Nadine, they held each other and wept. It was the only thing needed.

37

Nadine lifted the new stationary to her nose and inhaled. How could Nettie have known? It was so thoughtful. She'd awoken this morning with a purpose. She could write each piano student and include a few pieces of music they were working on. Rising to reach the oil lamp, she turned it up. It was a gray morning, making it hard to see all the music spread out over the piano. The beautiful instrument would go dormant once again. She sighed, gently pulling her fingers over the ivory. She looked up suddenly as someone knocked on the door.

"Hayes." She exhaled, stepping to unlock the door. He swept in, looking upset, and handed her a small card. *Nadine is leaving, Nettie,* it said. "This was on my desk this morning."

"I was going to tell you myself." She whisked around to the other side of the piano. "I wish she hadn't done that."

"What happened?" He followed her. "Did someone threaten you?" He touched her elbow.

"No." She turned quickly and backed away. "I just had time for…some soul…searching. I…I." She refused to allow her heart to constrict her tongue.

"Will you be back?" The muscle in his jaw flexed.

She stared into his eyes, waiting for something to change her mind "No. I won't."

He rubbed his temple, looking shocked.

"I would never have left without talking to you. I know how painful that was from-"

He huffed, interrupting, and shook his head. "Grace will be devastated. All she's talked about lately is having you for her birthday." He stalked over to the window and looked out. "When are you leaving?"

"Soon. The stage office opens again on Thursday." She walked up behind him. As long as he didn't look at her, her voice stayed steady. "I heard what you said. I will never feel safe here. My past has made that certain."

He stood staring ahead, shaking his head.

"I never wanted to hurt you," she whispered. "I take the blame for staying too long."

He turned suddenly. "Then stay until the end of the week. Come Saturday for her birthday."

Nadine rolled her lips and looked away from his sunken eyes. He was thinking of Grace. That's all she ever wanted. "All right." She turned to him. "But I want her here for a day. I don't want to ruin her birthday. I can tell her and…" She was an adult and didn't want to face the separation. What could she do to help a child? "…and help her understand."

"I'll bring her tomorrow. Thank you for waiting." He nodded.

The silence was lingering as they looked at each other. Nadine could feel her hand tingling to touch him, maybe the crease between his eyes, or the stubble on his serious face. She gripped the layers of her skirt.

"I'll see you tomorrow." He moved away and strode out the door, his absence bringing an instant emptiness.

The next day, Grace bound into the little store like a storm of sunshine. She rattled on and on about the dollhouse her papa had given her. She loved to move the little pieces of furniture around, making little things out of scraps of fabric.

She wanted to look for the other kittens, to see if Mittens had just gone back to his first family. Nadine took her next door, dropping into the back room chair as Grace called for the kittens.

"Not even lunch and you already look worn out." Nick walked by with a heavy bag on his shoulder.

Nadine smiled and nodded as Grace ran by. He set the bag on a pallet. "I wanted to tell you how sorry I am for everything. Nettie said you plan to leave and move back home?"

"Yes." Nadine sighed. "Maybe you could help me convince her it's not because of our misunderstanding." She leaned to the side, watching where Grace was off to. "I've had the money to go home for months. It's just that... that...now's the right time."

"Sure." He shifted foot to foot. "Must be hard being so far from family."

Nadine gave him a weak smile. If he only knew how these people had found their way into her tumbledown heart.

"You've been a good friend to her." He nodded.

"If *you* will be a good friend to her, I could leave in peace." Watching Nick's face flush, Nadine wished she could grab her words back.

"I will reassure you that is my intention," he said matter-of-factly.

Grace ran up to the table quickly, breaking the awkward moment.

"Can we make decorations now?"

"Yes, bug," Nadine pulled her onto her lap. She couldn't help touch the soft copper spirals around her angle face. When Nick walked out, she cradled Grace in the crook of her arm. "I want to tell you something important. First, I am very excited to come over Saturday and celebrate your birthday. But after that, I have to take a trip."

"Where are you going?" Grace sat up and looked up to her face.

"I'm going home to the dairy. In Wisconsin where I live."

"The dairy? Where the cows give milk?"

"Yes, that's the place. You remember me telling you about it?"

Grace's chin wiggled back and forth. "When will you be back?"

Nadine took in a steadying breath. "I don't think I will. I'm going back to live there. I...I... won't live here in Carver anymore."

"Why not?" she whined.

Her question so simple from a simple heart, and yet it was so complicated. "I...just...can't," Nadine whispered.

"Because you miss your mommy and daddy?"

Nadine wrapped Grace in her arms and kissed her forehead. "Yes, my love. I miss my home."

Hayes had quickly gathered Grace at the end of the day. He looked tired and told her he would be by at noon on Saturday to pick her up. After they left, she walked around the piano three or four times. Most of the music was sorted and put into envelopes for the children. She sat down on the bench, her fingers hovering over the keys.

She played a few soft chords. Nothing in particular, just allowing her heart to have its desired freedom. It was silly. Of course Hayes didn't understand. Truly, there was a freedom the first time she walked to the school, the first time she came to church, the first time she walked down to the Nickel Emporium and just browsed. There was freedom playing in the snow and chasing Grace. Her fingers seemed to quicken with the memories. There was freedom when she could have given into the desire in Hayes' eyes, but she didn't.

Her fingers jumped from the keys when she saw movement from the corner of her eye. Nick and Nettie clapped loudly, the sound echoing off the brick walls.

"That was amazing!" Nettie stepped forward. "Don't stop! I've never heard that before. Where's the music? You know that piece by heart?"

Nadine rose quickly from the bench. "I was just playing recklessly."

"Nell's Bells, Nadine. It was like something from a big city concert."

Nadine gave them a little curtsy.

"Come have supper with us," Nick said.

"Yes! We were hoping you would." Nettie held out her hand.

Nadine took it and walked out the back with them, such unexplainable comfort penetrating each step.

38

Hayes finished wrapping some small carved animals for Grace's dollhouse. With the curtains pulled open, the sun made a large yellow line across his room. It was unusually bright and warm for such a cold day. He looked out the window. He wished he could take the whole day for himself. He would walk the property and into the woods and do some target shooting. Really, anything that would keep his mind off this day. The last day he would ever see Nadine.

"Something for you today." He smiled at Grace as he set the package on the large dining table.

She put her drawing aside. "Can I open it now?"

"No. You have to wait for the party." He flipped her ponytail. "I think I smell something wonderful. I'm guessing -"

"A cake!" Grace shouted, jumping off her seat and skipping around the table, into the parlor and back around the table. His grandmother would never have allowed her to run in the house.

The child was happy, thank goodness, especially after a few nights of talking about Mrs. Von Keller leaving. She seemed to understand that she wanted to see her family. He waited, looking away until Grace was just about to pass him and he reached out, scooping her up into his arms. She kicked and giggled as he pretended to drop her and then lift her back up. She screamed as he tickled her and held her by her legs, finally leaving her in a squirming pile on the floor.

Mrs. Fox came around the corner, ready to reprimand her, Hayes guessed. "Nothing's broken." He tried to ward off a correction. "Just some birthday fun." He heard her huff as she went back into the kitchen. Grace had looped herself around his foot and calf. "How strange. There must be a large snake in the house." He tried to walk around like nothing was wrong. "I'd better go find some snake poison."

Grace shrieked and let go. "Goodbye," she uttered, running off.

"I'm going to pick up Mrs. Von Keller," he hollered after her.

Walking to the barn, he hesitated in front of the carriage. Without an ominous cloud in the sky, a horseback ride seemed needed. It was brazen—she would have to ride in his arms.

He could still remember pulling her from that smoke-filled room, his arms filled with her under a massive black coat. The thoughts still startled him as he secured the bridle in place. Laying her on the doc's cot and watching the soft brown hair fall from her face. His heart quickened, just like the first time he really saw her. She was young and incredibly beautiful.

He blew out a held breath as he cinched the saddle in place. The strong immediate attraction had increased month by month, but it wasn't just her beauty. From those first conversations, he wanted to know about her. Unfortunately, he hadn't been alone with a woman for years.

He swung his leg up and over the saddle, giving the horse a little kick. For a thirsty man, little did she know she was rushing clear water. But she saw herself only as a muddy pit, pushing him away and keeping the appropriate distance.

He shook his head and nudged the horse into a gallop. He would never judge her. He had his own reckless youth that haunted him. If anyone could love her and understand her, it was him. His horse was alive with independence, but he had to pull it back as he approached the town.

Love her and understand her. The words rang true all through him. Winded from the brisk ride, he vacillated making a formal declaration. What did love and understanding matter now? No words of poetry or persuasion were going to trump her desire to make her own choices. He knew that determined look on her face. She was leaving, and leaving for good.

Hayes held the door open for her as she walked out and turned to lock the door. Looking to the sidewalk and back at him, her brow furrowed. "I recognize your horse, but it's missing a buggy."

He smiled slowly and touched her arm. "The sun was shining, and I thought a ride would be nice."

"For you… and I am walking?" She stepped forward.

"No," he laughed, lightly placing his hands around her waist. "I will help you, and you can have the saddle. Do you want to ride side saddle?" The horse moved next to the sidewalk. "Grab the horn."

"I have Grace's gift." She turned around, and he instantly felt her chest brush against his chest. They were so close that he couldn't think, only wanting to press her warmth with his. She opened her mouth and turned back toward the horse.

"I'll hold it." She grabbed for the horn.

Quickly he lifted her up. She sat sideways in the saddle. Reaching for the tethered reins, he pulled them around as he swung onto the back of the horse. He heard her gasp as the horse moved. "We're good. I can reach the stirrups." His arms surrounded her, pulling the horse to the right. "Didn't ride much at the dairy?"

"Heavens no."

"So, what are you looking forward to when you get home?"

Her head shook lightly. "I hadn't really thought about it. I…I…" Her shoulder lifted and dropped quickly. "I'm… not…sure how they will react to seeing me."

"I understand." He paused, not wanting to make her sad. "I am guessing they don't know the details."

She leaned to the side, catching his eyes. "No." She looked out to the road. "I have an older sister, Margaret. She's a teacher at an orphanage school in Chicago. My mother treats her like she's signed up for the French Foreign Legion. She just can't understand her not being married or not living at home." She turned again, squinting up at him. "But then…" she bumped her elbow back into him. "What will you do when Grace wants to move from home?"

"Probably go with her." He exhaled, seeing they were outside of the town. After what seemed like a long silence, he wrapped his arms tighter around her, dropping his fore-head on her shoulder. "I want to thank you," he whispered, lightly resting his cheek next to hers.

"For what?" she murmured.

He straightened up, taking in a deep breath. "For every-thing. She's a great child, living right under my nose and I didn't even know her. What's worse is I didn't want to know her or care for her. I was so consumed with Molly's betrayal. I didn't see the gift right in front of me. It was almost like if I didn't accept Grace, I could wash my hands of everything Molly."

The clop of the horse's hooves kept rhythm in the silence.

"Then I want to thank you." She looked far off, to where the creek ran. "You allowed me to be in her life. She brought such comfort and sunlight to me, and yet I know you didn't trust me." She rubbed her brow. "And you shouldn't have."

"I trusted you. I knew from the first night I met you. Now, no one could talk in circles better than you." He nudged her shoulder. "But I could see you were lost and suffering. The way you looked past yourself to love and laugh with her. Watching you hold her hand and kiss her cheek goodbye. The things no one else had done."

They approached the dirt road to the Victorian. "I guess we've both been saved by grace," she whispered.

"I think you could say that." He led the horse into the yard and swung off. Nadine was still holding the package in a tight grip. He held his arms out as she slipped out of the saddle and onto her feet. It was obvious he didn't want to move.

"Are there other children coming today?" She looked up, soft brown eyes meeting his.

"You are the only guest." He still couldn't seem to move, holding the reins and her arms. "It really was her only request. I know you think I arranged it for me." His remark was rewarded with her flawless smile. "I wanted you with us at Christmas. I knew you were with the Wagners, but I still wished it was us."

Her expression hardened, and she looked away. "Shall we go find the birthday girl?" she said quickly.

"Thank you, Mrs. Fox, for the petite fortes. And your bean salad was delicious," Nadine said as Mrs. Fox cleared the dishes.

Hayes stood and placed Grace's gifts on the table. She jumped in her chair and began to clap. "Yip Yee!"

"This one is from Mrs.....Miss..." he stumbled. "Von Keller." Grace pulled the string off and pulled the soft stuffed animal out. "Ahh." Grace hugged it. "I love it. It's so soft."

"The last time I was here, I remember Mr. Pippy was losing his fur. Now you will have two to love."

"I will call this one Mr. Zippy." she said, bright-eyed.

Hayes pushed his gift over to her. She pulled the string and pulled out a wooden dog, cat, cow, and horse.

"For your dollhouse." He smiled.

Grace jumped from her chair and ran to him. "Can I get a barn house?"

Lifting her up into his lap, he laughed. "I guess I should have thought the horse and cow would need a barn."

She touched her little fingers to his cheeks. "Can we go to Mrs. Von Keller's dairy and see the cows?"

He gently set her down. "Only if she invites us." He gave Nadine a quick wink. "Let's put our coats on and go for a walk. That, is if you have time, Nadine."

"I do." She nodded. "Besides, I have to stay for singing and cake."

"Yes, yes!" Grace jumped up and down. They walked to the foyer and gathered their coats from the closet.

Hayes looked up quickly. "Wait a moment. I need to grab something." He took the stairs two by two. Nadine was tying a knit cap under Grace's chin when he came back down, a gift in his hands.

"Hayes." Her eyes flickered with confusion. "You shouldn't have."

"Just open it."

She drew in a ragged breath and pulled back the paper. 'They're beautiful," she said, holding up the new brown leather gloves.

"I wasn't sure of your size. I guessed a small. And thought to forgo the black ones." He gave her a lopsided grin.

She slipped them on and clutched them together. "They are perfect." She smiled, her eyes misting. "Thank you," she mouthed, blinking back the tears.

"You'll need them for your trip." He moved away, pulling his jacket on, wishing he hadn't stated the obvious.

The crisp air and brisk walk were enjoyable. No words were needed. They both seemed content to watch Grace looking for ice puddles to jump in, the bright sun warding off the bitter cold.

"Do you have someone in mind for Grace after school?" Nadine asked.

He shook his head. "I don't. I don't...want to picture walking up to those yellow curtains and not seeing you with her. It was the best part of my day." He looked out to the horizon.

"Well, you are a wonderful boss to work for." She smiled.

"You should tell that to George and Ralph," Hayes quipped as they walked on. Her foot caught on a rut in the road, and he reached out to steady her. She allowed him to tuck her hand in the crook of his arm. It felt so natural for them to walk together and watch Grace. He wondered if her insides were aching as badly as his. He contemplated dropping to one knee and proposing marriage. Anything to get her to stay. Looking at her, she seemed content. Making her own decisions; her quest for freedom.

"Hayes." She stared down the rugged dirt road. "I want to leave you my parents' address with one favor."

"Anything."

"Would you have Grace write me or draw a picture? Whatever she wants."

"Yes, of course."

"I will write her back." She swiped a loose hair behind her ear.

He couldn't guard his emotions anymore. Stopping, he pulled her in front of him. "What about me? Can I write to you?" He paused, smiling, waiting to gauge her reaction.

39

Hayes' blue eyes savored the moment. The way he had her hand locked under his arm. The way she felt when he brought his other hand around her. He knew she was melting next to him. He wasn't going to make this easy.

"Hmm. Let me think." She dropped her head to the side. "Probably only Grace should write. You don't really have any talent in that area."

He chewed on his lip, fighting a smile. "You don't say."

"Of course, I can't stop you from writing to me." She batted her eyes a few times. "Your dry and impersonal style would be good for putting me to sleep."

He straighten up, eyes going narrow. "There will be no cake for you."

"All right." She pushed against his chest. "You can toss a snippet in with hers."

Grace ran around them, her cheeks bright red. "I'm cold."

"Let's get back then." Hayes reached for Grace's hand as Grace gripped Nadine with the other hand.

Hayes put another log on the parlor fire as they stood near to get warm. Nadine walked over to their oak upright piano. She pinged out the simple notes to *He's a Jolly Good Fellow*. Grace joined her, and they played it together.

"Sing it, Papa," Grace said.

"Only with your help."

Grace stood up on the piano bench as Nadine played the song. They all sang, changing the words to 'she's a jolly good fellow' and held out the last word, as Nadine exaggerated the notes, playing up and down the keys for dramatic effect. They ended with cheers, and Nadine stood and wrapped her arms around Grace. "Happy, Happy Birthday my little bug." She kissed her ear. "Now ask your Papa if I can have some cake."

Grace licked the frosting off the bottom of all the candles.

"Germans like to take credit for birthday candles," Nadine said as she forked her cake.

Hayes nodded as he chewed. "Do they take credit for teaching their daughters to-"

Nadine shot him an evil warning.

"I...I was just going to say...play piano well."

She tried to appear stoic, but couldn't as Hayes began to laugh. A snicker flowed out, and she had to cover her mouth. It was the best day she'd had in a very long time.

Mrs. Fox came to clear the dishes. Nadine knew it would be dark soon. They all looked up when they heard a knock at the door.

"Who ya expecting now? Mrs. Fox grumbled.

"No one," he said as he stood and walked to the foyer. Nadine and Grace rose as Hayes opened the door and watched him begin to back away. Nadine's heart plummeted as his face went pale.

"Molly... what are you doing here?" Hayes had backed into the oak banister.

Nadine clutched her collar and grabbed Grace's arm, her mouth instantly dry.

"I came to find out what's wrong," Molly said, turning toward Grace. "Oh, Lord of Heavens!" Her hand flew over her mouth, and she dropped to her knees. "Are you Gracie?"

Hayes closed the door behind her and Nadine gripped Grace's shoulders with both of her hands. The reddish freckled resemblance was undeniable.

"Your grandmother's letters stopped coming. Tell me, Hayes, is that her?" Molly cried, never taking her eyes off Grace.

Nadine waited for him to answer. He couldn't seem to breathe or talk. "Yes, this is Grace," Nadine finally said. "Unfortunately Mrs. Burden passed months ago."

Molly's face contorted with of pain and loss. "Aye, my Gracie," she said, tears spilling down her face. "Sweet lass, you look so much like your sister." Her voice shook, and she slowly rose to her feet. "Your grandmother has always written and told me of her well-being. But then the letters just stopped. I tried to wait, until I could wait no longer." She eyed Hayes.

Nadine extended her hand toward him, trying to break him out of his shock. He seemed to follow her meaning and came to stand next to them.

"You could have written to *me*," he said, emotionless.

"I...I...didn't think you would want to hear from me." She looked down.

"Anything would have been better than just showing up."

Molly closed her eyes and exhaled. "I want...I need...to take her home with me."

Nadine jumped and grabbed Grace tighter by the hand. "I think we will go upstairs and-"

Hayes caught her by her arm.

"Please stay." He bent down to Grace. "Would you mind going to play with your dollhouse in your room?"

"Okay." Grace passed Molly wide-eyed. "Is she my mother?"

Hayes pointed to the staircase. "Just give us a few minutes, Grace."

"Today's my birthday," Grace called over her shoulder, climbing the stairs.

"I know, luv." Molly watched her.

"Would you like to come in and stand by the fire?" Nadine wondered why she suddenly sounded like the matron of the home. Molly walked into the parlor, and Hayes pulled his hands down his face.

"I'm sorry," he said, his voice sour. "I had no idea my grandmother was writing to you. Considering I am her father, it seems a bit offensive that both of you were keeping this from me."

Nadine loved how he claimed her as his child without hesitation.

"All the same, you know I don't have a good…standin' with your family. They think I am the devil."

"Not my grandmother, obviously," Hayes scoffed.

"I thought leaving her that day would be the death of me. I did. Aye I did." Molly looked at Nadine. "I know I shouldn't be talkn' of this in front of your wife. But I've married myself and have two more wee ones. My Clara looks the spit and image of that Gracie. We'd been savn' our pennies to make this trip. I want to take her home."

"Out of the question." Hayes walked to the piano and back. "This is her home."

Molly looked confused. "But I am her mam. I said I have a husband now and we will take proper care of her."

"She doesn't even know you, Molly." Hayes gritted his teeth.

"That's why I am here. Without your grandmother's care, she needs me now." She bowed to Nadine. "Pardon me, but Mrs. Burden didn't say anything about Hayes havin' a wife."

"She's not my wife," Hayes blurted out.

Nadine sucked in a quick breath. A sharp stitch pinched her stomach.

"That's correct." Nadine nodded, squeezing her icy hands together. "I need to be on my way, even now." Hayes went to open his mouth, and she raised her palm. "I've done it before. I can make it to town before dark. You need to stay here and…" She already moved to the hall tree to grab her cape. Hayes followed her.

"Please stay. I don't want you walking. It's not safe," he whispered.

"I can do this." She buttoned the top button, not looking at him.

"Please." He gripped her elbow.

"Y...yo...you." She rolled her eyes, willing her tongue to work. "Y...you have waited f...for this m...mo...moment f...for....years. I...I...d...do...don't b...be...belong here." She stepped quickly through the open door before he could stop her.

40

Hayes glared at the front of the boarding house where he'd watched Molly go in. He said he would wait in case they were full, but she hadn't come out. He gripped the reins tighter and tighter, not wanting to go home. There was only one place he wanted to be.

He couldn't let Nadine leave town like this. He didn't mean to say *she's not my wife* with such force. It sounded cruel, like they had no relationship. And the opposite fact was crushing his chest. He had to, like needing his next breath—he must to talk to her. Extremely unlikely that he going to convince her of anything, but he just wanted to hear her voice and apologize.

Leading the carriage toward her little store, he'd sworn he would never let his emotions have such control. His stomach felt like he'd eaten a barrel of green apples. Where was his philosophy on how to contribute to a peaceful life? Why wouldn't his favorite poets and prophets remind him of truth? Everything he prided himself on knowing logically had flown the coop.

He jumped down from the carriage and stared at the dark brick building. It wasn't Molly who had turned his world upside down tonight, it was Nadine. Nothing about seeing Molly had pulled his heart apart. She had moved on, she had a family, and he was happy for her. He didn't hold any bitterness against her. Every heart tie was gone. But the young woman with brown hair and soft round eyes was worth waking up the neighborhood for. Listening to her stutter tonight was like watching her insides crumble. He needed to make it right. Walking around the building, he saw a light on near the stables.

"Hello." He looked around.

"Can I help you?" A tall young man turned around from a work bench.

"Yes. I'm Hayes Sullivan, a friend of Nadine Von Keller. She was at my home this evening and unfortunately had... walked home." He looked to the ground. "I can't rest until I know she got home safely."

"I saw her around dusk. She was talking to Nettie. Some busy girl talk, so I stayed clear. But then she went up to her place." He nodded up.

Hayes nodded his thanks, biting down hard on his bottom lip. "I need to talk to her. I know it's getting late. But I also know she's planning to leave soon, and I have to talk to her."

The tall young man turned and placed some items on a hook. "Can't wait until the morning?"

"No." Hayes exhaled, watching the man appraise him

"I've heard Nettie talk about you. She thinks you and Mrs. Von Keller have a courtship going without much courting."

Hayes circled his head. "Sounds about right."

The man scratched his jaw. "Let me go knock on her door and see if she wants to come down. If she says no, then it's no. Are we straight on that?"

"Of course." Hayes nodded.

Hayes rubbed behind a tan sorrel's ears and tried to regulate his breathing. He looked up quickly when the back of the little store door opened. Nick held the door as she walked out, holding a lantern. Her eyes were weary as she spoke to him. "Let's go in the back kitchen."

Hayes followed with an overwhelming sense of relief. He watched as she lit the other lanterns illuminating the warm kitchen. She moved around with such grace and familiarity. This was her other world he knew nothing about.

"Coffee is still warm. Would you like some?" she asked, holding her hand on the pot.

"No, no…thank you." He pulled out two chairs from the table. She sat slowly, never taking her eyes off him.

"Where is Molly?" She pressed on her bottom lip.

"At the boarding house." He wanted to reach over and grab her hand, her arm, her…

"What did you two decide?"

"You heard." He dropped his head to side. "She wants to take her back East."

"But…you…won't let that happen." Her soft lashes blinked slowly.

He stood quickly and rubbed the back of his neck. "I don't know what to do. When I went to say goodnight, Grace had such a sweet curiosity on her face. So many questions—she wants to know her."

"That's only natural." Nadine piped in. "She can visit."

Hayes turned, blinking slowly, suddenly extremely weary. "Maybe she should go with Molly."

"Oh, Hayes." Nadine covered her face.

He walked over and knelt on one knee in front of her, gently pulling her hands off her face. "Please, listen to me." He whispered. "She won't have you in her life." Nadine met his gaze. "You have been her comfort and companion. As much as I love her, I'll never be a woman. I can't nurture her like you. And I'm not saying that to make you feel bad about your choice to leave here. Grace and I will always hold you in the best place in our hearts. Maybe it's just God's timing." He stood back up.

"God's timing?" Anguish laced her voice. "I feel like my heart is abandoning my body."

Hayes reached over and helped her stand. He wrapped his arms around her as she buried her face in his chest. Her body shook with her cries as he stared out into the back room kitchen of the Feed and Seed. A lone tear disobeyed the vow of every boy turned man, as it ran freely down his cheek. He would have to say goodbye first to Nadine, and then to his daughter, Grace.

41

The scent of cinnamon rolls met Nadine as she walked in the back store kitchen.

"I made these with you in mind." Nettie poured Nadine a cup of coffee. "Nick said Hayes was here last night. What happened?" She slipped a plate to Nadine and sat.

"Do you remember how I told you I needed to leave? That it just felt like the right time?" Nadine sipped her hot coffee. "Last night, Molly showed up."

"Who's Molly?"

"Molly is Grace's mother. You should see them, Nettie. Same hair, same soft green eyes."

"Oh Lordy." Nettie pressed her fingers over her mouth. "Did Hayes know she was coming?"

Nadine shook her head. "But he's considering having Grace go with her. To live, back east. Not like the next town. He will rarely see her."

"So how do you feel? Happy little Grace will have a mother? The timing and all that?"

"I...am...trying. I could barely sleep last night." Nadine stilled, searching for any words to describe her confusion. "I should be happy she has a mother that wants her. I judged Hayes unkind for not having an attachment to her. But you should see him now. He's fun and loving, and now that they have such a good bond my heart breaks for him."

"It's just a puddle of pain," Nettie whispered. "Maybe Grace won't want to go."

"Hayes asked if he could take me to the train station in St. Paul. Mrs. Fox has agreed to have Molly for the day and let Grace get to know her. He said if Grace wants to stay here, she's staying. If she wants to go, then they will all go."

"Him too?"

"No, I meant Mrs. Fox. The Sullivans have already provided a severance for her to live. Hayes wants her to travel back and retire."

Nettie pulled her hand down her face. "Poor Mr. Sullivan, to lose all his family in one week." She looked at Nadine. "Including you."

"I think I may be grieving for myself too. This little kitchen has been a wonderful home away from home. I have never experienced such hospitality and forbearance as I have here. I feel as if I'm losing my family."

Nettie reached over and squeezed her hand. "Nick and I are talking about things in the future."

Nadine sat up a bit taller. "That is good, right?"

"Yes, it's very good. But I never could have reached him without you. You think you gained all this love and forbearance, but I gained more by knowing you. I was drowning in my lack of confidence. I know I have it in spades in certain areas." She huffed. "But not as a woman. I didn't know how to show interest. I thought the man did it all. We'd still be talking about the price of grain right now if it weren't for you." She rolled her head. "We do talk a lot about grain though." She snickered.

Nadine smiled. "I will pray you have a lifetime of talking about it."

Nadine spent the afternoon covering the grand piano and cleaning out the little desk. She had taken her little sign down last week and informed all her students of her departure. She stacked the last of her personal things and carried them up to her little room. Her simple bag held her two extra dresses and the last of her things from downstairs.

She looked into the bag and saw the most prized possessions she had ever had—Hayes' letters. Just looking at her name scripted on the envelopes made her emotions rise. They'd brought life to her many days when she didn't know how to go on. They strengthened her faith in God and humanity when she had none to find. Many a lonely night she had read them over and over. He was not perfect, but an open soul that stayed growing and curious about life. Why do people think or believe as they do? Hayes awakened her beyond her scrambled lies and mistakes.

Clipping the bag closed she grabbed her cape and went down the stairs. Pulling her gloves on, she walked out her back door and looked up the hillside. One last walk. One last goodbye.

Nadine had promised Nettie they would all eat together this last night, but she wanted to catch Hayes before he left his office. She wasn't sure how early he would pick her up for the trip to St. Paul.

Most of the storefronts still glowed with activity as she approached the railroad office. She stopped to peek in the window to see if they were busy. Hayes had someone in his office. He was a large man with a baggy black coat. The man patted Hayes's arm and then shook his hand briskly.

Nadine waited, not wanting to interrupt. As the large man turned, she shot backward. It was Clyde from the Silver Holiday, and he was heading for the door!

Nadine turned and ran to the end of the block, hiding behind an alley fence. She clung to the wood and dropped her head, panting. It was Clyde. It had been months, but she would recognize that face anywhere. Why would he be in the railroad office? With all her fears, why would Hayes talk to him? Shake his hand?

Her legs gave out and she crouched down low. What if he was looking for her? Had Hayes told him this was the last day she would be in town? She prayed and moaned in the darkness. When she finally stood, her whole body was shaking. Nettie would be worried. She crept back down the alley until she saw their building and ran. Like the winner of a footrace, she practically fell into the back of the Feed and Seed.

"There you are." Nettie looked up and went back to the pot on the stove. "I know you said you loved my ham and potato soup. So I made that and I'm about to pull some yeast rolls from the oven."

Nadine leaned back against the door. She couldn't seem to pull enough air into her lungs. Had Hayes been scheming with Clyde all this time? Was Hayes in on her harassment? *N…never…trust any…* giant black spots blurred her vision, and she opened her mouth to call for Nettie when everything went black.

"Nick, hand me another cool rag." Nadine heard. She opened her eyes to see Nettie's face above her.

"Where am…what ha…hap…happened?"

"You fainted." Nettie's face was creased with worry.

Nadine looked around and saw she was lying on the edge of the gray and brown braided rug. "I'm sorry." She brushed her hand over her face. Nick was standing over Nettie. "This is embarrassing." She tried to sit up.

"I was just about to send for the Doc when you opened your eyes. Nick can still go fetch him." Nettie held her arms around her.

"No, please no. I'm feeling better."

Nettie scowled.

"Really, friend. I am." Nadine didn't know if she wanted to tell Nettie what she had seen. A better story was coming to mind, but she didn't want to lie either.

"I'm just a bit of a train wreck." Nadine chuckled, as Nick helped her sit in the chair.

"Don't say that!" Nettie laughed. "You're getting on one tomorrow. Take some deep breaths. You still look pale."

Nadine straighten up and inhaled. "So much going on, I didn't sleep much."

Nettie rubbed her back. "Do you want to try the soup?"

"Umm, yes. Something in my stomach sounds good."

Nettie turned to the stove as Nadine gripped the table, her body still swaying.

42

Had she lost all her good sense? Nadine walked in another circle around her bed. Somewhere a rooster crowed, reminding her it was the morning she was to leave Minnesota for good. Not a problem for most people, except that the one person she had grown to trust was not who she thought him to be. She felt the timing was right to leave. At least she could trust that.

She'd spent most of the night trying to figure out how to confront him, but now with the morning rays, she just wanted to get out of Carver. She'd said her painful good-byes to Nettie last night. With a quick cup of coffee and some bread, she would be ready to head down to the stage office.

Stepping out, she scanned the few people on the simple walkways of Carver. All she had to do was cross the street and keep her eyes on the stage office only a few blocks away. Her chest was already rapidly rising and falling as she pushed off the little brick store and walked across the street. Feeling like a nervous hawk, she turned at every dog bark or horse's movement. A sweet older woman nodded a greeting at her as they passed, and she realized didn't even offer a smile.

"Thank God," she murmured as she looked in to see the clerk behind the counter. Walking in, she set her case on a chair and pulled out her billfold.

"I need to get to Elbert County in Wisconsin."

"All right," the tall young man said. Pulling out some maps, he tapped a ruler over them. "I think we can get you there. These will be the stops." He turned the paper to face her and traced the stage route.

"That will be fine." Nadine looked back over her shoulder.

"The East by South leaves in about an hour."

Nadine squeezed her hands together. "All right. I'll wait." She paid and picked up her case and sat.

Looking around the small office, she wished every chair wasn't exposed to the front windows. She shook her head. Why had she agree to allow Hayes take her to the train station? It had been late, and she'd felt sorry for the exhausted look on his face. He'd said he had something to drop off for the railroad. That was probably a lie too.

Nettie had given her a lovely gray hat for today, something Nettie herself would never wear. Nadine loosened the pins and brought it over to the side of her face facing the windows. At the right angle, it looked stylish and also concealing.

Nadine watched the large pendulum on the clock swing back and forth. Losing two night of sleep was catching up with her. She felt her eyes droop. Her head bobbed forward, and she sucked in a rapid breath. She stood quickly, clutching her case. She needed to be alert. After looking around, she returned to her seat.

Opening her case, she looked down, Hayes' letters taunting her. Had Clyde assigned Hayes to watch her? Is that why he was at the Silver Holiday that night? Was watching Grace for him just a cover? Some sick plan to keep tabs on her? After the flood, he said he saw her through his gun scope. Obviously, he had many chances to see her harmed. What was their plan? Maybe she would have never made it to the train station. Maybe she would have been dead in a ditch somewhere. No one in Carver would look for her—they all knew she was to return home.

Nadine grabbed the letters and stood. A small pot belly stove burned warmly in the corner. She stared at the clock. Only twenty more minutes and all this will be over. Glancing at the clerk with his head down, Nadine moved to the little stove and pulled quickly on the hot handle. It swung open enough and bending near, she-

"Nadine."

Straightening quickly, she saw Hayes as the letters dropped all over the floor. Locking her jaw, she knelt down and picked them up. He was by her side in an instant.

"What are you doing?" Hayes touched the letters as they rose.

Nadine pulled them from him and went back to her case and dropped them in. Her lips would not move, and she was better off for it. There was nothing he could say, no amount of his confidence or deep blue eyes. Nothing. She would be gone in only a few excruciating minutes.

"Why didn't you wait for me? I said I would take you."

"I changed my mind." She watched as the stage rolled into the front of the office.

"Why? The stage is rough and crowded. I wanted to show you the line and the city. We can leave now. I'm sorry. Did you think I wasn't coming?"

She cinched her case up close to her body, watching as men unloaded and loaded boxes. She tried to get around Hayes, but three large men started walking in.

"This is what I'm doing." She waited and slipped through the door.

Hayes followed her, came around and grabbed her arms. "Please, talk to me. Don't leave like this."

Nadine jerked back from his grasp. "I saw you and Clyde." She'd rehearsed this a hundred times last night. "I know you are *not who* you led me to believe." She delighted that her words and tongue were cooperating. "I actually trusted you. Yes, you, Hayes, after I'd sworn to trust no other man."

He stepped back. "Can I explain?"

She turned around. Why wasn't the stage loading passengers? She felt him pull on her arm.

"Listen to me, Nadine."

She shook her head and looked at the ground. She would not cry, anger her needed fuel.

"I sold some of my family's wine to Clyde for the Silver Holiday. He has some customers who only want the good stuff. I only sell to him a couple of times a year, because it's very expensive wine."

"After everything I told you, you would still do business with him?" She refused to look at him..

"It was because of what you told me that I did business with him."

"You're talking nonsense." She scowled.

"I made him a deal. He wanted the money he was out for the gals that went with Marcus. I told him I would give him the wine in exchange for the debt. The debt he wanted from you."

A slice of cold air hit Nadine's face. "Why...why...would you do that? I am leaving Carver for good."

"Because you said you desired freedom."

"I do." Her chin quivered.

"True freedom is living with no regrets, never looking behind you. I want you to have that. You deserve it."

"You did this to have me stay—stay with you?" she whispered.

He shook his head. "No, I know you are going home. Otherwise I wouldn't have spent all night writing these." He pulled out a small stack of envelopes wrapped with a red satin ribbon. "They are numbered, by weeks. I know it might help to have some stiff philosopher boring you to sleep."

"Hayes. I don't know what to say."

"Leavin' in five minutes," someone yelled behind them.

"Don't look at me like that." He lifted his palms. "I have no perfection in me, no divine holes in my hands...or my feet. You know that."

She stared at him in the silence. "I'm speechless."

"Then just listen to me." In one swift movement, he closed the gap between them. "I love you. Beyond what I've ever known, I love you." He dropped his forehead down to hers, waiting until she smiled. His lips found hers, pressing eager and desperate kisses to her cheek and back to her lips. Joy ran through her as she returned his passion with her own.

She broke away, holding her hand over her tingling mouth.

"I love you too." She pressed her hand to his cheek. "But I have to get on that stage."

"I know you do." He smiled, handing her the stack of letters. "Go on now—go be free."

43

"O uch." Nadine grimaced as the stage bounced from a rut. Hayes was right. Hour after hour on the cramped stage left her backside sore. She tried to shift in her seat and found some relief staring out the small narrow window. She'd gotten a simple hotel room the night before and was told this morning it was only about a hundred more miles to Elbert County.

"Excited to get home?" the middle-aged woman sitting next to her husband asked.

"Excited to be off this stage." Nadine smiled.

"What progressive parents you must have." The woman smiled. "When I was your age, we weren't allowed to travel alone."

Nadine could only smile. Her parents were far from progressive. Something dropped in her stomach—she'd left home a foolish, rebellious girl. So much had changed. Would they see her for the young woman she'd become? Would they try to understand her independence?

She pulled Hayes' letters from her pocket. Her name was in the same graceful script, each envelope with large numbers. She wondered, why four letters? Perhaps because it took a month for mail to travel back and forth. Maybe that was all he had time to write.

With Molly's arrival, everything was turned upside down. What a shock to a fun birthday celebration. Chewing on her bottom lip, she wondered how Grace would fare this week. She was such a sweet and loving child. How could she not want a mommy who desired to make a home with her? Hayes could fight for her, but he wanted it to be what Grace needed.

Nadine exhaled. Hayes was incredible. He'd told her in one of the letters about his family's vineyard. He had found something Clyde wanted more than revenge. He did something for her she could never do for herself. At her first opportunity, she would write about it to Nettie. It almost sounded like one of Nettie's Bible stories. Jesus, who pays the debts we can never pay.

Unfortunately, it was already dark when the stage pulled into Elbert County. Stepping out, she grabbed her belongings and looked up and down at the town she'd grown up in.

"Hotel a block to the right," the man on top of the stage yelled down.

"Yes, I know," Nadine whispered back, stepping onto the wooden walkway. Saloon across the street, she mimicked to herself. Library across from that, a dairy about three miles down that road. She moved a few feet toward the hotel and waited.

Where was the guilt when she looked at the saloon? Where was the stomachache looking at the road that led to the dairy? Was she just exhausted? Had all her emotions been bumped out of her? Stepping slowly toward the hotel, she wanted a hot bath and good night sleep before going home. She approached the hotel and saw a few people sitting in the lobby. Putting her hand on the handle, she took one last look back at the light streaming from the saloon. *Humph - no guilt, no remorse, no desire to run. Interesting.*

Thanking the young woman who took her breakfast plate away, Nadine chewed on her bottom lip. She could walk the two or three miles or ask someone for a ride. She had walked back and forth from Hayes' home. Cold but exhilarating. When they walked the property on Grace's birthday, he'd talked about the need for air in his lungs, the expanse of the sky, and all the sounds of nature filling his being.

Freedom—he had left out freedom. Walking meant movement and connection with the elements. She would walk.

Nadine smelled the dairy. How funny she'd never noticed the smell before. The landscape around her two-story brick home was barren and cold. The swing Ben had made for Minna hung crooked and unused. Edda's garden was just frozen dirt and some bent-over vines.

Movement caught her eye down around the barns. Stopping, she willed her heart to quit beating so erratically.

Who would be safer to approach? Switching hands, she tried to relieve the ache from carrying her case so far. She gazed at the tree she used to meet Ben at. Surely he was long gone. Two men came from the end of the long cow barn. It looked like her father and Carl, his dairy manager. She pressed her hand down her skirt and straightened her hat. She thought about dropping her case and approaching them. But no, she stepped forward. The case was a sign. She was returning from the place she had kept from them.

Carl saw her first and touched her father's arm. Her father looked good. His leg had healed, and he stopped and jerked his head back.

"Nadine? *Tochter?*" His mouth hung open, and he touched his head. "Is that you?"

She smiled faintly and wondered if he would allow her to embrace him. He was barely stepping toward her. "Yes, it's me." She nodded at Carl. "You look well...both of you." She looked at her father, trying to gauge his reaction.

"You are home to visit? Your letter said you are married. *Ja?*"

Rolling her lips, she tried to find a calm expression. Her bottom chin began to quiver, and she swallowed hard. "I...I...n...ne..." her eyes rolled back, and she jetted her chin forward. "Nev...never was ma...mar...married. The man I le...left with end...ended up le...leaving me."

"I go check on the horses." Carl bowed before he walked away.

"Oh no." Her father's eyebrows wrinkled. "*Dat* is not *gut*." He shook his head. "Where have you been?"

"A ways from Minneapolis, in a little town near there. A week or so after I ran away from here, he left me to go to Montana."

"*Ja?* So what have you been doing?"

Nadine hated seeing his face still a mixture of confusion and disapproval. She knew this wasn't going to be easy.

"I got a job."

"What kind of job?" His voice was ridged.

"I taught piano lessons."

"A piano teacher. *Ja.*"

"They don't make much money." She tried to smile. "So it took me a while to save up to come home." She wished she could spill out every painful detail, but just the hurt on his face right now was choking her simple story.

He nodded in the silence, arms crossed over his chest, leaning back in his muddy black rubber boots.

"I know I don't deserve you and mother's forgiveness." She stared at the ground. "I understand if it is too much to have me here."

He took a step forward and grabbed the case out of her hand. "You will always be our *tochter...*" He squeezed her arm. "We welcome you home.

His grip on her arm helped steady her shaking knees. "Thank you, *Vater.* Your leg looks well."

He dropped his arm and tapped his thigh. "It gets stiff at night."

"How will mother do with seeing me?" she asked as they walked to the front steps.

"Ahh." He pulled his hat forward and scratched the back of his head. "She was very pained when you left. *Ja?* And how you left." He stopped at the door, still and quiet.

Nadine pressed her fingers against her mouth. She was so close to crossing the threshold and back to everything she had ever known. Yet it would never be the same. She had ruined that forever.

44

M inna poked her head out from the upstairs hall.
"Oh, my!" Her face flashed with recognition. "Nadine?"

"How are you, Minna?" Nadine took the pins from her hat and pulled it off.

Minna descended the stairs slowly. "Did someone know she was coming and not tell me?" She hit the landing.

'They didn't know." Nadine reached to touch her chin. "You have gotten taller."

"You look different too." Minna looked around. "Where's the husband you ran off with?"

Nadine plastered a smile. This was the Minna she remembered. "We never married."

"Never married?" a fretful voice behind her said.

Nadine turned. "Mother." She nodded, surprised when her back stiffened at the sound of her mother's voice. "That's right. I never married." She rotated the hat in her hand. "I was… ashamed to tell you the truth. So I made up the story about going to Helena. Well, he did go to Helena as far as I know. He just didn't want to take me with him."

Her father pulled off his boots and hung his coat. Thank God—it seemed he would be staying for this interrogation.

"I don't understand." Pain laced her mother's voice.

"It's a long story. Can we talk in the parlor or dining room?" Nadine sucked in a deep breath.

"*Ja.*" Her mother pointed to the dining room. "Minna, please finish what you were doing."

Minna dropped her head back. "Why can't I hear this? I want to know what happened."

"It does not sound appropriate for you. Go." Her mother glared.

Nadine rolled her lips closed and looked at the ground. Of course, they didn't want her wayward story to influence Minna.

Her mother's long thick gray skirts swished slowly as she walked into the dining room. Her father followed in his brown wool socks. The room looked just as it had the day she left. The four wide windows outlined with long cream colored curtains, the large cherry wood table centered in the room with the same lacey cloth.

Her father went to his chair at the head of the table. Nadine turned and saw the housekeeper Edda enter the room.

"Oh, miss!" Edda shook her head quickly. "Nadine, dear. How wonderful to see you."

"Frau Edda. You look the same as ever." Nadine wrinkled her nose, sounding so much like the thoughtless young woman that left months ago. "You and Carl are well?" She tried to sound sincere.

"*Ja, ja,* just more rickety." She smiled. "I will bring some tea."

"Helga." Otto held his hand out to her mother's usual seat. She slowly sat, looking tense.

Nadine pulled out the chair closest to her—the one Margaret used to occupy. "How is Margaret doing?"

"She's back in Chicago," Otto said. "Teaching at the orphan school and helping out with her other…activities."

Nadine smiled lightly. They'd never approved of Margaret living away from home. She had a sudden desire to reconnect with her sister. After resenting her sister's freedom for so long, her old feelings seemed to have vanished.

"And you…" Otto cleared his throat. "Tell us what happened."

Edda set the tea tray down. Nadine needed a moment, as she could not seem to look at her mother.

"I…" Her throat was locking up. She couldn't repeat the truth of the pregnancy. It would destroy them. "I thought I was in love with a man named Marcus. He worked at the saloon in town, and from the beginning, I knew you would never approve." Her mother rocked back and forth in her seat. "He made me a wagon load of promises." Her mouth went dry. "But then would not keep them."

Her father sipped his tea, helping her forge forward. "I did care for Ben Graham, and I rushed into the decision to marry him. I not only had one wrong, I…I was about to make it two wrongs. The day of the wedding, Marcus came to the house and begged me to leave with him. I guess you could say that was the worst wrong. A terrible lack of judgment on my part." She huffed and pulled in a slow breath. "I know I have dishonored my family. I understand if you do not want me here." She bit her lip and looked down. Her father reached over and patted her hand, the simple gesture touching her deeply.

"Tell your *mutter* what you have been doing."

"I've been teaching piano." Her mother's face stayed stoic. "In Carver, Minnesota. The pastor's wife helped me find a place with another single woman who ran her own business."

"What kind of business would that be?" Helga's disapproval radiated.

"Her name is Nettie, and she runs the Feed and Seed. Many of the farmers and ranchers in town get supplies from her. Her store."

"Humph." Helga pursed her lips.

"The store next door had the most gorgeous grand piano. It had been left by the last tenants." She looked to her father.

"Who would leave a grand piano?" Helga snapped.

"They got it into the building in pieces, but put together they couldn't get it out." Nadine felt the courage to sip her tea. "I put an advertisement on the door and had parents and children hire me for lessons."

"Why did you just not come home?" Helga huffed.

"I…I didn't have the money."

"We would have wired you the money. But the letter you sent said you were living in Montana. So you never lived there?"

Nadine shook her head.

"Minnesota is not that far. Your father would have come for you." She bellowed. "Why so long? Why didn't you just come home?"

"I was ashamed. I knew full well the reason you kept us so close was to keep us safe." She leaned back in her seat and then toward her mother. "I had done everything you had tried to keep me from doing. I didn't understand when I left, but I understand now. I thought I could be happy and free. I was hiding, mother. Can you try to understand? I'd made so many mistakes. I…co…could…couldn't face you."

"You think us so unforgiving?" Helga murmured.

"Can you, then? Can you find forgiveness for my reckless actions?"

Her mother and father looked at each other.

"*Ja.*" Otto nodded. "We are Christians. Christians have been forgiven by God, and we are to go and do the same."

Helga looked away, staring out the window. "It is not that easy." She pulled her hankie out and dabbed her eyes. "This God has taken our only heir, our only boy, so young. Then your sister wants to go off to college; leaving us, leaving the family. We find out later she almost died of typhoid from one of her mission trips. Then you, rush-rush, in such a hurry you were, to wed Ben Graham. And then you are gone, just run off. I understand why it is important to forgive. *Ja*, I do. But it does not just go away. My hurt is a deep thing…maybe even God cannot reach."

Nadine stared at her mother. All pain is such a deep thing. For the first time in her life she really heard her mother. Nadine had been annoyed every day of every year in this home. All Helga would talk about is the *loss of their boy*, as if her daughters held no value. Her mother was just hurting. She had felt the same ache, the same loss.

Rising slowly, Nadine came behind her chair. She wrapped her arms around her and leaned into her. "I am so sorry. So very sorry I have added to your pain." She placed a soft kiss on her mother's cheek, their tears mingling.

45

The door of her childhood room clicked closed. Someone had lit the lamps and sat her case on the bed. She could only stand and stare, feeling a lifetime of hurt and regret since she'd last stood in that room. The wonderful days of being in Grace's soft pink and white room came to mind, she had been her joy. Maybe she'd also been granted a lifetime of love and forbearance from the last time she'd slept in her bed. Everything was so ornate compared to her little room above the store. All her books and personal things were just as she had left them. Opening her wardrobe, she fingered her lovely gowns.

Her parents were subdued from the shock of her return, but overall the day had gone by with a polite peacefulness. She pulled out her hairpins and dropped them on the vanity. Dragging her fingers across the glossy finish, she remembered how she'd almost destroyed her room the night Ben Graham had found her on the floor.

Earlier that day, she'd confronted Marcus about the baby and marrying her. He dared to question if it was his child. He would help her get rid of it; seemed his only solution. A shiver ran up her spine. Would this room and that night haunt her?

She spread open her case and reached past Hayes' letters. At the bottom was the little Bible Nettie had given her. It seemed to bring comfort just being in her hand. Carefully she reached for Hayes' letters and set them inside the little drawer in her vanity. She felt too sensitive to read his words, his declaration of love so freshly wrapped around her heart. It would bring on melancholy she couldn't shake.

Willing her eyes to open the next morning, she looked around the strange angles of light in the room. The fireplace was already lit for the day, and she wondered how long she'd overslept. Gathering one of her pillows, she wrapped her arms around her soft pink bedding. The comfort of home was undeniable, but the thought of having nothing useful to do was daunting. How had she managed before? Would she get back to the oversight of Minna's care? She rolled back onto her back and let out a sigh. That held no appeal. Her parents might even want her to pick up her help with the literary society, but since that was her ruse for seeing Marcus, that had no appeal either.

What about the townsfolk who knew their family? Did she want to shame her family more every time someone asked an innocent question? No, she would stay close. She'd fallen asleep to the Psalms last night; God was her strength and very present help. He would guide her and help her.

After helping her with the bath, Edda had asked which dress to lay out. Nadine couldn't find the answer to a very simple question.

"Something from your wardrobe? The green emerald looks striking on you," Edda said wide-eyed.

Nadine sat on the stool in the bathing room, wrapped in her light blue robe with her mouth hanging open. "I'm sorry. I can't seem to…"

"Pick up your old life," Edda said, towel drying her hair.

"I think you're right," Nadine whispered. "I don't feel like the young woman who wore those things. Yet, I used to love those dresses."

"I can tell you've changed." Edda pulled the comb through her hair. "You have a calmness about you. Some of your determination has died down."

Nadine smiled and nodded. "You've seen a lot working for this family. I just want to say thank you for always being kind and patient with all the Von Kellers." Nadine stood and took the towel and squeezed her hair. "Now I have the challenge of staying my own person, and being helpful and respectful while living back in my parents' home."

The day before Nadine had stayed in and listened to Minna play violin and piano, but today she needed some fresh air. She found her mother reading in the parlor. "I'd like to go for a walk. Just around the yard." She smiled. "Nowhere too far." Her mother put down her book and took in a deep breath.

"I can't help but worry," Helga said.

Nadine braced herself for a lecture.

"Edda often told me after you'd left that you were meant for a big adventure." Her mother dropped her head. "The very thing I don't like to think about. Do you think Frau Edda is correct?"

Nadine sat on the corner of the brown settee. "If I wore britches, one could say I was just too big for them." She chewed on her bottom lip. "All the signs Marcus wasn't trustworthy were there. But I ignored them. I thought *we* would live some grand adventure. I'd have my own home, and my own say to come and go. I was sadly mistaken." She stared out the window, never realizing how peaceful it was here in the winter. It reminded her of another peace.

"The only adventure to claim is one to my heart. Nettie loved her Bible stories. We would read together in the evenings. I had never believed God could meet me in a personal way. I just pictured him up there with a glowing face and a gold rod in his hand. But when you read the Bible you find out that it might be describing Moses, not God." She chuckled.

"The life of Jesus reached me profoundly. Did you know there is a man named Paul who murdered Christians and then became an apostle of Jesus? I didn't know the Son of God would even speak to the outcast. Not only did Jesus speak to them, but he also ate with them and touched them and forgave them and rescued and healed them. So I guess you could say I had a divine adventure. And *mutter*, if there was anyone who needed all those things…it was me."

Helga eyes glazed and her chin quivered. "*Ja*. That is how Ben's *mutter* helped me, back in Ready Springs when you were small. She would say Jesus was that real to her. And you know I had to listen to her. She had lost a boy too."

Nadine nodded, realizing something profound—Laura Graham was her mother's Nettie Wagner.

"When the minister says God is always with you, we often don't know what it means." Nadine said wistfully." Really, all we had to do was look in the mirror and into the face of these dear caring ones."

46

Today made day seven. Nadine had survived a full week of adjustments living at home. She pulled out Hayes' letter with the giant "one" on it and sat it up against her vanity mirror. Tonight, this would be her reward. She finished dressing and peeked into Minna's room.

Her sister had turned fourteen while she was away. Minna was gone, but her things were strewn everywhere, covering the floor. She grabbed her sister's dirty underthings and dropped them down the chute. Her skirts and dresses didn't look dirty—probably just tried on once and discarded on the floor. She knew the routine from doing it many mornings herself. She hung each piece and noticed a big lump in the messy bedding. Reaching under the covers, she pulled out a thick sketchbook. Minna had clipped some ads of what looked like some kind of bicycle, pasted them here and there and done some drawings of-

"What are you doing?"

Nadine jumped. "Just straightening your room. I was going to make your bed. Is this your sketchbook?"

Minna grabbed it from her and held it to her chest. "Yes, and I would appreciate you not snooping around."

"I was trying to help you clean. I know how picky mother is about messes."

"That's what Edda is for."

Nadine pinched a frown. Her sister was often disrespectful and rude. Her being a year older hadn't changed much in that area. "Tell me about these advertisements. Are they some kind of new cycles?"

"Maybe."

"Is riding something that interests you?"

"Maybe."

"Minna, I'm not going to tell mother. It's important that you have your own interests. Even if it's a penny-farthing."

"It's not a penny-farthing. It's called a safety bicycle. They've changed the giant front wheel to two matching wheels."

"So…this is something that interests you."

Minna opened the door to her wardrobe and stuffed the book under a pile of things. "No matter, Nadine. Do you see mother and father allowing me to have one?"

"Humm. That is a fair question." Nadine held back the curtain and looked out the window. "I don't."

"Maybe I should just run off and join the circus," Minna grumbled.

Nadine walked over to her and touched her arm. "So many things Margaret tried to help me with, but I would never listen. So I doubt you want to listen to me."

"What do you want to tell me? How thankful I should be for a warm home and parents that care about me?"

"Yes, and I would tell you to be patient. Good things are coming to you. If you love cycles, do what you are doing now. Dream and clip advertisements and go to the circus and watch them. I thought if I didn't get what I wanted now, it would never happen. I didn't know how to trust in God's timing."

"God's timing." Minna sneered. "What does that have to do with getting a bicycle?"

"He knows our desires. All I'm saying is don't run after the counterfeit. Don't settle for a hundred horses if what you want is a bicycle."

"You are so strange now." Minna smirked.

Nadine chuckled and wrapped her arms around her sister. "I can't believe you are as tall as I am." Minna tried to wiggle away, but Nadine held her tight. "I've never told you this, but I love you and believe in you. Maybe not this year or the next, but one day I can see you riding down the lane on one of these. Maybe Margaret and I will be the ones to buy you one." Nadine nudged her, trying to get a smile. Minna rolled her eyes and Nadine kissed her on the cheek.

"Ouu." Minna slipped out from her grasp. "I think I liked you better when you were mean."

Later in the afternoon, Nadine took a hot mug of coffee to her father. He sat hunched over the ledgers spread out on the dining room table.

"*Danke, tochter.*" He smiled.

"Can I be of some help?"

"This would bore you, *tochter.*"

"I had some experience in payables and receivables working with Nettie."

"Really?" He looked up and sipped his coffee. "Her father let her run this Feed and Sack?"

"Feed and Seed," Nadine said. "Yes, Nettie did it all except shouldering the heavy grain sacks. I'm fairly good at my sums. Give me a chance."

"*Ja,* I will tell your *mutter* it was your idea. Here." He patted the table, and she sat.

Edda walked in later with the dishes to set the table. "Oh my. What do we have here?"

Otto looked up. "Nadine helped me find over four dollars. Some simple mistakes can add up. I guess I just needed another set of eyes."

Nadine gave Edda a wink. "Nothing wrong with my vision, and my ability to notice Elbert Mercantile never paid their October milk invoice."

"So." Otto closed the large ledgers. "We will clear out for supper." He rose and carried the ledgers out.

Nadine stood, helping with the silverware.

"Your parents, they appreciate your help, *ja.* I also appreciate your help, but you cannot stay here," Edda said, walking around her setting the table.

Nadine froze. "What do you mean?"

"You may think all your reasons for leaving here are gone." Edda lay the cloth napkins in place, just like she had hundreds of times. "But you were meant for more. Just take the time for that. Don't stay a day less and don't leave a day too late."

Nadine was still trying to figure out Edda's point when she crawled into bed. She gripped the letter from Hayes in her hand and brought it to her nose. She wished it smelled clean and masculine like him. But she had to be honest; it didn't. Pulling back into the pillows, she wondered if all they felt about each other would fade. According to Edda, she wasn't going to last long here. That brought no comfort. She rolled her eyes, remarkable how fast her mind would dip into despair.

She carefully pulled the parchment from the envelope.

My dearest,

May I take a moment to bestow my thoughts on this occasion of your departure? First, did you make it one week? Did you follow the directions? Either way, it means I have gone seven days without seeing or hearing or touching you. Nadine let out a sigh. *I selfishly devised these four letters to be in your thoughts as you will be in mine every hour.*

I am calling this piece 'Ode to Nadine.'

Like a rock dropped into a clear pond, you broke into my world. My deep was only shattered by your call to deep, your wound beckoning mine back to the surface. With God's light of Grace we had to look once again. When I finally had to see the pain, the most astonishing thing was revealed. It was beauty. By numbing what had hurt, I had numbed all that is beautiful. Grace is beautiful. You are beautiful. Love and forgiveness is beautiful. Seeing Molly again was a shock, but it didn't injure. For the first time in years, the well of my heart did not rattle with emptiness.

Tonight, when I put Grace to bed, she tried to sing a song Molly sang to her. I remembered it from when my sister would sing it to me. Too-Ra-Loo-Ra-Loo-Ral, that's an Irish lullaby. I fear she will want to be with her mother. That is the kind of pain that would have closed me off to God and man. But I also have a peculiar peace that I will survive. God gave me the grace not to tie you up and force your hand to see you stay. (I'm smiling) So I can only hope he will see me through these next days. I realize my ode to you lost its poetry. I apologize.

Let me leave you with a prayer: (for both of us)
Father, may all that feels unforgiven be released.
May our fears yield into our deepest tranquilities.
May all that is unlived in you, Nadine, blossom into a freedom graced with love.
Amen,
I will talk to you in a week-
Deep Warm Affections- Hayes

Nadine sunk lower into her bedding and read the words once again. She understood him, and he so tenderly understood her. She'd spent months in Carver trying to avoid anything fearful but had also pushed away from the beautiful things. She pondered on '*may all that is unlived in you blossom into freedom.'* Staring at the twinkle of the lamp, she wondered what was unlived. Edda pushing her toward what? If she had a sketchbook like Minna, she would paste all of his letters into it with pressed flowers. She'd told Minna to hold her onto her dreams. Would she take her own advice?

47

An eerie quiet hung in the house the following Sunday while the family was away attending church. Her mother didn't even make a fuss about Nadine not attending. She sat curled up in the parlor chair with her open Bible and hot cocoa.

Such a strange thought—she'd found her faith outside of the church. Sleet started to pelt the window. So many people in the Bible came to the Lord because of need. She felt a certain link to them. Hayes' letter swirled around in her thoughts. God can use all things. Heartache, betrayal, loss, all the things we would do anything to avoid—He uses for some good, some redemption. How would anyone know this side of God without difficulties?

Something dark moved quickly across the front lawn. Nadine set the cocoa down and stood to see through the blurry window. A man walked to the back of the house. It didn't look like Carl. He attended church with her parents anyway. Maybe a worker looking for...

She raced through the kitchen and back pantry. Grabbing the door knob she locked the bolt, then ran back through the front of the house and locked the front door. Her heartbeat was erratic as she came back through the kitchen. Spotting the high window off the bathing room, she pulled a chair close and stood on it.

The man wore a black coat and derby, and was too well-dressed to be one of the workers. He turned toward the back door and then looked out to the yard. He seemed confused, looking for something. When he turned again, she could make out his face.

She'd seen him before. In town…where? She needed to calm down. He could just be a customer of her father's. But why would he come on the Sabbath? He walked to his horse, tied up to a tree, and swung up. The horse turned toward the window and he spat on the ground, just like Marcus did.

His father. A shock rolled through her. It was Marcus' father. She gripped the window sill until her fingers cramped. She'd seen him a few times at the saloon in Elbert. He looked stern and angry as he turned to ride off. She stepped off the chair and plopped on it. Why would he be here? Of course, he was looking for her. Was Marcus back in town? Never in a million years did she think he'd come back here.

Her best plan for the quiet peaceful morning was now ruined. An hour later, she sat at the dining room table with the paper Nettie had given her for Christmas, hoping to pen one letter to Nettie and one to Hayes, but her hand would not quit shaking.

A knock at the back door made everything in her jump. He'd returned. Maybe he had wanted to speak to her father, thinking Marcus would be here. She would not open that door when she was alone in the house. She peeked into the kitchen and heard Minna's voice.

"Nadine! Open the door; it's freezing."

She let out a long sigh and ran to the door. "I'm so sorry." She unlocked it and held it open as her family filed in.

"Why did you lock the door?" Minna dropped her coat over a chair. "Don't prowlers observe the Sabbath?"

Helga pulled her scarf off. "It is a gut idea to lock the door when you are here alone, no matter what day it is."

Carl and Edda walked in and took off their coats. "I'll have some soup heating up in a moment," Edda said.

"Can we have those potato rolls with it?" Minna asked, the commotion in the kitchen a distracting relief.

Carl warmed his hands by the cook stove. "I saw some extra hoof prints when I brought the wagon in. Was someone here?"

Nadine looked around to make sure the others were not listening. "Yes," she whispered.

"A friend?" His eyes narrowed.

"I don't think so." She drew in a shaky breath, her parents still talking. "I think it was…you know… the man I left here with, I think it was his f…father."

"Are you in some kind of trouble?" Carl spoke with his back to the others.

"I don't…think … s…so." Nadine squeezed her hands together. "He owns the saloon and I haven't seen him in months."

"How did you get home last week?"

"I rode the s…stage into town and spent the night at the h…hotel because it was late. I ate some breakfast and then I walked to the dairy."

His brow crinkled. "So, many people could have seen you?"

"I guess so." Frustration made her voice drop. "All I thought to avoid was all the busybodies."

"Maybe it is nothing. I will go talk to him."

"No Carl, I…I…couldn't ask you-"

"Get away from my stove, you two," Edda broke in. "This soup isn't going to warm itself. Nadine, you keep Minna from filling up on rolls."

Nadine turned reluctantly. She didn't want Carl stirring up any trouble.

Rereading her letter to Nettie, she dropped it on her bed. Words full of niceties and everything about the first week. Now, however, her stomach knotted. Presently, it didn't feel true. Maybe she should go to see Margaret in Chicago. There must be somewhere on this planet trouble did not follow her.

She grabbed another piece of paper, thinking it was time to apologize to her sister anyway. Five or six lines in, she crumbled up the paper and threw it in the fireplace. It felt manipulative to invite herself to her sister's world just to escape her own past. She paced around her room and grabbed another piece of paper.

Hayes. Certainly she could pour her heart out to him. She sat at the vanity, but nothing would come. She wanted to tell him how deeply his prayer had touched her, but it felt like everything was crumbling on her again. She dropped her head on her arm, unable to focus.

Hadn't she just spent the morning understanding God uses all troubles? Why did each moment of understanding get tested so quickly? It was one thing to understand God had a plan for everything. It was another to be back in the fire.

48

The cold gray week dragged on. Every time she wanted to catch Carl, he was with her father or Edda. She didn't want him intervening. It would only make things worse. She felt distracted and almost dependent on looking out the windows.

The one day the weather cleared, her mother wanted to go shopping; something about her dresses from Carver being; what had she said? Somber? After wearing black for weeks on end, normally this would have made her beyond happy. But not now. Her mother knew the truth. She wasn't ready to be seen in town and answer the personal questions.

By afternoon, she'd gone upstairs and pulled out the piano bench. She sat and reminisced. This was no grand piano. How interesting that such a valuable instrument was left abandoned in Carver. How interesting that her fingers rambling back and forth on the keys would help her melancholy. She tried some simple chords and had to smile. It sounded nothing like the Steinway with the hardwood floors and tall brick walls. "I need thee every hour" emerged from her soft chords. Her voice could raise over the old piano. *I need thee every hour, most gracious Lord; no tender voice like thine can peace afford. I need thee, O I need thee; every hour I need thee; O bless me now, my Savior, I come to thee.*

"Are you dying? Is that why you came home?" Minna leaned into the music room.

The music halted, and Nadine tilted her head to the side. "No. I'm not dying, silly."

Minna smirked. "You had your eyes closed and were singing like some downtrodden maiden drowning in a lake."

"I'm glad to see you have been reading and feeding your active imagination." Nadine rose from the bench and went into her room. Losing the battle with her common sense, she watched out the window. From the second story, she could see the yard and barns, everything the same as last time she looked.

She was thankful she'd mailed Nettie's letter. But nothing would instigate the words for Hayes. He'd taken so much time to write her beautiful letters. Why couldn't she respond? He might even take her silence as rejection. Sitting at the vanity, she gazed in the mirror. Her reflection was as downcast as she felt. A drowning maiden. Dropping her face into her hands, she whispered, "What is it, Lord?"

'I have not given you the spirit of fear, beloved. Take up your shield of faith and stand.'

Nadine looked up. Hiding and fear were so familiar to her. She really was drowning. Slowly allowing fear to lock her in this house, she couldn't pen anything to Hayes because she was ashamed of how helpless she felt again. The very pattern she had run from in Carver! It didn't matter the person or the location. Fear was trying again to steal the very life Jesus came to give her.

She stood, new air reaching her lungs. She knew what she needed to do.

The next morning Nadine told her mother she would be going to town. She would stop by the dress shop as her mother wished. Helga asked if Carl could take her. Nadine said she'd prefer to walk.

"Nein." Helga piped in. "I want you to come home with a dress box. And the roads are frozen." She gave Nadine some money.

"I have the-"

"Please, Nadine." Helga put her hand up. "I need you to pick up a coat from Mrs. Bibbins. It's too much to carry."

"Yes, mother." She smiled, feeling undaunted.

An hour later she rode next to Carl, heading into town.

"Carl, I need to make one stop before I run my errands."

"*Ja*, fine." He nodded.

"I need to speak to Mr. Monroe, the man I believe was here last Sunday."

"I told you I would speak to him. You don't have to worry."

She noticed his face tighten.

"This is important to me." She saw the outskirts of Elbert. "Important that—I do it. Would you stop in front of the saloon?"

He gave a low groan. "I watch over you like a daughter, so I don't like this idea." He pulled the wagon to a stop.

"It should only be a few minutes. If I'm not out in a reasonable time, you may come find me." He offered her his arm as she held her skirt and let herself down.

Nadine straighten her back and tried to even her breathing. "Please Lord, no stuttering," she murmured, walking in the smelly saloon.

A woman emptying spittoons looked up. "Who you lookn' for?"

"I'm looking for the owner." She sucked in a quick breath. "Mr. Monroe, I believe."

'The woman rolled her eyes. "Well let me see…Miss?"

"Von Keller. You may tell him Miss Von Keller is here." Nadine pulled off the new gloves Hayes had given her and squeezed them. She looked back through the half-open front door where Carl watched. It had been a comforting idea to bring him.

"Miss Von Keller, is it?" An older version of Marcus walked toward her. He looked like the man from Sunday.

"Were you at my family's home, sir? Last Sunday?" Her voice worked, but her legs started to shake.

"Yes, I was." The corner of his mouth curved down. "I was looking for my son."

"You should know I haven't seen nor heard from your son in months. He abandoned me in a town outside of Minneapolis. I have had no word. Nothing."

"Why would he abandon you?" His brow creased together.

"Because I would not participate in his depravity." Nadine realized too late she was standing in the family business. "He made promises he never kept. He manipulated and used me. I would have never left here had I known how malicious he was." She swallowed and took in needed air.

"I'm sorry to hear you feel so poorly about him." His eyes drooped, looking bored.

"Is there any more information you need sir? I don't plan on ever talking to you again."

"Oh." He waved a hand in the air. "Won't that be a hardship? No, no Miss Von Keller. If he's not here, then he's not here."

Nadine nodded and turned on her heel. When she reached the wagon, she gripped the side. "Thank you, God… Thank you, God." She heaved a sigh. She bit her bottom lip as her smile exploded. "I did it. I did it." She reached her hand out as Carl pulled her up. "Thank you, Carl. I can't tell you how free-" she caught her choice of words. "Freeing that experience was. I needed to do it for myself."

He nodded and tapped the reins.

Taking her time looking around the dress shop, she smiled. She hadn't enjoyed an afternoon since browsing the Nickel Emporium.

The dress in the window was the one, somewhat mature, yet stylish. The bottom was a large black and white window pane design with a sheer white blouse under a smart fitting black vest. She fingered the hats and decided to let her mother buy the dress, and she would buy the matching hat.

As the woman boxed it up, she couldn't help but smile. God had told her to stand, not to live another day in fear. She would write Hayes about it. She felt proud of herself for the first time in her life. Carl met her outside and took the large box. Two doors down at Mrs. Bibbons' shop, a little bell rang as she walked in.

"Hello, Nadine." Mrs. Bibbons greeted her with a wide smile. "Your mother said you were back. Let me get the coat she wanted to be altered." She vanished around the corner and came back with a large box. "Do you want to try it on first?"

"Oh." Nadine was confused." I didn't know it was for me."

"That's what your mother said. Said you'd come dragging home in nothing but a thin cape."

Nadine rolled her lips. "That is true." She smiled, enjoying the honesty.

Mrs. Bibbons lifted the lid. "It is a beautiful coat. I added a bit of fur trim to keep your neck warm."

Nadine startled. "It's black."

Mrs. Bibbons came around the counter and held it out. "You want to see the back?" She flipped it around and then held it out for Nadine to try on.

"No the color…I meant…" Nadine slipped her arms in. It was at least a foot shorter than the other one. After exhaling, she breathed in a deep breath. "I…I think…it…is… perfect."

49

Nadine reached over and grabbed her mother's arm at the breakfast table. "I have received a very important invitation."

"What's wrong, *tochter*? You are smiling and crying."

"I know!" Nadine held the napkin to her wet face. "My dear friend is getting married. You've heard me speak of Nettie?"

"*Ja, ja.*"

"She's marrying a young man she has loved for years. I can't believe it." Nadine rose and walked around the table. "Well, I can believe it. God is so amazing." She waved the letter in the air, then stopped, looking at her mother. "I think you should go with me."

Her mother rocked forward. "Oh *nein*." She rose from the table, shaking her head. "That is too far for me."

"We could do it. We will take the train. It will be an adventure." Nadine wrapped her arms around her mother. "Please think about it."

"*Ja, ja.*" Her mother pushed away, smiling. "I will think about it."

Nadine watched her mother doze on the train as it crossed into Minnesota. Hayes had been right. This was much smoother and faster than the bumpy stage. She glanced down to re-read week three's letter.

Now sleeps the crimson petal, now the white;
Nor waves the cypress in the palace walk;
Nor winks the gold fin in the porphyry font;
The firefly wakens; waken thou with me.

Now droops the milk-white peacock like a ghost,
And like a ghost she glimmers on to me.
Now lies the Earth all Danaëe to the stars,
And all thy heart lies open unto me.
Now slides the silent meteor on, and leaves
A shining furrow, as thy thoughts in me.

Now folds the lily all her sweetness up,
And slips into the bosom of the lake;
So fold thyself, my dearest, thou, and slip
Into my bosom and be lost in me.

The author was Tennyson, but her heart swelled as if Hayes had written it for her. Which he had, in his beautiful handwriting. She smiled, holding it against her chest. She had letter four tucked safely in her case with one purpose—he could read it to her in person. Like Minna's sketchbook, she'd collected all his words and pieced them together for her dream. Hayes was strong and brave and honest and never despised her freedom. Spending the last hours on the train picturing Nettie and Nick standing at the altar warmed her to her toes. Knowing she would see Hayes again kept her heart fluttering in a million directions.

Nadine knew her mother was tired as they arrived in Carver. She got them settled in at the hotel and wondered about running down the street to the Feed and Seed. Would they be in the little back kitchen talking about the wedding? Being well past the hour for visiting, Nadine wondered if she could sleep at all.

Helga pulled the covers up to her chin. "*Tochter*, are you going to keep the light on all night?"

"No, mother. I just wanted to say how proud I am of you to take this adventure with me."

"*Ja*," Helga yawned. "I will get to meet all your friends."

"I do have one special friend… I want you to meet." Nadine sat in the chair, holding her breath.

"*Ja*. The one who writes you the letters."

"How did you know about his letters?"

"Minna."

"Of course." Nadine laughed. "I'm not sure he will be at the wedding. But when the newlyweds leave, maybe that day?"

"*Ja, ja*." Her eyes closed. "We will meet…him."

The next morning her mother waved her on to see to Nettie. "You are like a rabbit from a cage. I will see you later," Helga said.

Nadine grabbed her and kissed her cheek. '"I will be back." Threading her arms through the tailored black coat, she rushed through the hotel lobby. Stepping out onto the sidewalk, she wanted to throw open her arms and yell, "Well, Hello Carver!" Laughing at herself, she couldn't contain her quick steps up to the Feed and Seed. It appeared dark and locked up, so she sailed by it to the Wagner home.

Alma opened the door. "Mrs. Von Keller."

"I know it's early. Is she up?" Nadine walked in and heard a scream. Nettie raced around the corner, arms open wide, as Nadine screamed back. They fell into each other's embrace, laughing and crying off and on.

"This is a good look." Nadine flipped Nettie's rag curlers.

Nettie did a circle with her nightgown and robe twirling. "And this is what Nick's going to have to look at from now on."

"Oh please." Mrs. Wagner walked in. "Good to see you, Nadine. Maybe you can help her."

"Yes, please Nadine....*help....me...*" Nettie snorted and pulled her upstairs to her room.

Nadine dropped her boots, coat, and gloves on the floor. They both jumped into the bed and wrapped in the covers. "I only got one letter," Nadine said, wide-eyed. "I want details. Start from when I left and don't leave anything out."

"We need to be at the church in one hour." Mrs. Wagner knocked on the door.

"We are getting close," Nadine called back. She helped Nettie step into her bustle. Nettie looked to her backside. "Do I really need this contraption?"

"Today, yes." Nadine pulled her around, straightening her satin undergarments. "You're a beauty Betty Nettie, but this will knock Nick over." She held out the white satin and brocade dress. Nettie carefully stepped in, and Nadine helped her slip her arms into the sleeves. "Now we need the cavalry." Nadine stepped to upstairs hallway and called for Mrs. Wagner and Alma. After an hour of placing, pinning and buttoning and wiping the tears, stunning Nettie Wager was ready.

50

Thankfully her mother was waiting when Nadine ran into the hotel. She took a minute to freshen up and joyfully walked arm and arm with her to the church on the corner. She wanted to look around to see if Hayes was anywhere to be seen, but the church piano already played a song. They hustled in, and Mrs. Wagner waved them to the pew behind them. The pastor smiled and led everyone in "Like a Shepherd Lead Us."

Nadine's heart raced as the wedding march began. Nick, in his white starched shirt and brown vest, stood up by the pastor as Mr. Wagner walked Nettie slowly down the aisle. Nettie sparkled, beaming from ear to ear, never taking her eyes off Nick. The pastor prayed, and Mr. Wagner took his spot by his wife. Nettie's mom set her hand on her father's arm. Mr. Wagner moved to grasp her hand and pulled her close.

Nadine's tears rose fast and full. These parents; such love and excitement for their sweet Nettie. The ceremony was personal and spiritual, everything true to Nettie and Nick. The pastor turned them to face the gathering and

Nadine had to drop her soaked hankie. She wanted Nettie to see her delight in this amazing day.

The pastor smiled. "Before I introduce you, you may now kiss the-"

"Oh no," a little boy interjected and slapped his hands over his eyes. Nettie and Nick laughed, starting chuckles throughout the church.

"Kiss your..." Pastor Thomason tried again.

Nettie had already grabbed Nick by the shoulders and was kissing him. Nadine heard an unusual sound coming from her mother.

Nettie released Nick.

"I was going to say *you* could kiss your bride." Pastor Thomason shrugged at Nick.

"Yes, please." Nettie winked at Nick. Nick carefully touched her face and mouthed I love you before he set a gentle kiss upon his new bride.

Pastor Thomason shook his head at the couple, and everyone watching. Nadine looked over to find even her mother chuckling. She didn't know if she'd ever heard her mother laugh before. Nadine wrapped an arm around her shoulders. "That is my Nettie."

Nadine introduced her mother to the Wagners and Thomasons as they enjoyed cake and coffee in the fellowship hall. Without going near Edgar, she but couldn't help but notice him helping his grandmother get around. Nick and Nettie were circling their guests, receiving hugs and well wishes.

Mrs. Thomason asked questions about her adjustment back home. Nadine shared about the things God has helped her with in the past weeks.

"Sad time for Mr. Sullivan." Mrs. Thomason said.

"I assume you mean about Grace?" Nadine coaxed.

"Yes, it surely will be a change. But I believe he's doing the right thing."

"By letting her go?" Nadine felt her brows crease.

"Well, mostly because he's moved back east to be nearer to Grace. I think it speaks to his commitment as a father, don't you?"

"He's moved?" Nadine felt the room spin.

"Yes, I believe so. He resigned the commissioner job and sold the house."

Nadine couldn't breathe. Besides Nettie, every mile of this trip was to see him. Had she just imagined the words of love before she got on the stage? Was it more than a friendship? Isn't that what his kisses communicated? Why hadn't she written him her feelings sooner?

"You look a bit pale, dear." Mrs. Thomason touched her arm.

Nadine forged a smile. "I think I will take in some air. If you will excuse me."

Emiline rushed her at the back door. "Mrs. Von Keller."

Nadine looked back to see her mother talking to Pastor Thomason. Only one Mrs. Von Keller attended today.

"Emiline. How wonderful to see you again."

"I wanted to thank you for those extra pieces of piano music you left. I have been practicing at home." She held up a basket of little cotton bags. "Some oats and dried corn to throw on the couple when they leave."

"Oh yes." Nadine took one and could feel her eyes filling. "You'll have to excuse me, Emiline. Weddings made me cry." She walked out into the churchyard and looked up and down the street. Her eyes closed, she could almost see Grace running around the building and flying into her skirts. Her chest seized up as she tried to find a steady breath.

Someone made an announcement inside the church hall, and she wiped her eyes and sucked in a deep breath. This is Nettie's special day, and she didn't want to miss a moment of it.

Before they'd left, in a flurry of wishes and hugs, they'd agreed to have breakfast the next day in the back kitchen of the Feed and Seed. Helga wanted to stay at the hotel, and Nadine walked the familiar path to the back door. She tried to shake off her fretful night of sleep and focus. It was extremely generous of Nick and Nettie to add anyone into their first morning as husband and wife. She pulled the door open and smelled the bacon.

She hung her coat on the peg. "Nettie, I can't believe you are cooking." She looked back and forth to make sure Nick wasn't close. "You should be abed, wrapped up with your new husband."

"Who says I wasn't...already...*wrapped up*." She smiled, her brows rising quickly. Nadine laughed and had to look away as Nick entered.

"Good love and good breakfast. Am I forgetting anything yet, Nick?"

"Manners," he mumbled and kissed her check.

They passed around the food and bowed to pray. Nadine tried to swallow the emotions accompanying Nick's words of thanks over all their blessings.

"Nadine..." Nettie droned. "Why are you crying?"

"Because I am so happy for you two." She dabbed her nose. "And I will so...very much miss you all...again..." She chuckled. "My mother doesn't know all the details." She stirred her eggs around. "So many called me Mrs. Von Keller yesterday, yet I introduced my mother as Mrs. Von Keller. She doesn't know I lied about being a widow. Don't you think it strange no one caught the discrepancy? Forget that." She shook her head. "The glowing radiance on you two, really, was all people saw. It was the most beautiful ceremony ever."

"And a bride hungry for a kiss." Nick sent Nettie a sideways glance.

"That Rollins boy started it." Nettie shrugged.

"It was perfect." Nadine took in a deep breath.

They ate in silence, and Nadine asked about where they would live. Nick gave her a tour of the back rooms. She peeked in the little room, her first safe haven in Carver.

"We are going to tear out this wall and make one big room."

"With a big bed…" Nettie called from the kitchen. Nick shook his head, "Live here until I can build what she wants."

"Don't forget a guest room." Nadine smiled. "I plan on being an annoying house guest."

Nick smiled. "Nettie and I wondered if one day you might move back. She seemed to think you and Mr. Sullivan might have a future."

"I understand he moved back east." Nadine sighed.

"I saw him a few days ago."

Nadine stiffened. "You did?"

He asked me if I was interested in his stock. I bought one horse and I think he sold the rest to the livery."

"Do you think he's still in Carver?"

Nick shrugged. "I couldn't say. He said he had most everything wrapped up."

Nadine walked back into the kitchen. "Thank you two for a delightful morning. I suppose I should go check on my mother."

51

Nadine found her mother curled up in bed, reading. "Since we are leaving tomorrow, would you mind if I went to visit one more place? It was special to me."

"I don't mind. I can see why you enjoyed your time here." Helga nodded.

Nadine gathered her scarf and gloves and slipped on the black coat. She'd done this before and knew how cold it could get. The high clouds covered the blue sky, and a rare peek of the sun met her face. The solitude of Hayes' Victorian sat on the horizon.

As she neared, her heart sank. No livestock grazing or in the barn; no clothes on the back line. The snow ruts from the playtime in the front yard were all melted. Carefully, she walked up the front steps and looked in the side window. The furnishing and paintings were all gone, the grand dining table and piano missing from their assigned places. She tried the front door and found it locked.

Miserable and cold, she sat on the front step, wrapping her arms around her legs. Spying the open land around the home, the peaceful space reminding her of freedom. Freedom to make choices. How could God trust His fickle creation with such weighty things? The time and way the Lord reached her heart—so extraordinary and unexpected. Dropping her chin on her knee, she closed her eyes and tried to count her blessings. Memories of Grace, running and screaming in the snow; sitting in front of a crackling fire with Hayes, sweet angel asleep in her lap. These were also the pieces of her dream. How could she-

A loud crack rang out and Nadine jumped up. It seemed far away—somewhere in the direction that they'd walked on Grace's birthday. She looked and wondered. Hayes said he liked to target shoot.

"Hayes," she whispered and jogged down the steps.

"Hayes!" She yelled, running toward the area they had walked.

She stopped, huffing. Cupping her hands around her mouth, she took in her deepest full breath. "Hayes!"

She saw movement in a grove of trees in the distance. "P...p...please." She walked toward it, pinching the stitch in her side from running. Making out his face, she stopped. "Oh my Lord," she panted. "I can't believe it." He tilted his head to the side and smiled. His jacket was open, exposing his flannel shirt, pant legs tucked haphazardly into his boots, his gun strapped to his back. He looked so good.

Nadine tipped her head playfully. "Are you Hayes Sullivan?

"I am." He bowed slightly. "But you cannot be the woman I remember. She would never wear a black coat."

"Oh," Nadine puffed, holding her arms out. "Just to please my mother."

They stared at each other, the familiarity increasing but the pain of loss drying Nadine's mouth. "You are moving back east? To be closer to Grace?"

"Yes, I am." He nodded. "I have an agreement with Molly. I will remain Grace's father. If at any time Grace is unhappy, she will come back to me. I can see her whenever I want, for now every weekend. But to be her father, I need to live near her."

"Of course." Nadine nodded. "It sounds very reasonable and a…ad…dmirable." She looked down to the dried ground. "I was here for Nettie's wedding." She looked up, not meeting his eyes. "It was yesterday."

"Wonderful."

"My mother is with me. The real Mrs. Von Keller." Nadine chuckled.

"And how is your family?"

"Good. They don't know… everything." She sighed. "But they have slowly embraced me and the person I am now."

Hayes nodded.

"You have given up your post with the railroad."

Hayes rubbed his hand over his ear. "Yes. The rail lines are connected, it doesn't need three men. George can run it now."

"What will you do?"

"I've received an offer from Brown University." He started walking, and Nadine joined him. "I'm going to teach

Literature and Philosophy. See how many students I can torture with trochaic tetrameter or seventh-century French poetry."

Nadine smiled. "Perfect for you. I know you believe that every aspect of what happens to us is to become part of our life truth."

He pulled back, squinting at her. "Very accurate. I'm impressed."

"I read your letters... *a lot*. " She pinched her smile flat. "My favorite is when you told me to be patient toward all that is unsolved in my heart. You said to make peace with the questions themselves, for they will reveal their meaning in the perfect timing."

"Have you found your peace, your freedom you longed for?"

"I have and...I haven't." She drew in a shaky breath. Dare she tell him her heart was shattering? Should she leave him with her dignity intact?

"I heard the Lord's voice one morning."

He watched her as they approached the yard.

"I don't know how that sounds for everyone. But I think it was the Lord. He told me to stand up and be strong. I had gone home and sunk back into some of my fearful hiding."

Hayes nodded.

"So I stood up to a... problem, and I felt the most incredible strength in my soul." She shrugged. "It must be catching," She chatted nervously. "My mother agreed to travel with me." Hayes began to go up the front steps, Nadine standing at the bottom.

"Can you come in for a moment?" His eyes flashed his familiar sincerity. "I have something of my grandmother's I want to give you."

Nadine hesitated, looking up at him. Maybe a quick goodbye wouldn't hurt so much. Being inside the house would bring more memories. "Thank you for thinking of me, but all your grandmother's things should go to Grace and I've left my mother today...more than I should."

"Please." He came down a step and held his hand out. "Trust me." His roguish grin broke into her defenses.

"For a moment." She took his hand.

He unlocked the front door, and they stepped inside.

"You'll probably want to wait here." He set his gun in the corner. "What I have for you is in my bedroom." He headed up the stairs.

Nadine stood inches from the door, the emptiness filling her being like the cold, hollow home.

He came back down the stairs, and she looked at him questioning. He held no item. It didn't matter—she'd allowed her heart to be drawn in again. Frustrated that her affections were so gullible, she turned to grab the knob.

"Nadine, wait." He pulled on her coat sleeve. She turned, but he was too close. He pulled his hand down his face, eyes serious.

"I can't stay here," he whispered. "I remember when we were moving in. Grace was but two or three. All she wanted to do was go up and down those stairs." He smiled, looking back. "My grandmother was sure she would fall and break her neck. I had to go into town and get some bailing wire and build a little gate. I remember because I was annoyed. I was annoyed by everything Grace did." His jaw locked, and he swallowed hard.

"The night I came to the Silver Holiday, I wanted to find Molly." He shook his head. "I was irritated by this house, by living with two old women and a crying child. I wanted her to see my misery. I didn't want her back. I wanted her to have to live in my discomfort." He looked up and huffed. "But there you were in a room filled with smoke, wrapped in that long black coat," he said wistfully. "I needed a knock in the head. I'd become so self-assured of my philosophy of life and truth, that I'd let my heart go cold."

He pulled off her gloves and let them drop on the floor. He rubbed her hands back and forth in his. "I'd prayed and asked God for help, and then my grandmother died." He shook his head, his face troubled. "I thought my life unbearable until I saw your little sign on the door. I didn't know it then, but I know it now…you were my answer to prayer. You modeled how to love Grace. But without Grace or you here, I can't be here…" His expression dulled. "I can't."

"I understand." Nadine gently touched his face.

52

The warmth and familiarity were present again, connecting them like looking into the depth of each others' eyes. "I understand…I do." Just as he'd given her the ultimate gift of sacrifice and freedom, she intended to give it to him. She loved him so much.

"So, I guess you saved me a trip." Hayes smiled.

"How so?" She squinted.

"And you only brought your mother?"

"Yes… why?"

"When I leave here tomorrow, I have a ticket to Wisconsin. To an Elbert County. I understand there is a dairy there that Mr. and Mrs. Von Keller own. I have plans there."

"What kind of plans?" Nadine's' brows crinkled.

"I planned to speak to your father. Introduce myself. Convince him of my worth."

"Your worth?"

"Yes. He's never met me before, and I want him to know me. Know my character and honorable plans. I want your family to approve of me."

Nadine tilted her head and smiled.

Hayes pulled her in close and whispered in her ear. "I love you and can't live without you." He backed away slowly. "But since you are here…" He got down on one knee before her and pulled something from his pocket. "This was the ring my grandfather gave to my grandmother before he went to war."

Nadine's heart thudded out of her chest.

"Nadine, will you consider becoming my wife? I want to love you and protect you and hold you and love our children with you… while at all times protecting your freedom to fight your own battles. That last one is the hardest," His voice dipped. "I will be a husband of faith and prayer." He waited, the connection in their eyes overwhelming.

Nadine nodded up and down slowly, as the ring slipped on. "Hayes, oh dear Hayes…" Hope pulsed through her as he stood up, his lips finding hers. His kiss was so deep and without reservation, that passion resounded in her soul. A freedom finally allowing her heart to soar unbridled. She pulled back, breathless, resting her cheek on his. "Yes. I want to marry you."

He kissed her neck and nuzzled her cheek. "Can you live on the east coast?" He rolled his forehead against hers.

"Yes, I can. According to our housekeeper, I'm made for adventure."

He smiled and kissed her again. Pulling back, he laughed. "I would think so. Someone insistent, yelling my name while I was out thinking and praying this morning."

"I came for Nettie's wedding. But I came *for you* and for you to read me this last letter."

"Ah, number four. You never peeked?"

"If it contained any hint of marriage, I assure you, I did not know."

He laughed and held his hand out as she gave him the envelope. They sat on the steps of the staircase.

Opening the paper, he read, "The Black Coat, by Hayes Sullivan."

"Oh..." Nadine moaned. "He's my favorite."

Hayes bumped her shoulder. "This was written at four the morning before you snuck away for the stage. Don't expect much.

"The Black Coat

In the stillness of the night, soot and smoke covered the lovely rose, its fragrance hiding under the layers of darkness. Like a little child with stored up fears and tears, the cloak was its only protection. Created for perfection and light, the rose longed for love and grace. Salvation only a choice away. Fingers free to sing a new song became a strange garden of release, the blackness replaced by beauty once again. Tenderness and hope filled the garden until one day the black coat had to give way to the rushing waves of freedom. Surprised by the consequences of freedom, the rose often lost hope. Fire was made to refine, and the rose became glass. Beauty radiated from the diamond like hues. So fragile yet full, vulnerable yet alive.

'For there is nothing covered, that shall not be revealed-neither hid, that shall not be known,' Jesus said in Luke 12:2"

Nadine let out a long sigh and lay her head on his shoulder. "Thank you, Hayes. I will cherish it always." She hugged his arm. "I needed you to know me, and you needed me to know you, and we thought we could hide away from an all-knowing God." She laughed softly. "Oh, we did try, but we just couldn't."

He turned and whispered in her ear. "I don't think either of us fell from God's limitless grace. I think just like our mishap in the icy creek, we finally allowed His grace to soak us good."

Nadine nodded and held out the sweet rose cut colored diamond clustered ring. "I'm marrying the one whom my soul loves. Extraordinary Grace."

Black Coat

Into the Light   *Inspired me- (Nadine's song)*

You saw me broken. You saw me battered.
You saw me filthy. You saw me shattered.
You saw me wicked. You saw me lying.
You saw me failing. You saw me trying.
You saw me angry. You saw me jealous.
You saw me prideful. You saw me selfish.
You saw me wonder. You saw me lustful.
You saw me striving. Worshipping idols
You said; *I want her. I love her. She's the one for me.*
I choose her. I know her. My blood has made her clean.
She is my true love. Bring her to me.
Put a ring on her finger. Clothe her in my righteousnes
Shine my light all around her. Place a crown upon her head.
Keep her tears in a bottle. See her name upon my hands.
When she says: I don't deserve it. Tell her: I took the nails instead.
I took the nails instead.
Now she's always by my side. She stays in my arms day and night.
Out of the cage. Out of the shame. Into the light. Into the light.
She's finding her beauty. She's finding her grace. She's finding her
whole heart. She's showing her face. In the light. In the light. She's
pure in the light. She's home in the light.
Copyright: 2005 Laura Woodley Osman

Listen here:
https://www.youtube.com/watch?v=7iGfn4FduV8

Author's Note:

Thank you for your time joining me on the pages of the Mighty One Series, the Graham and Von Keller family sagas. Somewhere in between the plot and characters, I hope you saw the undeniable woman helping woman theme. I started my own journey ministering to woman *before* I could honestly say "I like women." At the end of ten years of focused woman's ministry, I left with "I LOVE women!" *Burgundy Gloves* introduces you to Laura Graham and her journey with God, family, and hardship. One of the women in her path is Helga Von Keller. Just in their short time at the same church, their lives were ever intertwined, beyond their children, in *Broken Chain*. One woman strong in faith, giving away the simple love of God – the other woman vulnerable enough to receive it, and now their influence reaches generations.

My fiction is based on many a woman's real life. I dedicated this story of grace to my best childhood friend Grace Kingsbury Ruddy. I was seven years old and new to the neighborhood. A sweet mama brought a plate of cookies and her little girl, Grace, over to welcome us. That freckle-faced girl and her family were the light and – through lots of rides- to church, camp, VBS –reason for my discovery of a God of love and family table.

Rightly so, Grace stood as my maid of honor. And my first daughter is named Rebekah Grace.

And I know I am just *one of many* the amazing Kingsburys have influence for eternity. And how could I list the other hundred women that have helped me, held me, taught me, and pulled me up? I would surely leave someone out, so I hold their influence close as I write stories with women reaching out, and pray I do them honor as they have honored my life.

Bless you, dear one, for all those **you** have touched.

Just a plate of cookies. I think I smell something baking in your oven.

All Glory to God, the Director of all our paths.

Julia

Please come visit at juliadwrites.com.

Encouraging blogs, inside thoughts on the books development, newsletters with giveaways.

www.ingramcontent.com/pod-product-compliance
Lightning Source LLC
Chambersburg PA
CBHW030553180626
46816CB00005B/1524